SILVER'S SECRET

SILVER BROTHERS SECURITIES

LACEY SILKS

"Everyone is a moon, and has a dark side which he never shows to anybody." ~ Mark Twain

"Look at us. Perfect on the outside, full of secrets on the inside. One's hiding a son and the other a fetus. No twenty year old could handle our shit, so be grateful our men are older."
~ Laura Young, Silver's Secret

FROM THE AUTHOR

Allie and Tristan's story was originally published as Layers Peeled in 2014 but their story evolved into a page turning romance filled with twists and turns.

If you've never read this emotionally charged romantic suspense, I hope these characters satisfy your every craving. The Silver family has my heart and I expect them to take you on a beautiful adventure filled with love, laughter, and plenty of smut.

Allie Green, a fresh recruit to Silver Brothers Securities, brings a new vibrancy and expertise as she's set to lead a division dedicated to rescuing women from the streets. Tristan Silver, her boss, finds himself not only safeguarding her life but also falling deeply in love. Their perfect future seems within reach, if not for the shadows of their pasts: Allie's relentless stalker and Tristan's haunted memories.

As Allie struggles to find the right moment to tell him about their unborn child, balancing a burgeoning relationship, demanding work, and the weight of her hidden reality, Tristan's nightmares become a reality. When a determined redhead threatens their budding happiness, Tristan vows to protect those closest to him.

Silver's Secret is the fourth novel in the *Silver Securities Family Saga* and should be read after *Silver's Pawn*. Intended for mature audiences.

Chapter 1

Allie

Tristan's words rang in my ears on a loop. "You're fired. You're fired. You're fired."

I rose from the couch in what felt like slow motion. The wrapped gift box with baby booties I'd set on my billionaire boyfriend boss's desk seemed completely inappropriate now. I'd timed that one like a bomb because he'd fired me before I could tell my boss I was carrying his child. How could he have fired me?

"What?"

"I said, you're fired."

Oh, my God. I can't tell him I'm pregnant now.

"Why? I don't understand. I thought—"

"Surprise!"

The office door flew open, and I jumped back. Laura, my mom, the Flintstones, and Emma walked through the doorway. What was Laura doing here? Behind the immediate family were more deliciously handsome men than I'd ever seen in one room in my life. I recognized the Silver brothers, but not the others. My mouth opened and closed and opened again. Someone popped a confetti wand. Laura glanced around as if looking for the same answers I was seeking, while Tristan's

1

father popped a bottle of champagne. I turned in a circle, searching for Tristan's face, but just as I found him, Emma slammed into to my side. She threw her arms tight around my leg, looked up, and batted her lashes.

"What's going on Ems? What is this?" I asked her.

"This is one less secret I have to keep, that's what it is."

Shit. Secret.

Laura hugged me next while my eyes grew wider and wider.

"Grab. The box. Off. The desk."

My ventriloquist impression must have failed because Laura's nose scrunched and she looked at me like I was losing my mind.

"What?"

"If you love me, you'll get that box with baby booties on Tristan's desk and run. I didn't tell him I'm pregnant yet."

"Allie, that's crazy. He loves you, and you're having his baby. He should know."

"I don't disagree, but right now is not the right time. I want it to be special, not in a crowd."

"All right, all right. I'll get it as soon as he steps away. You should preoccupy him. I'm sure you can figure something out with those hormones."

As if on cue, Tristan's gaze lowered to the box. The corner of his mouth lifted as he squinted and removed the gift off the desk.

"Shit, shit, shit. You have to help me, right now! He's gonna open it!"

Heat and cold passed through my body. The golden streams of sunlight filtered between the blinds like ribbons of silk. The sounds in the room mixed into one, lifting in tone, and my legs gave into gravity. The temporary weightlessness changed into a strong hold as Tristan caught me in his arms before I hit the floor.

"Are you all right?" His lips moved, but I couldn't hear him. A hum of concern hovered around me as I focused of faces until I found Tristan's face again.

"Are you all right?" he repeated.

He fired me?

The room stopped spinning. "Yeah, I think so. What happened?"

"You fainted. Did you eat anything today?"

"I did. I think I'm just a little overwhelmed, that's all. Can someone explain what's happening?"

Laura peeked from behind Tristan with a thumbs up. She stuffed the box in her purse as Tristan covered my head with his palm.

"I'm so sorry, Allie."

"I… I don't have a fever."

Someone set a glass with orange juice beside my head, and I sipped through the bent straw. My heart was hammering in my chest. Tristan helped me to the couch while everyone stared. The low conversation resumed when I sat down.

"Just checking. You look flushed."

Flushed?

But he'd fired me. I was much more than flushed.

"Help me up," I said.

Tristan lifted me by the elbow, and we walked away from the crowd. The conversation resumed, and the family's attention finally dwindled.

"Champagne?" Greg passed me a flute, but Tristan stopped him before I could remove it from his hand. The single moment pressed a panic button inside me. Did he somehow know I couldn't drink?

"I think she needs another minute."

"No, I think we're done here." I turned away and headed for the door, but Tristan was quicker and blocked my way before I reached the closing frame. A wave of attention flowed our way.

"Whoa, Allie, I beg you. Please let me explain. I have to fire you."

"You're the boss. You don't have to do anything you don't want to." The air I sucked in tiny breaths wasn't helping. "You clearly don't want me a part of Silver Securities."

The deafening silence in the room made me unaware of Tristan's guests. They stood frozen, staring at me like I'd lost my mind.

"Allie, baby. You don't know what you're saying."

When he said 'baby,' I broke down even further. I sucked in the sobs on short inhalations. My phone buzzed with a text from Emma. I reached into my pocket to read:

Emma: Don't be sad. I'm calling my niece or nephew Baby-Puss for now ;)

I looked across the room to where she was standing by the window, smiling. I wanted to be part of this family so much that it hurt. Tristan's little sister had helped me keep my secret by forging my blood work at the hospital in exchange for choosing the baby's name. So far, all of them had been from the Flintstones. And I loved that too.

I broke in half, and Tristan took me into his arms, holding me tight. "Allie, I'm so sorry. Firing you is just a technicality, so I can hire you for a new position."

"Technicality?" I blubbered through tears and snot and repeated, "Technicality for what?"

"I'm sorry. I should have known it would be overdramatic. It's been a long day." He blinked the clouds away and his whiskey eyes brightened. "Maybe surprising you with a new job wasn't a good idea."

I pulled in a weep. "A new job?" Then: "Overdramatic?"

If overdramatic had a face, yes, it would be Tristan's right now. But could this be true? I wasn't fired? Were we really going to work together again?

"Really? I still work for Silver Securities?"

"Of course you do. Like it or not, you're a part of this family for the rest of your life."

My chest warmed a little. When I'd woken up this morning, I was so sure of my path that I'd never have predicted a bombshell like losing my job. The moment he'd told me I was fired, that I could possibly be pregnant and out of work planted a seed of doubt I couldn't easily weed. I let go of his hand.

"I think I'm okay now. What's the new job?"

He cleared his throat and stood up. "Settle down, everyone."

Another moment of panic passed through me. Jesus, was he about to propose? I wasn't ready for that, but then again, I didn't think I was ready for this baby, either.

"Allie's fine, but I haven't told her about the new job yet."

"She should get checked by a doctor." My mother's brows lifted. She was looking at me funny, like she could see right through me and my temporarily flat stomach.

"No, really. I'm fine, Mom. Job? What job?" I focused on Tristan.

Shit.

I was so off my game. These hormones were not only playing with my body but also with my instincts.

The conversation silenced. Tristan turned around to face me again and took my hands into his. "If you agree, you'll head the new division at Silver Securities along with a new partner." He pointed to Laura, and my best friend grinned from ear to ear.

"What?" I gaped and turned toward her. "You're working with me? For Silver Securities?"

"Woot, woot!" She lifted her flute of champagne in cheer. "Can't argue that you'll get a better partner, can you?"

"And you've been keeping this secret from me?"

I saw Emma roll her eyes at my comment. All right. I was a hypocrite.

"Sorry not sorry."

"Wait a minute—what exactly will we be doing?"

"Silver Securities partnered with a local safe house to form a rehab team. The Green Team, will investigate, gather evidence, provide security, and hopefully, catch the criminals. The Wagner brothers formed a team to help you with the legalities."

"The Green Team? After me?"

He nodded, and my eyes welled. Oh, these new hormones were a real treat.

"After one of the strongest women I know. Sorry, Wilma."

His mother bent down and kissed him on his head like he was still her young boy, and my heart squeezed at the sight. "As long as you're happy, I'll be elated."

She then leaned in to hug me and whispered in my ear, "You look wonderful, Allie."

"Thank you."

Maggie and John Silver took such a liking to my mother that they'd asked her to permanently move into the guesthouse, and she agreed. Tristan was right. I was part of this family, and I couldn't wait to tell them all the good news.

"Tristan, this is wonderful. I can't believe you did this."

"I know how hard the past couple of months have been. I'm sorry for everything, Allie. Once you're well, Silver Securities can't wait to have you here permanently."

Tristan's phone beeped, and he checked his message. He stiffened and stared down the long hallway, eyeing the exit.

"Grab something to drink and eat up. Mom made coconut sweet buns, and she won't leave until they're all gone. Excuse me."

He kissed me on the cheek and left. I followed his quick step out the door to where he disappeared down the hallway. The smell of sweet pastries and roast beef sandwiches brought my attention back to the room. My mouth watered and my stomach grumbled. The delicious aroma overpowered my resistance, and the next thing I knew, I was sitting behind Tristan's desk with a plate full of fruit, sandwiches, and pastries. I stuffed them in my mouth one after the other.

Emma sat on the mahogany desk, swinging her legs. "So? What do you think?" she asked.

"They're delicious." I bit into a cream-stuffed puff ball.

"No, silly. I mean about Baby Puss."

"I think you should keep trying. Tristan won't go for it."

"Let's ask him, then." She wiggled her brows.

"Let's not." I rammed the remaining cream puff into my mouth. "I'm gonna need you to hold onto that little secret for a while longer."

"But that's not fair. Do you know how many secrets I have to keep?"

"A lot?" I shrank my neck back like a turtle. "But that's what makes you so special."

"One day, when I work here, I'll make it a rule to have no secrets."

My stomach turned, and Emma whispered, "But don't worry. I won't say a word about Baby Puss."

"Shh."

Laura hopped up on the other side of the desk. "I think this is the only time Mr. Silver will let me sit here. But don't tell him I did."

Emma jumped off the table. "That's it. I'm full. This is too many secrets, and I have phone calls to make."

She strolled out of the office like she owned the place, and Laura frowned. "I don't think she likes me."

"It's not you. It's all the secrets she keeps. Besides, she adores babysitting Foxy," I said.

"Have you ever thought asking her for other secrets she might know? You know, like about James?"

"You think he's hiding something?"

"I don't know, but he goes to the doctor every month."

"Why don't you ask Emma to help? She loves investigating."

"Maybe."

I jabbed my finger into her arm. "I can't believe you kept this surprise from me. You knew I was going to the office this morning."

"And you know how good I am at keeping secrets. It had to be a surprise, so don't shoot the messenger. And I was sworn to secrecy with a mighty sword."

"Would that sword happen to be James's dick?'

She coughed into her hand and looked at me like I was the one losing my mind. James was the only decent guy she'd ever dated. Getting stuck together during an avalanche was the best thing that could have happened to them, they just couldn't see it yet.

"It's not his dick. Emma has a new obsession with sword collection. You should see them. I literally mean she swore me to secrecy about this job with the sword."

"Oh, sorry."

"No, things are good with James. Real good. He's a good father."

"So maybe it's time to tell him?"

"But things are good now," she whined. If it were up to Laura, she would keep Foxy's paternity a secret forever, just to avoid conflict. But the longer she waited, the larger her lie grew.

"You're not digging yourself a grave, my friend. You're already on the other side of the planet! What the fuck, Laura?"

"I'm trying to tell him, but now we'll be working together, and that comes with a lot of benefits I'm not ready to part with."

"What benefits?"

"His dick." She shrugged. "Or, at least, the potential of his dick."

"So you haven't slept with him yet?"

"Please, don't rub it in. I've rubbed it out enough. Don't get me wrong, I'd love to, but I can't get myself to do it because"—she curled her shoulders in and bent at the spine—"Because…"

"So what benefits are you taking about?"

Her mouth curved. "His arms, his smile, and I already know what's under those clothes even if I haven't seen it all for three years. But hell, it doesn't stop me from imagining all the naughty things we could be doing."

Yeah, I knew exactly what she meant, and so did my hormones. Before I'd arrived tonight, I'd had the silly image of Tristan grabbing me into his arms and spinning me high in the air. He'd be elated about becoming a father and would grin with that cute dimple. The scar on his upper lip would twist into one of those sexy daddy smiles. God, he would look good on a playground with his little one.

Guilt chewed at my patience. I'd have to tell him I was pregnant as soon as the opportunity presented itself. I glanced over to the window where he was standing, tall and wise, talking to one of the Wagner brothers. I still couldn't believe the man who walked into the auditorium was my man. When I weaseled my way inside the company for revenge, I'd had no clue he'd become a permanent part of my life. A life which had changed so quickly the past couple of months, it was difficult to predict the upcoming winter. Chills swept over my arms.

The dimple sank into his cheek and the scar on his upper lip twisted his smile into a sexy lopsided grin. Ah, how I wished I could touch that lip with my mouth and pussy. His whiskey eyes caught my stare, and my nipples hardened.

"You have to tell him." Laura urged. "You two are meant to be, no question about it."

"And you can't keep your secret forever. Foxy's growing up."

"That's not true. I didn't think I could introduce him to James, but it's worked so far. And Ems is keeping the secret."

"Until she blows."

"I may have not made the connection, Laura, but James would if you stopped dressing Foxy in costumes."

"Laila loves clowns. We went to a park to feed the ducks, and we even went to the aquarium. See? Quality time. Things are working out. Sort of."

"You put makeup on Foxy so his father wouldn't recognize him," I loud-whispered.

"Says the woman who hasn't told her boyfriend she's carrying."

"Shh." My mother side-eyed me from the corner. I'd visited with her yesterday to see how she was settling in, and she absolutely glowed. The move and safety the Silvers had given her was something I could never pay back. Nor did anyone make me feel like I had to. I would tell Tristan about our baby when the time was right, no sooner and no later. And that time wasn't right now.

"It's still early, but I'm telling him soon. There's no way I'm keeping this going for as long as you have."

She sank into her seat and reached for a marshmallow-topped brownie.

"That's what I used to say. Then I met James, and I really got to know him... and everything changed. He's an amazing father. And those eyes..."

She sighed like I'd never heard her sigh before. I wasn't sure whether she was talking about her son's eyes or James's, but it didn't matter—because they had the same eyes. The fact that James hadn't caught on boggled my mind. Then again, Laura had done a great job covering up her truth. Did she regret not telling James earlier? A good father had missed out on two years of his son's life.

I touched her arm. "Laura—"

"Did you see that beard? I mean, how many twenty-year-olds could pull off that growth?"

"I know exactly what you mean. The stamina, the experience, no bullshit. All the more reason you should tell him sooner than later."

"Look at us," she purred. "Perfect on the outside, full of secrets on the inside. One's hiding a son and the other a fetus. No twenty-year-old could handle our shit, so be grateful they're older."

Tristan would be happy once I told him I was pregnant, wouldn't he?

"I don't think they have a clue what's coming their way."

Laura laughed, and I slouched into the couch. I turned my head toward her. She reached to the side table beside her and passed me a chocolate praline truffle. I bit into the sweetness, and the chocolate melted on my tongue. The custom-ordered chocolates with a Silver Brothers logo stamped into the cut were always set in a bowl at Tristan's penthouse, and they were officially my favorite.

"Who's the redhead?" Laura asked.

"What?"

"Tall, thin, and territorial."

My back straightened. I scanned the room, but couldn't see the woman Laura had described.

"Territorial over what? Has Foxy kept you up at night?"

"No, but his daddy did." She winked. "Do you realize if we marry them, we'll have the same last name?"

"Marriage is not on the table."

"It's hypothetical, silly. It's not like I want that piece of fine man to wake up next to me every morning just so I can pick out a leftover crumb from his beard."

"Eww, gross. I'm glad Tristan's growth is not long enough to catch food."

"You'd disagree if you actually saw James in all his glory. They don't make boys in his shape. Those years of experience are hard-earned."

"Can we please stop talking about growth and men in

general, at least, until you actually sleep with him? I'm horny enough as it is. Now, what were you saying about a redhead?" I sipped my water. I was carrying the bottle everywhere with me because the doctor said hydration was important.

"I saw her earlier in the hall by the bathrooms. I thought she was Tristan's secretary because they were talking."

"Tristan's secretary is blond, and he's over there." I pointed to Greg, who was chatting with one of the Wagner brothers. The lawyers were sitting in the waiting area outside, enjoying what looked like a rare moment of peace. I took in the gathering. This company and all its employees blew my mind. The teamwork and diligence, brotherhood, friendships, close relatives, and trustworthy workforce worked for a reason, and I could see that reason playing out right in front of me. They trusted each other, and it was one of the many reasons I trusted Tristan.

"No, the redhead was definitely a woman," Laura said. "The oversized hat didn't catch your attention?"

"No, the chocolate croissants did."

She looked me over and smirked like she knew something I didn't. "I know they say you're eating for two, but the daily amount of calories required during a pregnancy is not that high."

"Shut up and don't judge. It's the only thing that will keep the hormones at bay for now. They don't tell you about this part in the books, but I googled it."

"You googled it? You could have asked me, you know. Seventy-three percent of pregnant women experience an increased sex drive."

"You were younger. I'm older."

She laughed. "I got pregnant three years ago, babe. Welcome to the knocked-up-in-her-early-twenties club."

"What happened three years ago?" James handed Laura a

glass of wine. The color drained from her face, and she took a quick sip.

"We were reminiscing about our Christmas in Colorado three years ago."

Laura took another sip, glaring at me to shut the fuck up.

The corner of his mouth lifted. "Yeah, that was a life-changing night, wasn't it? It's a miracle everyone came out alive."

"Hey, who was the redhead talking to Tristan earlier?" I asked him.

"Redhead?" His brows furrowed, and for a split second I thought he knew exactly who it was. "Not anyone I'm aware of."

"It must be his mistress." Laura lowered her voice, and I rolled my eyes.

"Tristan doesn't have another woman." I said.

"It was hypothetical."

"Well, he doesn't have a hypothetical woman either."

James shook his head. "You two crack me up."

"Why would he take her inside a conference room?" she asked.

James looked over his shoulder to the main hall. "Redhead, you say?"

"They went in the conference room together?" I mouthed.

The news dropped into the pit of my bottomless stomach, convincing me I needed another croissant.

"It's probably a client."

"On the weekend?"

"There are no weekends when you own a business."

"Laura's right. Our work is part of our lives, and business hours are all hours. With perks. Excuse me for a moment."

James left Tristan's office, and quickened his step down the hall.

"Is it normal for James to leave like that?" I asked.

"No, it's not, but I'm sure it's nothing."

"That's exactly what you say when it's something."

Tristan returned later that afternoon, but I didn't see James again. I drove home with Laura, and we picked Foxy up from the babysitter's on the way home. While my godson settled into his routine, I couldn't shake off the gnawing dread that had snuck up on me out of nowhere. The uneasiness only got worse, so I showered and decided to surprise Tristan. I changed into sexy lingerie that left nothing to the imagination, threw on a long coat, and left for Manhattan. Something had to give, and I prayed that something was my hormones.

Chapter 2

Tristan

I arrived at the Marina half an hour before our meeting and didn't expect Simone to be there already. Her element of surprise had *Hartley* written all over it. I swallowed the bitter taste in my mouth. She was sitting at a private table near the balcony end overlooking the docked boats. A seagull landed on the railing, and she threw a piece of bread in the air. The bird rose and caught the treat. Simone laughed, and the sound of her voice tore through me like a grenade. A flood of memories rushed back all at once, and my heart opened with all the pain of the happy years we'd shared and lost.

Yachts bopped in the water. The sound of metal clinking against metal echoed through the port. Simone sipped on a drink and looked out across the cove to where the Silvers lived. I had so many questions for her, I didn't know where to begin, but I needed the answers, because Allie deserved them as well. We all deserved them. The warmer fall day carried a crisp sense of change in the air.

I cleared my throat at the tableside, and she turned in her seat in what felt like slow motion. "Hello, Simone."

When she finally faced me, time stopped.

How can this be possible?

The fifteen years I'd thought she was gone were wiped away, and I was once again that young man who had fallen hard for her freckled face. Time had served her well. Her red curls spilled over her ample cleavage.

"Tristan." She smiled, rose from her seat, and walked around the table while I remained frozen in the spot. She wrapped her arms around me until my limbs gave into an embrace I'd never thought I'd feel again.

When she'd surprised me at the cemetery this morning, the moment had not felt real, and I couldn't make sense of anything she said. From the brief explanation about her captivity in her father's house to her gratitude for his death, it sounded like she'd come back from hell.

I blinked repeatedly, trying to process the situation I thought yesterday was impossible: *Simone was alive.*

"I can't believe I finally get to hold you." She tightened her arms around me and snaked her hands around my back and up to my neck. Her body pressed to mine like it was meant to be there forever. Her warm breath sent a trickle of nerves along my spine, the hair stood tall at the back of my nape. I had no right or business entertaining her body's power over mine. I loved Allie. Precious time had passed, and the clock that ticked away in my heart could not be turned back. I lowered her arms from around my neck, stepped back, and pulled back her chair.

"I assure you no one is more surprised to see you here than me."

She took her seat and crossed one leg over the other. "So, you got me chrysanthemums? Should I have worn pearls and rose perfume?"

I rubbed my chin.

"Just kidding. I'm sorry, I shouldn't have shown up like that. I worried when you ran off this morning."

"I didn't expect to see you at *your* grave."

"Right." The same defiance I remembered sparked in her eyes. Simone did things her way, though it seemed Hartley had robbed her of that—at least temporarily.

The server brought my drink. Our glasses clinked, and I emptied the whiskey in one swig, ignoring her lifted brow.

"The party at work went well?"

I squinted. Her out-of-character visit to Silver Securities had taken me by surprise. Then again, rising from the dead was out of character as well.

"It did. We celebrated."

"New hires?" She tilted her head.

"Yes. The work has grown. Your father has kept us busy."

"I bet. Your business is not the only one that has grown."

I leaned forward. "What do you mean?"

She waved her hand in dismissal. "Nothing. Just family crap I've had to deal with after his passing."

"Can I help?"

I was about to serve legal papers to her uncles; the Wagner brothers were moving forward with the case. It was time they took responsibility for the damage. Without the Hartleys' funding, corrupt congressman Donaldson wouldn't have the backing to fight the proposed sex trafficking legislation.

The corner of her mouth lifted, and she eyed me. "Possibly. You know, for the first time in my life, I can finally look ahead."

She reached across the table and covered my hand with hers. I pulled away, and she noted my discomfort. She withdrew the offer and clasped her hand around the wineglass.

"Simone—"

"I don't expect you and me to go back to the same place where we left off." She took a calculated breath, shifting her weight, and leaned forward. "But I need to thank you. If it weren't for your work and your team, looking for Kendra and all the others... What I'm trying to say is that I would have never been freed from my father's grip if it weren't for you,

Tristan. Whoever killed him deserves my full gratitude. Now I get another chance, and that's all anyone can ask for."

I'd sealed off the case documents. Simone could never find out Allie was there that night. " I'm sorry about your father."

"Thank you, but it's a little difficult to feel pity for a man who kept me away from the man I love."

"Simone—"

"I get it. You probably moved on. But I never stopped hoping that one day I would, at least, have a chance to see you again. To explain." When she reached forward the second time, she cupped my cheek. I lowered her hand back to the table with unease.

"What happened? How is this possible? They told me you were dead. I went to your funeral."

She tipped her wine glass back. When she lowered it to the table, her eyes glossed over. "Why don't we start with the appetizers?" She smiled, and my breaths slowed as memories of time when the same smile took over my life rushed back.

"Yes, of course."

I wasn't hungry, and Simone choose a tapas board to share. She didn't seem hungry either, just eager to remain in my company. I couldn't deny a similar need. I had too many questions and not enough answers.

"I can't tell you how happy I am to see you here. All these years, I thought you were gone. I… I thought I killed you."

"What happened was not your fault. It was my father's. He told you I was dead, but clearly I wasn't."

Bastard.

"For the longest time, I thought he'd cut the brakes or something, but the forensics came back negative for tampering. And that made sense because you were his daughter. He wouldn't have hurt you."

A distant, dull, empty stare shadowed her face. "I'm not sure about that."

"What?"

"You think my father actually cared about me?"

"You were his only daughter. Of course, he cared."

She shook her head in denial. "My father cared about his bitches and money. Nothing more and nothing less. He couldn't give a flying fuck if I were in that car. He wanted the perfect revenge against you and Silver Securities, and when they found me alive, he got what he wanted and more. He kept me to himself."

A sickening feeling swirled in my stomach. "Did he hurt you?"

"He kept me locked up for most of my young adult life. He kept me away from you."

Right. Of course, he'd hurt her, but that wasn't what I meant. Maybe I wasn't as ready for all the details as I thought I was.

"The funeral and your tombstone?"

"It was all for show."

"Who else knew?"

"My mother is the only one in my family who didn't know. Everyone else is loyal. When Father broke the pact with the Silvers and Wagners, he made a vow to break us up. You know he hated the idea of us together."

Poor *Candice*. Simone's mother….

"Your father trafficked minors," I reminded her.

"Allegedly. He hasn't been charged with anything."

Because he was dead. Was she defending him?

"We were closing in on the case, but I guess not fast enough."

"You wouldn't have gotten him." She straightened and squared her shoulders. "He was calculating, and always twenty steps ahead. It took his death to free me."

I leaned in. "What about your uncles? How did you get out?"

"The murder distracted them, and I finally found my chance."

"And now? They're not looking for you?"

"Don't worry, Tristan, they won't touch me. I carry their last name."

I shifted in my chair and leaned back. The server brought the tapas board and a fresh drink as I took the last sip from my glass. That first buzz of relaxation I'd been expecting wasn't anywhere close. Simone, on the other hand, looked like she hadn't missed a second of life. From her caramel tan all the way to her manicured nails, I searched for traces of pain and stress, but couldn't see them. Then again, not all pain presented physical symptoms, and I knew that better than anyone.

"Dig in." I pointed to the food.

She poked a fork into the fried eggplant with honey and rosemary.

"What would have happened if he hadn't died?" I asked. "I mean, for fifteen years, no one knew you were alive. He must have had a plan."

Her gaze lowered to the plate. She searched over the eggplant as if it held all the answers, hesitating to take a forkful. When she looked up again, the shadow I thought I had seen on her face disappeared.

"If he had a plan, he never shared it with me." Her tone lifted, and I was glad we'd chosen a secluded area.

"Honestly, Tristan, his only plan was to make you suffer. That's all. But I would rather not talk about my father, and as hard as it may be, the sooner I can forget it all, the better. I want to leave the past where it belongs. Now that he's gone, I can move forward with my work."

"Work?"

She took a deep breath in and exhaled. My instinct awoke as I recognized the slow building smile. Hartley's plan might have died with him, but Simone's was definitely alive.

"I know things."

"What kinds of things?" I held her stare until the world around us disappeared and it was just the two of us, sharing secrets and making future plans. Almost like back in the day; but not quite. As I searched her eyes, I realized they weren't the same ones I remembered. Something had changed; if she thought she could hide the trauma, she was wrong.

"Things he's hidden and kept from the world. Houses, hideaways, paperwork."

All right. I couldn't deny she had me hooked.

"Everyone feared him. He had this company, registered under an LLC in Mauritius. Untraceable and unbreakable."

She was lying. I could tell. A familiar smile lifted the corner of her mouth. I remembered that cocky confidence from when she threw uncontrollable parties.

Her phone pinged, and I waited as she checked the notification. The wind blew, and Simone tucked her red hair behind the ear. I'd seen women leave their pimps, flee abusive relationships, and escape captivity more than I'd like to admit, and for someone who'd been held against her will for the past fifteen years, she sure looked good.

She set her phone on the table. Her cheekbones lifted, and eyes sparkled like she'd just won the lottery.

"Everything all right?" I asked.

"Wonderful, actually. The charity where I volunteer just received a donation."

"That's great. You're working already?"

"Figured I'd lost enough time." She shrugged half-heartedly, then leaned forward and reached across the table, taking my hands between hers. "Speaking of which, I wanted to know whether there's a possibility we could ever make up for that time as well."

I slowly removed my hands from hers and swallowed hard.

"Oh." She lowered her hands beneath the table. "I'm sorry. I should have realized you would have moved on."

I still couldn't believe she was alive and sitting in front of me. When I'd woken up this morning, Simone hadn't even run across my mind; and now she preoccupied most of its space. Not because I loved her — at least not like that. I cared for the woman I thought had died. My grief had healed with time, though, and I'd already let her go.

"Don't be so sad, Tristan. Now we have the chance to work together."

I dropped my fork and fumbled to pick it up. "What do you mean?"

"I heard Silver Securities has formed a new department." She smiled. "Your fight against human-trafficking inspired me to volunteer at Hope for Hope."

And there it was. That devious spark I remembered flamed in her eyes. Silver Securities worked directly with Hope for Hope, and it shouldn't have surprised me Simone would find a way inside my life—just like that.

"I figured I have expertise in the area, you know. I know what those women have gone through. I can help them."

"I'm sorry to tell you I'm not the one you'll be working with. The department has new staff."

"Great. I can't wait to meet them at the fundraiser next week."

"What?"

"The dinner you're organizing next Friday to bring aware-ness to women's causes? I'm one of Hope for Hope sponsors."

I leaned back in my chair. "You've been busy since Jeff died."

"I find it's better to lose yourself in work than dwell on what can't be fixed. I'd rather focus on the positives, where I can contribute and what I can control. And that's our future."

Our future?

Her stare bore through me, keeping me rooted in the spot until a seagull flew by.

I swirled the ice in my glass and checked my watch, even though I had no plans for the night other than to find Allie, get lost in her pussy, and forget this day ever happened.

"I'm sorry to cut this short, Tristan, but I have to leave. Duties call."

"You just buried your father."

I stood up alongside her. She searched through her purse for her car keys, and when she found them, she stepped closer and looked up.

"No, Tristan. My father died the day he chained me up. It's time for me to live, not mourn. I'll see you soon?"

"I'm happy to see you well, Simone."

"Me too, Tristan. Me too."

She lifted her toes and gently touched her mouth to mine, where she left a bitter taste.

Chapter 3

Allie

"I should be in bed." I screamed over the loud music, checking at my phone every five minutes as my hours of sleep ticked away.

Laura wrapped her arm around my waist. "The only bed you should be in is Tristan's, and since he's not available, you're stuck with us."

The girls from our force threw us a 'good luck' party – otherwise known as an excuse to go out – and the four of us had ended up at Kissed, Kendra's nightclub. She was still recovering, but Julian had asked me to take her out to the gun range sometime soon, so I knew she was progressing. I sat at the bar drinking soda while Laura sipped on a beer.

Our friends were dancing somewhere in the buzzing crowd. The music's tempo prompted a sequence of waves, followed by a lot of moves I didn't recognize. Jesus, how fast time changed. Above the dance floor, half-naked women in body paint swung on swings overhead, like pendulums. Metal cages stood tall near the dance floor corners. Inside, twisted limbs, twerking asses, and bodies that bent in ways I wished I could pull off in the bedroom, danced to the music. It was all very erotic and definitely didn't help my hormones. A deep yearning tightened in my stomach. I missed Tristan and wished he hadn't left the office early.

Further away, in the second cage, a sculpted hunk grazed his slick hands over a girl's body. Oil dripped off her as she lost herself to his touch. The bikini top barely covered her nipples, and her bottoms had found a hiding spot in her ass crack.

"I don't think this place is good for me. The hormones are driving me crazy."

"I know exactly what you mean."

"I thought things were great with James."

"His little girl's been getting sick. We haven't had much time together the past couple of weeks."

"Something serious?"

"I'm trying to figure that out. He's pretty closed off when it comes to her, which makes sense."

"This would be a great time to tell him about Foxy."

She sagged back in her seat, hands falling to her sides. "I want to help him, not give him a heart attack. I totally get why most single fathers are divorced."

"Why?"

"So they don't have to deal with our shit."

"Oh, stop it. He'll be elated. He'll hate you, but this could be the little bit of happiness he needs to get through whatever he's dealing with."

"Thanks, but it's not the right time—which you should understand."

"It will never be the right time. That's why I'm telling Tristan tonight."

"No, you have to wait right now."

"What?"

"Well, did you find out anything about the redhead?"

I rolled my eyes. "I should get a new best friend. You give the worst advice."

She lifted her two shots of tequila, one in each hand, and

brought them together. "To your health and mine, when the Silvers come after us."

Laura swung the first shot back, shook through the alcohol, and then the one I couldn't drink. I yawned, and Laura followed. "Stop that."

"I can't help it." I laughed. "I'm tired."

The song changed, and my arms prickled.

"If you're tired, come home with me." The deep voice startled me.

I whipped around and bumped into Tristan's hard chest. He looked at me from above. Water dripped down his face. The open leather jacket stretched over his shoulders was soaked. A memory flashed in my mind of the night he'd found me at the bar, drowning in a bottle of tequila. Wet hair stuck to his face, and his brown eyes darkened to the shade of desire. A desperate ache flashed through my body, and my nipples bunched.

I swallowed hard. "Jesus, what happened to you?"

"Come home with me."

I touched my palm to his chest. His heart was beating hard, and his breaths vibrated with a worry I hadn't felt before.

"Help me forget."

"Forget what?"

"Everything."

"Something happened?" I asked.

"Yes. But right now I need to lose myself inside you."

His invitation washed away a little bit of my worry and awoke all those hormones I'd been suppressing since this morning. I turned to Laura, who immediately waved me away.

"Go, be with your man. I can, obviously, handle the drinking for the two of us. You've been horny all day."

Tristan remained in his spot, staring into the distance. His slouched shoulders and clouded eyes revived my worry.

"Yeah, thanks. I don't expect I'm coming home tonight?"

Tristan shook his head.

I hugged Laura in a hurry and took Tristan's hand. He gripped my hand harder than usual and led me out the back door. I'd never seen him this way before. We stepped out into the pouring rain, and he pulled me hard into his body. He lowered his open mouth to mine, and I got lost in his need. The world disappeared from around us. His hard dick pressed against my belly, heating down to my groin. The sound of pouring rain mixed with the uneven pounding of his heart echoed in my ears. The deep kiss knocked me off my feet, and I could barely catch a breath when he pulled away.

"What happened?"

"Not now," he grunted, and opened the passenger door to his parked Bentley and ushered me in. Tristan hurried to the driver's seat and swerved out of the alley at full speed. I gripped the seat sides.

"Jesus, Tristan!"

His hold tightened on the wheel until the knuckles whitened. I hadn't seen him drive this fast before. Despite the high speed, he steered easily around other vehicles, paid attention to the road, and checked the side and rear-view mirrors. We passed every car in our way, and I realized that he could weave among them like a professional. It was rough and sexy and a total turn on.

"I'm a good driver." He broke the silence, and I turned my head his way.

"Of course, you are. Why would you say that?"

"It wasn't my fault."

"What wasn't your fault? What happened? Tristan, talk to me. Please? I'm worried."

But he shook his head. "I need you to help me forget. Please?"

We were stopped at a red light, and he turned his head toward me. The tears there definitely surprised me. I nodded in slow motion and lowered my hand to his grip over the gearshift. "Yes, of course. I'm here."

It felt like forever until we reached his building, parked, and took the elevator to his penthouse. All in silence. I removed my heels and turned around to meet his deprived mouth. He could barely get enough of me—not that I minded — but this raw desire was new and very unexpected. I pulled away.

"Hold on, babe. Let's get inside."

"You're reading my mind."

"No, no. I have a better idea."

"Nothing can be better than being inside you."

"How about I prove you wrong, Mr. Silver?" I playfully pushed at his chest and finally got his attention. His crooked smile elevated my heart rate. I sauntered past him and gripped him by the slack in his shirt. My hormones danced and tingled in all the right places. I removed his phone from his back pocket and guided him to the plush lounge chair, where he sat. I switched on the fireplace app, and the darkened room lit up. Cold shadows from a warm glow danced along the walls and furniture.

I grasped my tank top hem, pulled it over my head, and shimmied out of my jeans. Tristan took in the matching set of panties and bra.

"Wait, wait." I turned around and gave him a nice look at the back of my g-string as I strode to the hall where I slipped into my heels. I returned to the family room and then strolled the rest of the way in my best sexy imitation of what Portia had taught me on the street.

He sat open-mouthed. I gave him a smug look, lowered my gaze to his hard dick, and dropped to my knees.

"Are you ready for me, Mr. Silver?" I fluttered my lashes and drew my hands along his muscled thighs and over his straining erection. He straightened his legs, and I unfastened the bulging zipper. The tighter fit tested his patience, and he jerked on the pants, having difficulty to lower them.

I giggled.

He burst through the suppressed laugh but stopped as soon as my hand reached for his tented boxer-briefs. I watched his face and grasped his thick cock in my cold hand. Tristan's head fell back.

"Fuck."

"Not yet. Later. MTC care first."

"What?"

"You'll figure it out." I winked and eyed his thick cock with a grin, drawing my thumb over the predominant vein. A drop of pre-cum glistened on the cock's tip, and I licked over the cap with my full tongue.

He groaned and pushed higher, begging for more. I closed my lips around his crown, his hot rim right against my gums, and began the torturous up and down motion.

"Oh, God." His ragged voice was barely a whisper and hardened his breaths.

I looked up, and he leaned back in the lounge. I lowered my mouth to his base and then slid my tongue up his shaft before taking him again. His veins rippled under my lips. He gripped the blanket at the side. I controlled the rhythm and depth, teasing him with each suck. My grip tightened and my hand sped. My mouth sank deeper, and I lowered my other hand to his balls. When he pinched my nipple, I almost bit him, but didn't.

"You're indestructible."

He was playing with fire, but whatever the fuck I was didn't matter because the same hormones which organized my daily wet dreams were finally in their element. I sped up my strokes. He hit the back of my throat, and I realized I'd never enjoyed cock as much as now. Perfectly seasoned with estrogen, his cock tasted like pleasure. His hands lowered onto my shoulders and his fingers dug deeper into my skin, sending a plea for a quicker release. I lifted his balls higher in my palm, and his skin contracted. I tightened my lips around him, and he groaned.

"Fuck… Allie…"

He filled my mouth, and my pussy clenched. I milked every last drop from his dick, finally releasing him with a quiet pop. I reached for a tissue and wiped my mouth.

Tristan relaxed in the chair. The fireplace cast its orange glow over his naked chest. I watched his heavy breaths slow and yanked at his jeans, pulling them off him. The corner of his mouth lifted into a lazy grin as he stood up like Adonis. Still on my knees, I looked up at the glow of satisfaction on his face, plus more. And that more was enough to get me so horny, I couldn't wait to do it again.

"It wasn't supposed to be like that."

My brows furrowed. "You didn't like your mouth-to-cock care? You should file a complaint with the 'I don't give a fuck' department, because I know you loved every stroke and every suck."

"That was incredible." He lifted me to my feet and lowered his hand to my soaked pussy. The barely-there panties I wore were pointless at this point. Tristan must have thought the same because he pulled harder at one corner, breaking the fabric, then the other. The panties fell to the floor, leaving me naked in front of him. I lowered my bra cups and freed my aching breasts. I could only have pictured this moment better if I had already told him about the baby. And I would tell him, right after he fucked my brains out.

"I want to fuck you, but I can't," he said, like he couldn't read the hunger on my face.

My brows rose as I lowered my gaze to his stiff cock. "He disagrees."

Tristan laughed and gently touched the spot where my wound from the shooting was healing.

"We have to be careful." He skimmed his finger over the yellow skin. His smile faded when his hand grazed over my discolored ribs. The bruises from my fight with Jeffrey Hartley were nearly gone, but not yet.

"Between the shooting, your hospital stay, and the new department, I haven't had a chance to tell you about a charity fundraiser we're attending. We'll be serving the Hartleys that evening. Hopefully, we can get a quick trial."

"No, no, no, Mr. Silver." I wiggled my finger. "Tonight you're mine, and we're not discussing work or anything else other than how much I'm going to enjoy you until the morning. And vice versa. I need you and my body needs you and I know you need me too."

He lowered his mouth to my neck. I closed my eyes and followed the path his lips danced over my skin in my mind. Shivers scattered over my body. The three weeks without his touch had felt like forever.

"I missed you so much," I whispered.

His hot breath traced down through the valley between my breasts, but I didn't think he'd noticed. I froze as he lowered to my belly and kissed me there, but relaxed when he continued lower.

Oh, God.

But just as I was anticipating all his MTP care tricks, he stood up and lifted me into his arms. I wound my legs around him and bit my lip. Tristan walked across the room to the floor-to-ceiling windows overlooking Central Park. My heated body pressed against the glass, and I yelped. He lowered my feet to the floor. I stood with my back plastered against the window and in front of him, acutely aware of the exposure. It felt like forever passed before he stepped forward and kissed me again. The slow longing in his mouth shot just the right amount of limpness through my body. He held me against him, tracing his hands up and down my side curves before finally resting them on my tender breasts. They hadn't filled yet, but my pregnancy hormones made my nipples more sensitive than usual.

I closed my eyes, and Tristan kissed his way down my body, finally letting go of my breast when he reached my pussy. His lips hovered a breath away, skimming my clit.

"Tristan…" I breathed out his name low and heavy, and looked down to where his mouth curved with mischief.

"It's my turn." He smirked and dove for my pussy, licking over the slit. My ass and back pressed against the cold window.

"Someone's gonna see me."

"The only person who will ever see you come is me, Allie."

His tongue resumed the torturous strokes and I lost the will to argue, completely submitting to the passionate kisses he left below my belt. The perfect licks and sucks intensified until pleasure won over and I no longer cared whether anyone saw me. It took him seconds to bring me undone. My body fell into his hold, and he carried me to his bedroom, where I'd dreamt of a day when all the secrets I carried could be revealed.

Chapter 4

Tristan

I devoured her delicious pussy for three days straight and made love to her for three more. Her soft curves and pleasant moans drove me crazy and helped me forget exactly what I had to forget. But that also meant I hadn't told Allie that Simone was alive.

Sated, Allie had been sleeping in my bed since seven last night and it was already noon. I sat in the living room, facing the window, where her ass print reminded me of our first night here.

I stood up, stretched my arms out, and twisted my torso until my back cracked and released the pressure.

"Okay, Good evening, ladies and gentlemen." I paced alongside the window from one end of the room to the other. "I would like to thank you for joining me tonight at this once in a lifetime event….no, that's wrong… Thank you for joining me tonight and for your generous contributions…. that's not right either."

I fucking wished I could just skip to the part where I served the lawsuit to the Hartley brothers.

Allie tiptoed from behind me and glued herself to my back. "Are you practicing for tonight?"

"You're awake." I turned around. Her pebbled nipples grazed against my skin.

"I slept like a rock."

"You're still recovering."

"Are you surprised? You have a vicious mouth and a hard dick all the time." She giggled and bit her lip. "Don't I have to go to work?"

"You start Monday."

She grinned and wiggled her brows. "Sleeping with the boss is finally paying off."

"It's nice to have you here, Allie, and since we're out of the office, I prefer boyfriend."

"Sleeping with your boyfriend doesn't sound as exciting." Her gaze fell and she hopped up on the couch, where she sat cross-legged. Her perky nipples poked through the t-shirt she was wearing, *my t-shirt,* and what appeared to be a pair of my boxer briefs. Allie was as wild a woman out of uniform as in one. It would be impossible to keep my hands off her during lunch hour.

"Are you wearing my underwear?" I asked.

"I've been wearing your underwear for six days. But don't worry—I changed them daily."

It's been almost a week?

"How have I not noticed?"

"Because I've been naked ninety-nine percent of the time. Speaking of which, I should get back home."

"Why?"

"Because that's where I live."

"No. You'll live here. It'll be a longer commute to work from Long Island." My brows furrowed. Unfortunately the same would be true if Allie moved to our new house I had yet to tell her about. If I couldn't get her to stay here, how would she agree to live in Oyster Bay Cove? I sighed.

"I'm a Long Island kind of girl, you know. I enjoy my train

rides and the sound of my thoughts. Manhattan is work and play. Long Island is home. I'd like to keep work separate from life. Something you could practice more often, Mr. Silver."

Did that mean she would consider moving to the new house I'd bought?

"Would you live with me on Long Island if my penthouse were there?"

"The odds are in your favor, but please don't go buying condos on Long Island."

I chuckled and decided to wait to tell her about the house. Better yet, I'd take her there and hand her the keys. There was no way she'd say no to a house on the cove, next to my family. The renovations were underway and would be complete in a couple of weeks. "Okay, no condos."

"Go on with your speech. I want to hear it."

"All right." I cleared my throat and stood in front of her, pretending she was the audience. "Good evening, ladies and gentlemen. Thank you for joining me for tonight's fundraiser. Your company and your support is greatly appreciated and will never be forgotten."

She snickered.

"What's so funny?"

She covered her mouth with one hand and pointed at me with the other.

"You look like you're about to deep-throat."

"What?"

"The way you hold your hand in front of your mouth."

"That's a microphone."

"I don't see a microphone. All I see is a dick in your fist."

"Come here." I lunged her way and pinned her on the couch before she could get away. She squealed in my grip, and I shut her mouth with mine. A desperate whimper escaped between her lips and I broke the kiss, skimming my finger over her brow.

"I'm so madly in love with you, Allie Green."

Her head lifted and she kissed me. "I love you too, Tristan."

She shimmied out of my boxer briefs and I lowered my jogging pants. Her legs parted, exposing her sleek and ready pussy. I hovered above her, centered, and slipped the tip of my cock an inch inside her.

"How do you want it, Ms. Green?"

The freckles on her face pushed past the brighter tint on her cheeks.

"I want it nice and slow, Mr. Silver. I want some PTC care."

I frowned.

"Pussy to cock, penis to cooze. It doesn't matter what you want to call it. I just need you."

She wrapped herself around me, pushing her heels into my ass until I sank deep inside her.

"Ahh…" she exhaled. "Just like that."

I kissed her hard and rolled my hips with every forward move. Her breaths shortened, but I couldn't stop kissing her. She turned her head sideways, dodging the fervent need on my lips.

"Are you all right?" she asked.

"Perfect."

She looked like a fucking goddess below me. Battered yet unscathed and strong. Her trustworthy eyes and heart had never failed me.

"I love you." I groaned and pushed deeper and quicker, grazing against her clit, watching her eyes watch mine in wonderment.

Where had she been all my life?

My next thrust sent her flying upward on the couch, and she gasped. Her mouth opened and lifted at the corner while her full breasts bounced underneath my t-shirt. I drove harder on the next one, and she whimpered. I finally found a steady pace, but that same steady pace threatened to betray me. I pulled out, and Allie's eyes flew wide open.

"What's the matter?"

"Patience, baby. Patience." I gripped my cock in my hand and slapped the head over her clit.

"Ahh!" Her lips parted. She absolutely glowed.

I slapped her clit repeatedly and watched her eyes roll back. Her pussy swelled underneath the assault, and I rubbed my thumb over her engorged lips until she positioned herself underneath my finger, begging me to get her off. So I did.

I hooked a finger inside her and rubbed on the upper wall. Her ass clenched and her mouth opened. She writhed underneath my touch, hair wild and skin flushed. Beautiful, loyal, and smart. I lowered my other hand to the swollen need between her thighs and massaged her pussy lips, brushing back and forth over her clit. The first shudder of pleasure spiked through her body, and my mouth went for the kill. I lowered my head between her legs, pushed on that spot with my finger inside her, and strummed my tongue over the protruding nub until she squirted.

"Jesus!" She screamed and opened her eyes in shock. "What was that?"

"Relax, Allie, you're about to cum."

I forced her down with one hand but she insisted. "I want to see."

"You want to watch me eat you out?"

She bit her lip, and I went back to her pussy. Three tongue strokes later, the orgasm consumed her. She shook underneath me, her body spasming and pussy pulsing in my mouth like a ripened fruit. She fell limply to the couch, and we stayed like that until I nuzzled my nose in the crook of her neck, and she turned to face me.

"Are you really going to out the Hartleys like that at the fundraiser?"

I nodded. "We've been waiting to do this for a long time."

"You don't look ready."

I ran my hand through my hair. "Why would you say that?"

"I don't know. It's just a hunch. Something's holding you back."

My forehead crinkled. "There is actually something I need to talk to you about."

My phone rang with Simone's old number, and my focus flew from the screen to Allie and back to the screen again.

"I'm sorry. I have to get this."

"Of course. I'll go shower." Allie hurried to the bathroom, and I waited until the shower turned on. I returned the missed call.

"Tristan, good morning," Simone chirped.

"You have your old phone?"

"New phone, old number. I was hoping we could meet up at my house to talk."

"What can I do for you, Simone?"

"Meet me at the Hartley cove house."

"Your father's house?"

She'd loved the house across the cove from my parents and had hoped her father would gift it to her one day. That was before the tragedy. Frank Wagner, the patriarch of the law firm, got the Hartleys out of trouble one last time—something about a favor he owed. The Hartleys turned after then: dirt surfaced in the media, the Hartleys accused their lawyers of leaking personal information, and the war began. The media angled the fight from a comedic angle. In truth, the Wagner brothers had so much more on their shoulders. But nobody's family was perfect. Everybody had problems; just different levels of problems.

"Tristan, are you even listening to me? Father left me the cove house in his will."

My gut turned each time Simone mentioned her father.

"Tonight's the fundraiser, remember?"

"Oh, right. How could I forget?"

I was certain she hadn't.

"Maybe we could meet up on Monday? Today's a busy day."

"Monday sounds great. I'll see you tonight."

"See you."

By the time I finished, the shower stopped running. I paced to the bathroom where I found Allie dressed in jeans and a cropped sweater. "I have an appointment at Grace's salon. She's doing my hair and everything else. I'm not sure what that means, but it sounded like it would take a while."

Grace Wagner owned an award-winning beauty salon, and it showed by her lack of time and long waiting list. But family members had their perks. Allie and Grace had become best friends ever since Emma introduced them.

I leaned against the doorframe. "Something tells me there's more."

"My dress is at the apartment."

"I'll have it picked up for you."

"How about we play a little game, Mr. Silver? I know you have a busy day ahead. Why don't I meet you there? I can come with Laura."

"I'll have a limo sent your way ahead."

"We can drive."

"I'd prefer you took a limo over Laura's Wrangler. The event is important."

"Sounds good. I'll see you tonight." She stepped up on her toes, kissed me on the cheek, and disappeared out the door.

MY FAMILY GREETED the guests near the entrance. Almost all the Silvers lined the foyer. The Wagner brothers, our company lawyers and partners, stood nearby. Cameras flashed, and the bright spotlights blinded me. I could barely tell who had arrived. Chad and Craig Hartley, Jeffrey's brothers, had showed up half an hour ago with their nephews. Silver Securities had announced the sponsored event in the media, and the affair felt like a royal wedding.

Everyone and anyone noteworthy had purchased a ticket in support of Hope for Hope, including Simone: New York's newly resurrected citizen. She sauntered toward me in her sparkling evening gown. Diamonds covered the thin strips of fabric hanging over her body, which didn't leave much to the imagination. Strategically sewn gems concealed her nipples, ass crack, and crotch. She looked like a fucking Jessica Rabbit in diamonds and stole the room.

"Hello, Tristan."

"Simone. You look stunning." I kissed her hand. "Thank you for your support."

"Thank me later when you hear what I've got for you."

I rubbed the back of my neck. In a matter of seconds, we became the room's focal point. Sweat dripped down my spine. I'd hoped to tell Allie about Simone already, but the subject of my dead fiancée coming back to life somehow never came up.

"Of course. Let me walk you inside."

She hooked her hand into my offered arm and we crossed the foyer, swerving into the side hall just before the ballroom entrance.

I stopped. "Are you all right, Simone?"

"Yes, but I have something urgent to ask of you."

"What do you mean?"

"You can't serve my uncles tonight."

"What?"

"It's not the right time, Tristan. I have information. On everything and everyone. And I'm willing to share it." She breathed heavily.

I gripped her by the arms, not meaning to be harsh. "What are you doing, Simone?"

She stepped forward, the bare toes in her high heel sandals touched mine, and her entire body challenged me. What the fuck was happening here?

"Do not serve the Hartleys tonight. They're ready for you, but I don't think you're ready for them."

"How do you even know we're going to serve them?"

"I had a hunch, but you just confirmed it."

Fuck.

"I'm not playing games, Simone. You know exactly who your uncles are, and somebody's got to pay. Your father held you captive."

"Well, I wouldn't call it captive."

"What?"

I had no time or patience for this conversation, but I certainly wasn't prepared to walk away either. "I don't understand."

"Wright snitched to the FBI, and they'll kill him before you take your seat in court. My uncles have no idea I know."

"Are you in danger?"

"I don't think so."

I sighed and removed her hand from my arm, but she reached back and squeezed my palm.

"Thank you, Tristan." Her sultry whisper carried a hint of satisfaction.

This was madness. The evening was not starting out on the right note.

Fucking Simone and her cryptic information.

Simone stepped up on her toes, kissed the corner of my mouth, and slowly let go of my hand.

"I'll see you inside. I can find my seat," she whispered against my lips. Then she turned around and left me stunned.

"Ahem."

Someone cleared their throat, and I whipped around. Allie was standing beside Laura with her arms crossed in front of her. Her dazzling silver gown, which outlined her every curve, did not match the disappointment in her eyes.

"Allie? What are you doing here?"

"Apparently I'm watching another woman flirt with my boyfriend."

"I'm sorry. That was one of the sponsors for Hope for Hope." I gave her half truth. Maybe a quarter truth.

"Do all your sponsors kiss you like that?"

"No, of course not. She… Ahm…"

"I'll leave you two alone." Laura threw me a dirty look and left.

"Allie, I've been meaning to tell you this earlier, but honestly I haven't been able to come to terms with the news myself."

Her posture perked up.

"That was Simone."

Her brows drew together, and I waited until she made the connection.

"As in Simone Hartley? Your dead fiancée?"

"Not so dead anymore. It's a long story."

"Obviously too long to have mentioned earlier."

"I'm sorry."

My head whipped to the ballroom at the ten-minute warning bell. My speech was scheduled prior to dinner.

"You have to go." She straightened my bowtie, and I breathed out a wave of nerves. "You have a busy evening, Tristan. We can talk later."

"Are you sure?"

"Yes, of course. Tonight's important. We can't let Hope for Hope down. Good luck on your speech."

Allie lifted for a quick peck on my cheek, wrapped her arms around me, and pressed herself to my chest. I kissed the top of her head and inhaled her scent. My nerves calmed. Her ear rested over my heart.

"Thank you for understanding. She took me by surprise."

"Does she know you're taken?" She looked up, then shut her eyes. "You know what, it doesn't matter. Hurry or you'll be late. I'll see you at the table."

Truth was, Simone had ambushed me.

Allie pulled away, turned on her heel, and left. The three-minute warning bell rang, and I hurried to the side stage, where Greg was waiting for me with cue cards in his hands.

"What's this?"

"Last minute addition. I got it from the stage manager. He said it's a thank you to our one-million-dollar sponsor."

"One million?"

He nodded.

"And that?" I pointed to the compact in his palm.

"You're shiny. Close your eyes." He powdered my nose and forehead.

"Thanks."

"Thirty seconds, Mr. Silver." The stage manager motioned, and I acknowledged.

The tension in my shoulders wound into tight knots as I walked forward. A few heads turned to the stage. The bright lights heated from above, and I hoped Greg's powder wouldn't turn into paste on my face.

I tapped the microphone. "Good evening, ladies and gentlemen."

The room fell quiet.

"It gives me great pleasure to welcome you to tonight's fundraiser. Silver Securities has been proud to sponsor Hope for Hope's for the last ten years. We've watched the foundation grow, fight, and prevail through challenging times, and most importantly, we've been able to provide direct assistance to the cause. Thank you for your generous donations and for joining us. Your support frees many from violence and oppression." I flipped the cue card Greg had given me and read, "A special thank you goes out to Simone Hartley from the Hartley Foundation, for their one-million-dollar donation to Hope for Hope."

Fuck me.

Chapter 5

Allie

"We're going to be late." I hurried down the sidewalk. By the time Laura was ready, we were fifteen minutes behind schedule, and rush hour had begun. The limo driver dropped us off at the building's side, avoiding the long line of other limos. I still couldn't understand how spending money on expensive venues and food was better than giving that money directly to the cause. Then again, I wasn't a billionaire.

"It's not my fault."

"I'm not saying it is. I just don't like being late."

Neither did Laura, but we had no time to dissect her earlier breakdown at home. We made it to the building's side entrance, but it was locked.

"What now?" I looked around. The front entrance would take too long. "Kitchen door. There must be, at least, one open in the back."

We lifted our gowns knee high and walked up to a guy in a chef's hat, who was vaping outside.

"Allie? Is that you?" I froze at the familiar voice I hadn't heard in years. He was older, but still wore the same kind smile I remembered.

"Cameron?"

"Who's Cameron?" Laura whispered.

"Camelot Cameron," I said between my teeth. I hadn't seen the man who'd taken my virginity since the night we'd agreed to the deed because neither one of us wanted to finish high school a virgin. So we'd hooked up on our senior trip to England.

"Oh, hi." Laura's awkward wave had me rolling my eyes.

"What are you doing here?" we asked at the same time and in that nerdy way.

"I'm the sous-chef. Looks like you'll be enjoying my food tonight. You look great."

"Thank you. I work with the sponsored charity. Hope for Hope."

"It's a great cause."

"It is. We're running a little bit late, actually. Do you mind if we sneak through the back?"

Cameron opened the back door and held it for us. "I'll do you one better and show you a shortcut."

A delicious aroma wafted through the kitchen, and my stomach rumbled. "So you finished culinary school after all?"

"And pastry. Let me guess. You're a cop?" he asked.

"Yeah, something along those lines. Please tell me you're not single."

He lifted his left hand and wiggled the ring finger. "Two years married and going strong with one-year-old twins."

"Aww, congratulations."

"Thanks. Are you expecting?"

"What?"

"You're not? I'm sorry, I shouldn't have said anything. It's just the way you're holding your stomach—"

"I am expecting. No need to apologize," I said.

"Take the second right, then left. The hall will lead you to the main entrance."

"Thanks, Cameron."

"And I highly recommend the lamb for dinner. It was lovely seeing you again, Allie. Have a great evening."

"You as well. Thank you."

He winked before leaving.

Laura elbowed me in the side. "What was that about?"

"What?"

"The flirting."

"There was no flirting. We were good friends."

"Friends with benefits."

"No. Friends with one benefit. It happened once, and we both promised to never talk about the awkward night, so I'd appreciate it if I didn't have to talk about it with you either. Now let's find the Silvers."

We stopped before the turn. The sound of soft jazz played overhead.

"We're going to make it." Laura tiptoed in place while I fixed her hair. She absolutely rocked the couture suit. The front was taped to her skin in a *V* all the way down to her navel.

"Okay. It's all good. You look stunning."

"I think tonight is the night I'll tell James about Foxy."

"Really?"

"Yes. You were right. He deserves to know."

"You should. You two have been meant to be since Colorado."

"Fifty percent of couples who fall apart get another chance. Hopefully, we're on the right side."

A warning bell rang overhead. We had only a few minutes left. Suddenly we stopped. My body went cold as I took in the image in front of me. I stood frozen in my spot, afraid to move and spook Tristan and the redhead. Laura stayed silent beside me. They were standing face to face, legs, their chests and hands touching. Tristan stood rigid as she clung to his body.

"That's the redhead," Laura whispered.

No shit.

Her snaky fingers rubbed over his hands, and the revealing gown held my attention. She dragged her hands up his arms and stood up on her toes, kissing him.

"Eww gross," Laura blabbered. "Make sure you bleach his mouth."

I didn't find her joke funny, and my heart dropped into my stomach, right above where my Baby Puss nestled in my uterus. My knees wobbled as the woman turned to the main entrance and left. I marched over the thick carpeting, heels digging in.

"Ahem." I cleared my throat, and Tristan turned around. For the first time since I'd met him, he stared at me like a deer caught in the headlights. Worse yet, his eyes filled with not only fear but also worry.

"Allie? What are you doing here?"

"Apparently I'm watching another woman flirt with my boyfriend."

"I'm sorry. That was one of the sponsors for Hope for Hope." He pointed to where the woman had left.

"Do all your sponsors kiss you like that?" Laura frowned.

I whipped my head to Laura.

"No, of course, not. She… Ahm…"

"I'll leave you two alone." My best friend eyed him from the bottom up and back down before leaving.

"Allie, I've been meaning to tell you this earlier, but honestly I haven't been able to come to terms with the news myself."

My nose wrinkled, and I straightened.

"That was Simone." His shoulders dropped.

My mind raced, searching for the name until I hit it, face first. "As in Simone Hartley? Your dead fiancée?"

"Not so dead anymore. It's a long story." His sidelong glances to the ballroom gave me the shivers.

"Obviously too long to have mentioned earlier." I crossed

my arms over my chest.

"I'm sorry."

The warning bell rang again, and Tristan adjusted his tuxedo.

"You have to go." I reached up and straightened his bowtie. "You have a busy evening, Tristan. I don't want to keep you here. We can talk later."

Sweat glistened on his forehead. I removed a tissue from my purse and wiped it off.

"Are you sure?"

"Yes, of course. Tonight's important. We can't let Hope for Hope down. Good luck on your speech."

I kissed him lightly on the cheek for reassurance. I hugged him right back underneath his arms and pressed harder. When he broke the heated kiss, he nuzzled his nose into my hair and inhaled. I pressed my cheek over his chest and listened to the calmer beating.

"Thank you for understanding. She took me by surprise."

"Does she know you're taken?" I looked up, then shut my eyes. "You know what, it doesn't matter. Hurry or you'll be late. I'll see you at the table."

I turned around and didn't look back. I couldn't because if I did, I'd break. Instead, I held my head high and boobs even higher, concentrating on the glamour around me. Gowns glittered, jewels sparkled, and the men looked like a family of lost penguins. I needed tequila, but I couldn't have any. When I caught up to Laura by the bar, she handed me a glass of sparkling water.

"Thank you. You were right about the redhead. That was his dead fiancée."

"Come again?"

"You heard me right. Simone Hartley."

"WTF."

"I know. He said she surprised him."

"I bet she did."

I eyed the table where Simone was greeting some people I thought were her family. Tristan planned to serve them tonight. The Hartleys had played a heavy role in last month's auction.

"I was going to tell him about my pregnancy tonight."

"Was?" Laura asked.

"I think I should wait until the first trimester passes. You know, for the baby's health. He has a lot on his mind as it is."

"Shit, Allie. Are you sure you want to do that?"

"The first trimester's only a month away. It's not like I'm keeping his two-year-old son from him."

"Touché."

"Sorry. You know what? I'm not sorry. I passed you pissing cups and toilet paper, and the day Foxy was born I saw things no best friend should see. It's your turn to be there for me. I'm telling Tristan when I'm ready. On my terms. It will be the perfect Christmas gift."

"All right. I'm with you, babe."

"How's the other Silver table?"

"As distraught about the evening as your table. Teresa's on her third glass of wine, Jacob resumed smoking and James thinks Silver Securities is at risk. Did you know the trifecta had a pact with the Hartleys?"

"No. Where did you hear that?"

"From my Bond." She giggled. "The one who hasn't figured out I'm hiding his son. I'm gonna tell him about Foxy tonight. I mean, I have to, right?"

I smiled. "You should. He'll be ecstatic."

"Or he'll kill me."

"Well, then he'll have to deal with a vengeful best friend. Teresa Silver is waving at me. At least, she adores Foxy. I think she may know."

"She's pretty smart. She probably does.

"Funny."

I gave Laura a quick hug and crossed the room to the table at the front.

"Hey, how are you?"

I kissed Wilma on her cheek.

"I would be better if she remained dead." Tristan's mother grumbled under her breath, leaned back in the chair and eyed the Hartleys.

What?

Tristan's father stood up from the table, embraced me, and kissed the top of my head. My heart warmed and nerves settled.

"Your seat's beside mine." Emma pushed the chair away from the table, making room.

"Thanks."

Julian sat across from me, beside a man about my age whom I didn't recognize.

Emma leaned in to my side. "Allie Green, meet Eric Waters. He's a family friend." She grinned.

I reached over the table and shook his hand. "It's nice to meet you."

"You as well."

"Eric just finished a tour in Afghanistan." Wilma beamed from ear to ear, like he were one of the Silvers.

"Thank you for your service." I said.

Another warning bell chimed, and the room fell quiet.

"They're best friends." Emma whispered.

"Who?"

"My brothers and Eric."

"Oh, okay."

"And he's a cowboy." Her dreamy tone matched the mellow in her eyes. She rested her chin in her hand, leaning on the table.

"Sit up, Ems, or he'll notice," I whispered.

She straightened her back and squared her shoulders.

"You're not taking the empty seat beside him?"

"Nah, I get a better view this way. Who knows when I'll see him again?"

"Isn't he a little old for you?"

"Ten years is not a lot. Tristan's older than you by much more."

Right.

"I'm not saying he's ready for me right now, but he will be one day."

"Feels like I've been meeting a lot of your brother's friends lately."

"Who else have you met?"

"Unofficially, Simone Hartley." I pointed to the woman at a table on the other side of the room.

Everyone's head turned in a wave. By then, Tristan had walked out on the stage, and their attention wavered from Simone's table to him.

Tristan tapped the microphone.

"Good evening, ladies and gentlemen. It gives me great pleasure to welcome you to tonight's fundraiser. Silver Securities has been Hope for Hope's proud sponsor for the past ten years. We've watched the foundation grow, fight and conquer through challenging times, and most importantly, we've been able to provide direct assistance to the cause. Thank you for your generous donations and for joining us. Your support frees many from violence and oppression."

Wilma beamed with pride as she looked at her son, stage front. I doubted she'd heard a word he said. Fred's focus remained on the Hartley table, his stare hard and cold.

Tristan flipped a cue card he held in his hands and continued. "A special thank you goes out to Simone Hartley from the Hartley Foundation, for their one-million-dollar donation to Hope for Hope."

The Hartley table broke out in applause, but the sentiment wasn't shared where I was sitting.

My gaze skidded to Simone Hartley. How could someone come back to life fifteen years later? And with so much triumph?

Why now?

Tristan rarely mentioned their past, though Wilma had filled me in on the accident's details. Hartley hadn't let him say goodbye, and Tristan didn't work for a year afterward. He left to Austria, where they had a vacation home in the Alps, and grieved.

"Please enjoy tonight's entertainment, food, and drink. Bon appétit." He finished his welcome, applause exploded, and I watched Simone watch him with the kind of intensity that made me uncomfortable.

Oh, my God!

I covered my mouth with my hand. She wanted him, and she'd stop at nothing to get him.

Tristan walked off the stage and joined us at the table soon after. The servers busied themselves pouring wine and champagne.

"Tristan, what's going on?" his father asked.

"The evening has gone to shits, that's what's going on." He loosened the bow tie around his neck. "The Hartleys found out Wright snitched, and they'll kill him if we proceed. We have to find the bastard before serving them."

"I'm fine if Wright dies." I leaned back in my chair.

"If he dies, we have no defense for Kendra."

"Then we should find more defense," Julian growled.

"Isn't anyone going to mention the fact the bitch is alive?"

Everyone at the table turned Julian's way. Kendra was still in rehab and staying away from family events. His brows furrowed and nostrils flared. Tonight was the first time I'd had any indication Tristan's beloved and dead fiancée wasn't the angel I'd made her out to be in my head. And not so ethereal, either.

Emma gently elbowed me in the ribs, and I whispered, "Be careful. Baby on board." I doubted Tristan would hear anything anyone said because he was staring at the Hartleys as well.

"Well, this sure took a turn." Emma chuckled. "I bet nothing this exciting happens in your neck of the woods, does it, Eric?"

The man shifted at Emma's love-struck puppy look.

"Can everyone please calm down?" Wilma tapped a fork on her wine glass. "You're all sitting like stiffs, gawking like amateurs, and making a scene. Now, let's celebrate the success of this fundraiser and discuss the rest in private."

"Tristan?" his father asked. "What do you know?"

"Hartley kept her captive, and she's grateful he was murdered. Wright snitched to the FBI. Jeff's brothers have him and will kill him if we serve them. That's pretty much all I could get out of her. She's Hope for Hope's sponsor now." He rolled his eyes. "And I fucking have a feeling more's coming."

"I guess we know the woman from Magnet. Big hat, big glasses, bigger boobs, and Botoxed face, as Walter said. Sound familiar?" Julian finished his champagne and turned to Eric. "Sorry you have to be part of this drama, buddy."

This crack in the Silver family was new. Simone Hartley singlehandedly unnerved every single person at the table, including me. Well, maybe not Eric.

"There's no drama like family drama. You should see our Sunday dinners at the ranch."

I forced out a laugh. Emma proceeded to ask Eric all sorts of horse-related questions while I lowered my hand to Tristan's leg underneath the table, smoothing over his strained thigh.

"This was planned. Her return, the new found love for philanthropy, and one-million-dollar donation were all planned."

"The Hartleys eat that for breakfast, but it's shady as fuck." Julian cracked his knuckles.

"Sounds like work for a private investigator." Emma perked up.

"Jesus, Emma. You're fourteen. This is serious business."

"Why does everyone keep saying that? I'll be fifteen on New Years day."

"Emma's right." Everyone's attention darted to Eric. "You should investigate it. But tonight you should celebrate the success you've all achieved. It doesn't come without a price." His gaze shifted to the Hartleys. "But imagine the world without your work."

The silence stretched across the table. Fred lifted his glass in a toast, and I had no choice but to lift mine along with everyone else.

"May Silver Securities shine brighter and throw more motherfuckers behind bars than it has till now."

My mouth dropped open, Emma laughed, Wilma rolled her eyes, and the brothers replied at the same time, "Amen!"

Everyone sipped on their champagne while I lowered my glass to the table.

"You can have that," Emma whispered with a snicker. "It's non-alcoholic."

"Seriously?"

"I filled your glass with the one I snuck under the table."

"Emma—"

"You're welcome."

I felt Tristan's attention shift my way and rubbed my hand over his palm. "Are you okay?"

"I feel like someone's pranked me."

"Is that someone Simone?"

"She ambushed me in that hallway."

"Today should be a good day, Tristan. Hope for Hope has enough funds to operate for years. The Hartleys can't turn back all your hard work."

"Thank you. I'm sorry. You're right. Today *is* a good day."

He refilled everyone's champagne glass except mine, which was still full "Are you not drinking?"

"Nothing hard tonight. To Hope for Hope."

I lifted the glass and tipped it back. The apple cider, identical in color to champagne, fizzed along my tongue. "But I do need to use the ladies room. Will you excuse me?"

I pushed my chair back and kissed Tristan on the cheek, hoping he wouldn't notice I'd left for the bathroom right after Simone stood from her table. I didn't notice when Emma left our table either because she headed for the bathroom door twenty feet ahead of me. She held a linen napkin in her hand and concealed her face before entering.

"What are you doing Ems?" I weaved between the last three tables and made a bee-line for the bathroom door.

Simone was standing in front of the mirror, reapplying her lipstick. She stopped and turned my way as soon as I entered.

"I've been wondering when we'd meet."

The comment took me aback, and I went completely still. Her cheekbones lifted.

"Allie Green. Tristan's girlfriend."

She tilted her head while I waited for the awkward moment to pass. The five stalls in the bathroom had their doors open, and Emma was nowhere in sight.

"Then you must know I'm Simone, his fiancée."

She was around Tristan's age, but looked gorgeous. My heart beat a little faster. Not only did she look beautiful, but my freckles had nothing on hers.

"I pictured you a little more—"

"Dead?" Her shoulder lifted with sass. "That's what my grave says, but not everything you see should be believed."

Her focus returned to her reflection. She over-lined her lips with Jessica Rabbit red. It matched her hair.

"I can't deny I'm shocked you're alive," I stuttered.

She lowered the liner to her pouch and removed a lipstick. "Thank you. My father was a bastard and spared no mercy."

"I'm sorry. Thank you for your kind donation to Hope for Hope."

"It was my pleasure. Tristan always had a heart for the underprivileged." She looked me over, up and down, and my stomach tightened.

"I—"

"My father's captivity taught me the importance of helping. His wrath is done."

As much as it would be nice to apologize for killing the bastard, the voice inside me said to keep my dumb mouth shut. Exactly like that. So I did.

She finished with the lipstick and turned away from the mirror, facing me. "So, what are we going to do about our Tristan situation?"

"What do you mean?"

"He can't have a fiancée and a girlfriend at the same time." The over-confident, powerful smirk trickled with territorial aggression. I gathered my thoughts, but Simone was quicker.

"I'm kidding." She waved her hand. She did that a lot. "Obviously, our engagement expired when my father kidnapped me."

Ya think?

"But I would love to get to know you. I think we have a mutual friend, Marissa."

How did she know about Marissa? Tristan certainly wouldn't have disclosed such information; but Wright would.

My heart stopped. "Marissa?" *The missing girl from the auction.* "Do you know where she is?"

She laughed. "Well, of course, I do. I saw her when I visited Hope for Hope."

"Oh."

"Our charity has a lot in common with Hope for Hope. I

was going to actually talk to Tristan about working together, but maybe you're the better person to speak with?"

Maybe I was wrong about Wright; and oh, so wrong about Simone. I could see why she was a handful.

"That's wonderful. So she's safe? She's not with this this middle-aged man?"

"She looked well to me."

"Good. That's great."

We stood in an awkward pause for what felt like forever. If there was anything I'd learned in life and my line of work, it was to keep your enemies closer than your friends. Although I wasn't sure which category Simone belonged to just yet, I decided it was wise to get to know her.

"Do you shoot guns?" I asked.

"No," she laughed.

"I go to a range with a friend. You should join us. It's fun."

"My definition of fun usually involves shopping malls, but I'm always game to try something new."

I scratched my cheek. Simone removed a card from her clutch and handed it to me. I turned the card from her name and phone number to a black infinity symbol on a white background.

"You've had time to set up a company?"

"It's a non-profit. Infinity helps women leave dangerous environments and relationships. Our program ensures they're safe forever. We have a lot in common with Hope for Hope. I was actually going to talk to Tristan about working together, but maybe you're the better person to speak with?"

I steadied my shaking hand and removed my card from my clutch. The prenatal bottle and my strawberry lip gloss rolled onto the counter. I quickly stuffed them back inside, hoping Simone hadn't noticed.

"Yes, it looks like we have a lot in common," I said.

"Wonderful. I should go. My brothers aren't happy with this

philanthropic journey of mine, but I figured my father's death and this new life is my new chance to get back everything I lost. So why listen to them?"

Cold shivers ran down my spine. Why did it feel like she was including Tristan in the *everything*?

"Right. Well, call me. We'll set the details for the meeting."

As soon as Simone left, a stall door opened.

"Emma?" I didn't think anyone was here.

"I stood on the toilet."

"Why did you eavesdrop, Ems?"

"Because my gut told me to follow that woman into the bathroom as soon as the commotion started. I never met her, but I heard she's caused a lot of drama in my family. Her father didn't like Tristan, but my parents never liked her either."

"Oh, Ems, I don't want you involved in this. It looks—"

"Dangerous? Should a pregnant woman be working alone?"

"I need you to hold onto that baby secret a bit longer for me. At least, until I figure out Simone's intention."

"I can find out stuff. What do you need?"

My brows lifted. "Maybe you should stay away from this one?"

Simone was Hartley's daughter, and I couldn't underestimate the name she carried.

"Nobody's gonna know. I promise. I can start with medical records. We already know those are easy. And then we can go from there."

I bit my lip. "All right. Do it. But this is top secret."

She grinned. "I excel at top secret."

We left the bathroom separately, and when I returned to my table, Simone was sitting in my chair, chatting with Tristan. Wilma had her arms crossed over her chest, Fred was frowning like he owned a trademark for the look, Julian had disappeared somewhere with Eric, and I had the urge to strangle somebody.

Chapter 6

Tristan

Simone fled the table before Allie returned. The dinner had barely passed down my throat. The lights had dimmed, and we were swaying on the dance floor to soft jazz. I held Allie close to my chest. While the fundraiser had been a success, there would be nothing easy about working with Simone Hartley. I hadn't seen her since the ambush in the hallway and she'd tricked the stage manager into giving me the cue card.

Allie's finger smoothed over my chest. "Are you okay?"

I looked down at her soft cheeks and freckled face. "Honestly? No."

She pouted. "I wish I could do something to help."

"You can. Just stay with me."

"How about some fresh air?"

I stopped and removed her hand from my chest, slipping it into my palm. "Best idea I've heard all day. Come on."

I crossed the hall to the adjoining empty ballroom, which had a balcony on the other side of the building.

"Are we allowed here?" she asked.

"Where's the brave cop I met at a burned strip club orgy?"

"I hope that's not the story you're going to tell our children." Her voice broke with nerves.

"How about I tell them I met their mother saving people from a burned building?"

"That's a half-truth."

I pulled open the balcony door. "How about we don't mention it unless they ask? Or we could make up a story how I met you at a ball. I saw your green eyes across the room and you spun in a beautiful gown, like a princess."

We stepped out onto the balcony overlooking Central Park. A gust of cold air blew by, and Allie shivered.

"Now, that's just telling fairytales."

I removed my jacket and draped it over her shoulders. "Nothing wrong with fairytales."

She leaned on the railing, smiling. "It's beautiful out here. Nice and quiet." She yawned.

"Tired already?"

"I had an early day with Laura. We went over a case, and… well… I think she's going through stuff with James."

"I had no idea. She's told him about Fox?"

"Not yet, but she's planning to."

"Good. That's really good. Secrets always have a way of coming out."

Her back stiffened before it relaxed against my body as I stood behind her. Manhattan life buzzed on the streets below. "What's going on with Simone?" she asked.

"I don't know. All I'm getting are… vibes."

"Vibes?"

"And a bitter taste in my mouth. That donation to Hope for Hope was timed."

Her green eyes darkened. "I know it's not what you want to hear, but Wright should have been six feet under years ago. Whoever takes the bastard down will ease my worries. My mother says people like Wright eventually get karma, so I'm really counting on karma at this point."

I puffed out in exasperation, and Allie turned in my hold.

"We need Wright for Kendra's case, but we're also looking for new evidence. I know it's out there."

"What is she facing?"

"Allie… I can't even utter the words."

"What are you gonna do about Simone?"

"Simone just opened a truck load of questions I need answered. I grieved her and I grieved us until all that grief dissipated into years of work, and I moved on. All that's left is shock and I guess a little bit of suspicion."

"Simone wants to pick up where she's left off," she said. "I ran into her in the bathroom. She saw Marissa at Hope for Hope."

"That sounds—"

"Suspicious? I thought so too. Do you think Simone's aware of her family business?"

"I'd bet both my kidneys on it. She's well adjusted for someone who just escaped captivity and lived through significant trauma. I mean, look at Kendra. She's under constant care, and she still won't talk."

Allie shivered, and I pulled my jacket tighter around her.

"I may have invited Simone to the gun range."

"What?"

She looked up. "I'm trying to keep my friends close and enemies closer."

Was that what Simone was? An enemy? The carefree woman who'd rebelled against her father had always calculated every move. And she never made a move without a reason. I brought Allie closer into my hold.

"Hartley had an unnerving look in his eyes. She has that same look—like nothing's a challenge."

Allie freed herself from my hold. "I didn't want to say

anything and sound out of line, but I got the same impression. Also, she's after you."

"It's been fifteen years. She knows I've moved on."

"She called you her fiancé." The light tremble in her voice sent a sprinkle of nerves down my spine.

"What? That's ridiculous."

"She corrected herself, but it was obvious she said it on purpose. Twice. Jesus, look at me. I'm snitching."

"Trust is underrated in life, just like instinct, and I completely trust you."

"Just like that?"

"Just like that."

I lifted her chin with my fingers so she could meet my lips. The strawberry taste on her mouth momentarily erased all worry.

"Come home with me tonight. I've been dreaming about you in my bed. On my dick."

She bit her lip and made puppy eyes. "I have a doctor's appointment in the morning. Routine physical."

Damn it!

"I'm sure I can take care of your physical." I groaned, rubbing against her. "They say MTP care is essential."

"Who says that?" she laughed.

"I don't know, but I'll make it essential if you come home with me."

"It's an early appointment and makes more sense to stay on Long Island." She lifted to her toes and kissed me. "I'll take the nine o'clock train and come to work right after."

I should have told Allie about our new house sooner, because if I had, we'd be fucking there tonight.

"Work." I pulled my fingers through my overgrown hair. "I need a fucking vacation."

"What are you going to do about the lawsuit?"

I tightened my fists. My blood boiled, my muscles flexed,

and my body heated from the inside out. Fucking would have felt so much nicer.

"I don't want negative publicity for the charity because the assholes who donated are the abusers we fight. If Simone's father kept her captive, she should want to stay clear of her uncles and brothers—yet she's here making a donation in their name." My nostrils flared. "The moment was lost tonight, and we need to reassess. We're meeting with the lawyers first thing tomorrow. "

"You're right. Nothing about her resurrection adds up."

I rubbed her hands over my arms, giving me an idea. "Want to take on a new case with me?"

"What case?"

"One where we work together to find out what she's up to."

Allie grabbed onto my arm and held tight. Excitement sparkled in her eyes, and she bit her lip. "Of course, I do!" She jumped up into my arms and kissed me hard before sliding down my body.

"I know you're still recovering, so it won't be anything physical."

She grinned from ear to ear like I'd just given her the best Christmas present of her life. "Even better. What exactly are you thinking?"

"I don't know yet, but be on guard. I'll also add this to one of the many reasons you should live with me."

Allie wrapped her arms around me and squeezed hard. "Soon. I promise." She yawned again.

"You're tired."

"A little. Foxy kept me up."

I gave her a knowing look.

"I said soon. She'll tell him soon."

"All right, all right. I get it. Soon. I think Laura left with James."

She frowned. "Crap. I like riding the train with her."

"You're not going on the train in a gown." I shook my head. "Come on."

I walked Allie downstairs to the front and kissed her good-night at the limo.

"How long do you have to stay?" she asked.

"Until the last guest leaves. It's part of the job as a host."

"So I'll see you tomorrow at work?"

"I'll be in just before noon."

I kissed her once more and held open the door. Watching Allie drive off in the opposite direction where I needed her to be ached in a way I hadn't felt before. I squeezed my eyes shut. The night of obligations finished well after one in the morning, and I walked the four blocks home. Crisp winter air cut my breath in half.

"Evening, George." I tipped my head to the concierge at the front desk.

He held the door open. "Good morning, Mr. Silver."

I pulled my hand through my hair. "Is it that late already?"

"It could be early if you're a morning person."

I chuckled. George was the glass half full kind of guy, and more importantly, someone I could trust. "You're right. Have a great morning, George."

"You as well, Mr. Silver."

The lonely elevator ride took much longer than when Allie was here. I set the car keys in the hallway basket.

"Rona. Soft jazz please."

A low saxophone tune played overhead, and I removed my shoes.

It didn't take long after I arrived and made myself comfortable with a glass of whiskey in my hand before George rang from downstairs.

"Yes, George?"

"I wouldn't normally disturb you, but since you're awake, I

thought I'd ring to tell you I'm either seeing a ghost or I've gone mad. Ms. Simone Hartley is here."

"Right. You're not mad, and she's not a ghost, George. Send her up." I emptied the glass in one swig, and a rush of valiance expanded my chest.

"Right away, sir."

I sat by the fireplace. The ice cubes in my empty whiskey glass melted. Two minutes later the elevator door opened, and I listened to the sound of her approaching heels over the marble floor. She stepped out into the living room in the same revealing ball gown she'd worn to the fundraiser, removed her heels, and sauntered across the carpet barefoot. She stopped in front of my chair.

"Couldn't sleep?" I asked.

"Do you know how hard it was watching you dance with another woman?" She tilted a hip sideways.

"Allie is not just another woman." I lifted my glass and spun the ice cubes around.

"I didn't see a ring on her finger, and I'm the one at your penthouse instead of her."

She removed the empty glass from my hand and strolled back to the alcohol cart, where she refilled the whiskey and poured herself a drink as well.

"What you did at the fundraiser was underhanded, Simone. It won't stop me from serving your uncles."

"I stopped you from embarrassing Silver Securities in front of hundreds of people. You should be grateful."

"Where's Wright?"

"Probably hiding. Your girlfriend could get him out. He's into her, you know."

"He's a sick creep. My evidence shows your uncles don't have him."

"I know that."

"Then why the fuck would you have told me not to serve

them?"

"Because my father's house shows evidence Wright lived there."

"At the cove?"

She nodded. She strolled toward me like she owned the place, handed me the drink, and sat on the chair across from me, holding my gaze.

"You could have told me at the fundraiser."

"If I had, you would have fucked up, Tristan, and I would have had no reason for coming here tonight."

Why exactly *had* she come?

"It's two in the morning. What can I do for you Simone?"

"I think a better question is what I can do for you."

"Our paths aren't aligned. A trial is inevitable. You should cut your ties while you still can."

"You're not listening to me, Tristan. I have access to Donaldson. I can get you that same access."

I couldn't deny her offer was tempting. The information could solve a lot of Silver Securities' problems. But there had to be a catch.

"You're telling me you'd betray your family?"

"My family is the one who betrayed me. They kept their mouths shut while my father conditioned me to his ways. At least, he thought he did. You remember the constant surveillance, lies, and manipulation, don't you? I had no way out until my father found himself six feet under. Which reminds me, I must thank the brave person who killed him."

Allie.

I cleared my throat. "What about your uncles?"

"They're not the ones running the show."

"Who is?"

"A new successor. Something about operating through the dark web without ever being spotted."

I sat up straight. "But you know who it is."

She smirked and was taking her time dominating the moment. "I'd prefer to leave business matters for the week."

"Then we should meet at my office. Just name the day and time."

I sucked an ice cube from the drink and bit through.

Her face reddened. She was upset.

"Or you could come to my house. We don't have to be so formal, Tristan," she offered.

Maybe Allie was right. Perhaps I was approaching the situation from the wrong angle.

"Your house? Where are you staying?" I sat back in my chair. The room warmed, and my legs relaxed.

She grinned. "Long Island. Across the Cove."

My brows lifted. "Not the old cove house?"

The Hartleys had used the cove house as a vacation home. Simone had always been a daddy's girl, and Hartley promised her the property when she'd asked at the age of ten. That's what her mother had told me. Candice Hartley—Watson now —was everything I had hoped Simone to be: a total opposite of Jeff Hartley. But history had proven Simone's wilder side flourished with every bribery Jeff Hartley mastered.

We spent the summers diving off the dock, racing jet-skis, and throwing the biggest parties in the state. So much had changed since then.

"Tristan?" she asked. "Did you hear a word I said?"

I didn't remember her talking. Her mouth curved lightly on the left, and my breaths slowed. My mind gave into the memories. I saw us playing volleyball on the beach again. It was all before Hartley fell rogue.

When I opened my eyes again, Simone was kneeling on the rug in front of me. She lifted and raked her fingers through my hair, gently scraping along my scalp. Unable to lift my hand, I looked sideways, pulling away from her.

"Do you remember the long summer nights and cool

autumn evenings by the bonfires?" Her breath flowed over my cheek, then my mouth. My arms and legs pinned me in the chair. "They were the best nights of my life."

I opened my mouth but couldn't speak. The smell of her overpowered the room, and when I closed my eyes again, I was there, on the beach, making out with Simone. Except she looked like Allie and tasted like strawberries.

My eyes flew open.

Where's Allie?

I blinked, and Simone came into view. She stood up, lowered her mouth to the corner of mine, and whispered. "I'll let myself out, Tristan. I'll see you at the office this week."

She sauntered out of the room, her ass swaying back and forth. I sank deep into the chair and leaned my head back, jolting at a noise from my bedroom. When I opened my eyes again, I thought I saw Allie pass by the door.

"Allie?" My mouth moved, but I couldn't hear my voice.

"Allie?" I called out again.

She appeared out of the corner of my eye. Her strawberry scent wrapped around me. I searched for her eyes, but her face was covered with her hair. She focused on my dick instead, lowered to her knees, and unzipped my pants. Her hand rubbed over my apparently stiff cock, sliding up and down my boxer briefs. I rubbed my forehead and shook my head. The room spun quicker with every stroke.

She used her free hand to pass my whiskey glass and held it against my lips. I tilted my head back and finished the bitter alcohol in one swig. My cock sprang out hard and stiff, which was odd because I hadn't thought about a hand job until her warm hand curved around me.

I closed my eyes and gave into her rhythm. She gripped my cock in flawless strokes. My ass tightened and I pushed higher into the seat, each painful thrust begging for a release.

"Stay still, stay still, stay still…" her voice chanted in my mind.

The relentless tugs sent me into a daze. Her voice sounded from somewhere far away until I gave into the pleasure. I came hard and fast and didn't get up again until the sun shone bright through the window.

"What the fuck?"

I pulled my hand over my eyes and sat up in my bed, naked and alone. Twisted sheets were wrapped around my leg and half my body. My cock was still fucking hard as a rock, but there was no sign of Allie.

I lay back on the bed.

Fucking wet dreams.

The clock showed seven in the morning, and my memory from last night was gone. My head pounded with a rare urgency. I pulled my fingers along my aching scalp, massaging the pain away, then popped two Ibuprofens. A shower eased the ache, but the fog from last night still hovered. I dressed in comfortable slacks and a sweater, and texted Allie to meet me for coffee before work. If I couldn't convince her to move in with me to the new house today, my dick would break.

Chapter 7

Allie

"Thanks for coming with me." I parked in front of my doctor's office.

"Foxy can't wait to see his little cousin." Laura unbuckled his seatbelt and settled him in the stroller.

"Second cousin. And I'm not sure we'll be able to see much. It's the size of a cherry."

"Sherries," Foxy squealed.

"They're not in season, baby. Here." She gave him one of the oatmeal cookies Mrs. Brewer had baked over the weekend.

"Allie? Well, what are the chances I would run into you here?"

I turned around at the familiar voice and nearly bumped into Cameron. "Oh, I'm sorry. Hi."

"Small, very small, Mr. Camelot." Laura tilted her head, and his face turned beet red.

"Hi. What are you doing here?" he asked.

"A doctor's checkup. Baby's first ultrasound." I rubbed my belly. "This is my partner, Laura. Well, not life partner, work partner, but you've already met… and I'm babbling"

"It's nice to see you again." Laura waved.

"First ultrasound? That's exciting. Can I walk you in? Betty's already inside. I forgot her water."

Betty. I'd have to tell Emma to scratch that name off the list because the last thing I wanted to think about when I looked at my baby was my ex's wife.

"I thought you said you have one-year-old twins?" I asked.

"I do. And another pair on the way."

Wow! Cameron from Camelot had been busy.

Cameron's wife glowed with pride the moment he walked through the door. He kissed her and then her heavy belly. She was carrying high, and Cameron couldn't stop talking about the twins' upcoming arrival. They looked like they would make a perfect family.

I took a deep, pained breath and closed my eyes, promising myself to tell Tristan about the baby as soon as possible. The feeling continued through the ultrasound when I heard the galloping heartbeat. My eyes welled, and Laura held my hand the entire time while Foxy pointed to my tummy, repeating, "Sherries."

I stuffed the black and white photos of the fruit in my womb in my purse. Today was my first official day at work, and I'd planned on reading through all the cases, right after Tristan showed me around. We dropped Foxy off at Mrs. Brewer's and took the train to Manhattan.

"Do you think he remembers the box with the booties?" I asked Laura as we stood in the line for coffee. "He's been preoccupied with Simone."

"All the more reason you should give him the booties—but those are at home."

My chest deflated.

"You know you don't need booties to tell him. Whatever you do, don't pull a Laura. It's harder to get out of that pile of crap than crap itself."

I chuckled, and Laura checked her watch.

"Tristan's running late."

"He never runs late. It's almost ten o'clock. Maybe he went in earlier?"

Outside, the first snow had covered the sidewalk. The fresh layer of fluff brightened the city, forecasting a long winter.

"May I take your order?" the barista asked. I jerked my head back at the familiar voice. After a double-take, I asked, "Portia?"

"Hi, Katie. It's actually Michelle. What can I get you?"

"And it's actually Allie. Not Katie. A pumpkin spice chai tea and a cappuccino. It's so good to see you here. How are you doing?"

"Better now than ever before. If it weren't for you, I would have been stuck in that alley until my roots turned gray."

Michelle neither sounded nor looked anything like the red-haired Portia I remembered from the street. Her brown ponytail bounced with her step as she prepared the drinks.

"I'm not sure what I did, but you look great."

"Thank you. I called the number on the card you gave me. Hope for Hope enrolled me in a rehab program, found me a job here, and everything else is history." She walked around the counter and hugged me before passing me the cups.

"Thank you. I owe you much more than a tea and a coffee, so these are on me."

"Thank you." My phone rang with Tristan's number. "I have to get this. It's nice to see you here, Michelle."

"Don't be a stranger." She smiled.

I slid my finger across the phone screen and walked to an available booth. "Hello?"

"Hey, it's me. I hope you're not waiting. I'm at the office already."

"Everything all right?"

The brief hesitation in his voice gave me the shivers. "Yeah, come on up. I can't wait to show you around."

"See you soon."

Laura left for our office while Tristan gave me a tour of the top three floors.

"You know, I had a naughty dream about you last night."

"Is that something we should be discussing on work hours?"

"It's gonna be a long day. I can't wait to tell you I wish you could be in my bed in the mornings."

"Soon, Tristan. Soon. We're still on for lunch, right?"

But by the time I returned to my desk, it was already time for lunch, and I couldn't pass up the chance to show Tristan the sonogram. I turned on my heel. "Look at that. Time flies when you're having fun. Where do you want to go for lunch?" I rocked from left to right. "Of course, his phone rang with perfect timing, and his face fell flat.

"I have to skip lunch."

"Everything all right?"

"Yes, just doing some old-school detective work with James. Laura should be able to catch you up on everything."

He kissed me quickly and disappeared behind the elevator door.

"He does that a lot," Greg said from behind the counter. "It comes with the territory. The Silvers are always busy. Always running around town."

Maybe a baby wasn't fit for this lifestyle. My stomach rumbled. I ordered takeout for lunch and stayed in the office with Laura, flipping through the files from Hope for Hope. Nothing said welcome better than work.

"I've seen nothing on Marissa."

"The girl from the auction? Didn't Simone say they rescued her?"

"Yeah, but do we really trust Simone?"

Laura laughed just as my phone rang with Emma's number. "Perfect. I'm about to get some answers."

"Answers to what?"

"Hey, Ems. What do you have for me?"

"I checked the medical records. Simone Hartley was pregnant at the time of the accident. There was a doctor called out to the house two weeks later."

"She had a baby? Tristan's baby?"

"What?" Laura perked up, but I pressed the phone harder to my ear."

"I don't think so." Emma breathed hard. "Sorry, I'm just leaving the hospital now, and it's lunchtime, and I have to make it back to class."

"Why do you not think so, Ems?"

"Records say she had a miscarriage."

"Oh, okay."

"But Simone has visited an OB recently."

"How recently?"

"Ahem, this morning. I saw her at the hospital. Total coincidence. Allie, I think she's hiding more, and you should definitely tell Tristan about the baby because I'm holding onto too many secrets. Too many, you hear me?"

She was a balloon ready to pop.

"All right. Soon, Ems. I'm doing it soon, and you'll be the first to know. I promise. Thank you for your help."

"No problem. See you at Thanksgiving."

She hung up before I could ask her about the upcoming holiday. From what my mother had told me, the Flintstones had been getting ready for the event for weeks.

"We definitely don't trust Simone. Emma says she miscarried after the car accident, but she's seeing an OB now."

"Wow."

"I know. I think I need some air."

"Want me to come with?"

I shook my head. "I won't be long."

White flakes drifted lazily to the ground stuck to the sidewalk and streets. A cold gust of wind messed my hair. I sipped on my tea in the cafe when a familiar voice shook me awake.

"A tall black," a customer barked at Portia, and I froze.

That voice.

I shut my eyes and my head sank into my body like a turtle's. I turned sideways enough to catch Wright's reflection in the glass refrigerator.

Shit.

I glued my back to the cushioned seat in the corner, the same way I had as a little girl when I listened to him rape my mother. I lowered my hand over my stomach, covering my bump. What the hell was he doing here? *I thought the Hartleys had him!*

David Wright grabbed his coffee and left. He walked to the front window near where I was sitting, and I watched as he scrolled through his phone. I lowered the jacket hood over my forehead just enough to see his hurried walk across the street.

Vengeance returned to my veins with a force, and I quickly typed a message to Tristan.

Allie: Spotted Wright at the cafe. Following.

The piece of shit might be an important witness, but he had yet to pay for my father's and sister's deaths. I slid out of the booth, zipped up my jacket, and walked out of the café. I watched from across the street as the old man stepped inside a convenience store. He paid for a purchase, came outside, and lit a cigarette. I spun around on my heel to face away from the bastard, spotting him in a storefront reflection. The snow fell harder, and the thickening flakes obstructed my vision. I checked my phone, but Tristan hadn't replied. A stench of cigarettes paralyzed me, and I checked the window's reflection again, where his wrinkled face appeared next to mine. I lowered the hood further down and adjusted my scarf upward, covering my face. He turned to the right and continued down the sidewalk.

Cold and hot sweat trickled down my back. I gripped the handrail and followed him down the stairs into a subway heading north. Wright turned the corner, and a scrap of paper fell out of his pocket on the way. My knees wobbled and my heart pounded in my chest as I hurried down the corridor. I picked up the paper and focused on Wright near the end of the tunnel.

The approaching subway thudded on the tracks, and ten seconds later, the wind blew my hair as the train came to a stop. I ran across the middle of the platform, pushing through the crowd. The train doors opened. Three cars down, Wright stepped inside. I pushed forward and stopped a dozen feet from the door and watched him. The hunched man stood with his back toward me. My breath locked in my lungs, my palms tingled, and my body shook. The morning commotion settled as people boarded the cars. I pulled my hand across my eyes, and the jacket's hood fell off my head. I, obviously, couldn't go in the same car with Wright because I had no plan. What would I do if I went in? Murder him? Go to jail and give birth to a child only to give it up?

No. I can't risk this baby.

I stepped back and lowered my hand over my stomach. So much had changed since I'd met Tristan. He'd given me something to hope for. While I hated Wright with a passion, I was ready to leave him in my past. Tristan Silver had replaced the fury and anger with new hope and a baby. I couldn't afford to apprehend Wright. I had too much to lose, and I would never allow the bastard to take that away from me. The door closed, and I let go of a long held breath.

Another subway approached on the tracks behind me. The wet piece of paper I'd picked up flopped against my palm, and I flipped it over. The air stilled, and the howling winds stopped time. Blood drained from my face as I stared at a photograph of my young mother. I looked just like her.

"What the fuck?"

More than one and a half million people lived in Manhattan, and he'd found me. My throat closed up.

Wright turned around in slow motion and looked right at me while I stood frozen in my spot. As the subway rolled, he stepped forward, pressed his palms and nose against the door, and smirked.

The cold sweat turned into chills over my spine. The train left, but I remained standing for a long while. At least, that's what eight hundred and fifty-seven heartbeats felt like. The day Tristan had driven me to the mountains this fall flashed in my mind, and for the first time since then, I regretted not taking the shot. I should have killed Wright when I had the chance. Instead, I'd cowered. But if Wright was supposed to be imprisoned by the Hartleys, what was he doing here?

My phone rang with Tristan's number, and I slid my shaky finger over the screen, barely controlling the trembling.

"Allie?" Tristan asked. "Are you all right?"

"He's here," I whimpered.

"My ping's coming up at Eighth and Broadway. I'm almost there. Stay put."

I shuffled my feet along the wall, never breaking my back's connection with the tiles until I found a bench. A homeless man tucked his feet in so I could sit. A blink later, Tristan rushed down the subway steps, almost slipping on the wet ceramic. Out of breath, he took my hand in his and crouched in front of me.

"Allie, look at me."

I blinked past the tears and wiped them away.

"He sought me out on purpose. The Hartleys don't have him. Wright is free."

Tristan cracked his knuckles, and his nostrils flared. He took my hand in his and helped me off the bench. "I know, baby. I know. Simone said he escaped after the fundraiser, but she lied." A vein twitched in his neck. He wrapped one arm around my shoulder, while his other hand went for my belly. At least, I thought it did, but he gripped my coat instead and pulled it over the front, covering us. Protecting us.

"Isn't that convenient?" My voice shook.

"She's playing a fucking dangerous game."

"She's cunning and manipulative. That's what she is, Tristan, and if you don't see it—"

"Shh." He pressed his finger over my lip. "Of course I see it, baby. She's scheming and shrewd like—"

"An obsessed bitch?" I filled in.

The corner of his mouth lifted. "I was going to say her father, but that works, too. Come on. Let's get out of here. I'll get a team to check the CCTVs." He tightened his hold around my body, and we hurried to the Silver Securities offices.

I sat in the conference room, numb and shaky, as Kendra's team gathered around the table. Gabriel Silver joined in on a call from Austria.

"Priority one during the operation will be Allie and the team's safety. If we've learned anything from today, it's that Wright is dangerous and we no longer need him."

What?

"We've recovered a hard drive from Simone's with fresh evidence. As of now, Wright is a liability. Priority two, we're left with a small window of opportunity before Kendra's trial in January, but don't hold your breath. There's a chance the judge will move the trial if we bring this in." Tristan waved a black hard drive in his hand.

Julian mumbled something underneath his breath and shook his head.

"I don't believe I need to remind everyone that Simone Hartley and her family cannot be trusted. The judge has frozen some of their assets, but not all. Donaldson's working hard on overturning the ruling."

"If Silver Securities is looking for Wright, I bet the Hartleys are as well. He snitched, and Ms. Resurrected is setting a trap. You do the dirty work to find him, she kills Wright, your evidence is inadmissible, and you have no case. Again."

Heads turned Laura's way.

She twirled a pen between her fingers and rolled her eyes. "Are they aware you took a hard drive?"

"Of course not."

"Are you aware it will be inadmissible in court without a warrant?"

I looked at Laura like she'd just passed the bar while Tristan looked over to Axel Wagner, who concurred with a nod.

"I recommend asking your lawyers before solidifying plans. They're pretty good lawyers. Some say they're the best." She winked. "I also recommend keeping Wright in your back pocket. You know, just in case the hard drive evidence falls through. So, all we have to do is figure out where the Hartleys are looking for him, and voilà."

"Set our own trap." The attention shifted my way. "We all know who Wright wants. I'm the perfect bait."

"I'm not using you as a pawn again. That's out of the question." Tristan's chest shook. "The Hartley circle has tightened, and we don't have enough information for a definite decision. James and Gabe will check security for leaks, flaws, and breaks in all systems, Hunter's at Rebels with Scar Wagner, keeping an eye for extra activity, and I'll talk to George at Magnet. If the Hartleys are making a move, it will be at the club."

"What about Simone?" I asked. "She's joining me and Laura at the gun range this week."

Tristan frowned. "I'm going on my gut right now. Cancel the date."

"But—"

"Make up whatever excuse you need to stay away from her, Allie."

The request didn't come from Tristan Silver; it came from my boss, and negotiation would be pointless. Tristan was right: pawning myself was one thing, but risking my baby was another.

"There's been no activity at the cove for months. At least, none they'd want us to see." James cleared his throat. "I've had Scar Wagner surveying the place since Kendra's kidnapping."

"Someone's getting on that property to feed the bird. Find out who that is."

James quickly typed in his phone.

"What bird?" Laura whispered, and I shrugged.

"Thank you, everyone. We'll reconnect in the afternoon. " Tristan turned my way. "Allie? Can you stay behind?"

Wonderful. My cheeks flushed with heat. Day one and I was staying back in the boss's office.

I nodded and waited as everyone left the conference room. The door closed, and Tristan rolled back in his chair.

"I know you want in on this, but I'm not a fan of you and Simone spending time together."

"Whatever do you mean? She's a gem." I rolled my eyes.

"She's been following you."

"What?"

"She checked the security cameras at the hotel when you snuck through the back kitchen, and she followed you to the doctor's."

"I guess I haven't had a chance to keep my enemy as close as I should have."

"Point is, I need you on guard—which goes along with the surprise I have for you." He checked the time. "Today, after work."

I tilted forward and groaned. "Oh, you have to go?"

"Anticipation is the best part of the surprise. Be patient."

I rose onto my toes, leaned in and whispered, "I'll remind

you of that same patience when you're deep inside me, almost ready, and I will tell you about Emma's crush on Eric."

His brows furrowed. "That's cruel. She has a crush on Eric?"

"Please don't mention it, but that's not my point." His little sister would be so disappointed in my slip up.

"I promise my surprise will be worth it. I hope you'll like it." He rubbed the back of his neck. Was he nervous?

He leaned in and kissed me. Maybe tonight was the right time to tell him about the baby? I needed the baby booties in a box from Laura.

"Anything else I should know about?" he asked. "You seem off."

"I may have a surprise for you too. Also, I ran into the man who murdered my father and unborn baby sister."

"Right. I'm sorry. You have every right to be off. This wasn't the way I wanted your first day to start. Are you feeling okay?" He looked me over as if he wanted to ask me a question, but refrained.

"I'm fine."

His forehead creased. "When women usually say that, they mean the opposite."

"No, really. You have to go. We can talk tonight over dinner."

"Sounds great."

"Why are you looking at me like this?" The worry in his eyes stumped me.

"What is it, Tristan?"

"Don't worry about it. Should I pick you up after work?"

I cranked my head sideways. "All right. See you after work."

He lowered for a delicate kiss and left me more confused than before. I returned to the stacked files on top of the desk between mine and Laura's, noting Portia's closed file, and I smiled.

"Thanks for helping Michelle." I pointed to the picture, and Laura looked up.

"You're the one who gave her the card. No one gets far without that first step."

"Did Tristan seem off to you?"

"What do you mean?"

"He seemed… off. Like he wanted to ask me something." I bit my lip. "I don't think I can wait until Christmas. I think it's time I tell him I'm pregnant now."

"You should."

"Are you gonna do it?" I asked. "You know, finally tell James about Foxy?"

She removed the pen from behind her ear and lowered her head. "I want to, but now is not a good time. He hasn't been feeling well, and it's not flu-like. I work a lot, but he works all the time. I do not know how he finds the time to spend with Laila, and the constant fatigue is worrying me."

"He's a single father. You know what that's like."

"I think this is more. I may have to do some investigating."

"Tell him the truth instead. He'll be elated."

"Or he'll want to murder me."

"Laura—"

"I know, I know. The sooner the better; but what if the sooner is already too late?"

"There's only one way out of this, and you know exactly where it starts."

"I don't want to adult," she whined.

"Nobody does."

We spent the remaining day organizing cases for priority. Tomorrow we'd go to Hope for Hope to confirm job placements and interview the girls to search for new trafficking cells.

James and Tristan left the office right after the meeting and didn't come back. I stared across the Hudson River for the first time, wishing the distance between home and work wasn't so great. Tristan loved Manhattan, and this was his turf. The already-short days were becoming shorter and darker. There was something beautiful and peaceful about looking at all the buildings and houses, and knowing people were gathering for dinner. Yet there were those on the streets without homes, like Marissa. No one had seen her or heard from her after the auction, except for Simone.

"Are you in Lala Land again?" Laura asked.

"What does that mean?" I turned away from the window.

"You're daydreaming."

"I'm not. I just wish there was more I could do. We need to go to Hope for Hope tomorrow."

"Tristan said to stay away from Simone."

"He didn't say to stay away from Hope for Hope." I wiggled my brows. "Besides, I doubt the beauty queen actually gets her hands dirty. At least, not the way we do. You really think she even stepped inside the charity?"

"I don't know, but chances are the answer is no."

I rubbed my rumbling belly. Baby Puss was hungry.

"I feel limited with the baby. Everything I do, I think about my little cherry nesting in there, all safe and secure."

My best friend smiled. "That's your motherly instinct. It's telling you to limit yourself. Welcome to adulting."

"But I don't want to," I whined. "I want to go out there and—"

"You don't want to be out there, Allie. You've already seen what's out there. Your work here accomplishes much more than giving out speeding tickets."

"Want to take a walk with me?" I asked her. "I need to stretch my legs."

"Last time you took a walk, you ran into Wright. You're like a magnet for all the wrong things, so yes, I'm coming with you."

We took the elevator down, grabbed a tea, and walked

around the block. On our way back to the building, a familiar face flashed from across the street. She lowered her head when she saw us and hastened her walk.

"It can't be," I said to Laura, and then raised my voice from across the street. "Marissa?"

Her head jolted up a fraction, but she continued at her fast pace.

"Let's go." Laura took my hand like I was Foxy and guided me across the street.

"What are you doing?"

"Being maternal."

"Stop it. I'm not a baby." I hurried to the middle of the road, bumping into a taxi.

"You were saying?"

I threw her a dirty look as the cab driver rolled down his window, "You're going to get yourself killed, dream girl!"

"Sorry!" I waved an apology.

"Come on. She's getting away."

Laura grabbed my hand again. We pressed our feet harder, jogging forward.

The crisp air filled my lungs. Marissa's dark silhouette, a long coat and a hood over her head, seemed to get further away. We weaved between the few people on the street as she turned the corner. The sound of a siren howled in the distance.

"Marissa, wait!" I yelled out after her.

She halted, but it wasn't for me. She waved at someone, and the headlights of a parked car flashed. The vehicle pulled out of its spot and stopped at her side. Was that her pimp? Marissa got inside the back seat of a plateless black SUV. A man wearing sunglasses and a hood drove past us.

"Who the hell was that?" I asked.

"Marissa in a luxury car. Could be her pimp."

"Wright was the one who bought her."

"Could be Wright again."

I shook my head. "I don't think so. The bastard already accomplished what he intended."

"You mean, scare the living shit out of you?"

"Something like that. We have to find Marissa before he gets to her."

"We do, but not out here. Come on. It's getting cold."

The SUV's taillights disappeared, along with my hope for Marissa.

"Don't worry, babe. It will all work out."

"It takes three hundred and fifty-eight days on average to get a woman away from a sex-trafficker," I said.

"Hopefully, we can lower that statistic," Laura whispered.

Hopefully.

Sometimes hope was all you had, and if you didn't hold on to that, what else could you hold on to?

Chapter 8

Tristan

We parked at Scar Wagner's house and crossed the forest connecting to the Hartley property at the cove. The house was overgrown with shrubs and vines, and no longer resembled the coastal mansion with white trim. Overgrown trees and bushes covered the area, emasculating the estate I remembered. Dying vines hung over the exterior walls. The second- and third-floor windows had been shattered, but the locks placed there years ago remained.

"I can't believe they just left everything to rot."

"I thought Simone said she was staying here."

"She obviously lied. I think she's at a decoy condo. Who's got eyes on her now?"

James checked his phone. "She's at Magnet."

"Good."

We crossed the lawn, and memories flooded back like a tsunami. I remembered my last night here like it was yesterday. Simone had thrown the biggest party of the decade to spite her father. The organizer set up a carousel, a petting zoo, and camel rides. Performers, caterers, and guests filled the property. Alcohol flowed, and a distinct taste of cocaine drifted in the air. It all got out of hand so fast, I barely made it out with her on a boat.

Jeffrey Hartley softened on me for a while after the incident because I got his daughter out. With a team of reputable lawyers and crafty paperwork, Simone's alibi in the Bahamas kept her out of jail. Eight people overdosed that night. The fireworks misfired, killing three more. And when time came to pay, the phony LLC on title was a ghost company. Jeff Hartley vowed to never step a foot on this soil again and swore no one else would either.

"Are we breaking in?" James snooped through every window as we rounded the house from the back. Waves lapped at the shore, and the boathouse squeaked as it swayed.

"No need. I know a way in."

Simone and I used to sneak in past curfew from the back. The latch on one window never worked, and I didn't expect it had been fixed. The frame squeaked on its way up as I lifted the window.

"Watch your step. There's glass everywhere." The cracking underneath our feet echoed through the house.

"What's with all the sand?"

I skimmed my foot over the powder and glanced out the window to the docks.

"Simone had an indoor beach party." I pushed open the door to the enormous main hall, where they'd set up an above-ground pool. Remnants of its broken frame were scattered through the house.

"Why was I not invited to this party?"

I recalled the night a monkey got loose and the black puma freaked over the noise, injuring her trainer.

"I wish I could say you didn't miss anything, but that would be a lie."

"And you had no clue she was throwing this party?"

"Of course, I had no clue. She organized the whole thing in eight hours."

Simone had traveled to Costa Rica the week before. She wanted to clear her mind, and said she'd experienced the unique euphoria of her life after drinking Ayahuasca. She'd started experimenting with mushrooms shortly after, and Hartley blamed me for the behavior. I was the boyfriend who couldn't stop her from being stupid. She'd agreed to rehab, though, and six months later we were stupidly happy again and on our way to the altar. We'd planned the trip to Austria to celebrate our engagement. Instead, I lived through a nightmare. The accident broke me. I thought I'd lost and failed her. I thought she'd died because of me.

"What are we looking for?" James brought me out of the daze. Dust lifted along lazy ribbons of light filtering through the broken windows.

"I'll know when I see it. Look for anything out of the ordinary. The usual."

A high-pitched squeak sounded from the kitchen.

"That's impossible."

"What?" James hurried behind me to the sunroom. The bird cage stood a foot higher than my head, the same way it had years ago.

"What the hell is this, Tristan?"

"Fuck Tristan," the bird squawked, and James laughed.

"That's not funny."

"It is when my name is not Tristan."

"Fuck, Tristan."

James bent in half. "What's his name?"

"Freddie. I can't believe he's still alive."

The old parrot had a few bald spots, had lost a handful of wing feathers, and had a growth on his foot.

"Parrots live a long time."

"He looks ill. But someone must be feeding it."

"I have a feeling that someone is Simone."

"Fuck, Simone."

I looked at James, and he looked at me.

"Maybe not." His nose wrinkled. He was right; the place reeked.

"All right, let's split up."

We combed through every room until I found one tidier than the rest of the house. Someone had made the bed, wiped the windows, and swept the floors. An acoustic guitar hung on the wall, and fishing gear had been laid out on the bed. While I wanted to believe this room was Wright's, it looked more like a teenager's. Nature Polaroids were strung on an old Christmas light string. I opened a drawer filled with pens, blank paper, and a hard drive.

"Well, what do you know?"

"Hey, Tristan," James called for me from downstairs.

"Fuck, Tristan," Freddie screamed.

"I think I found what you're looking for," James yelled out.

I stuffed the hard drive in my jacket pocket and hurried downstairs to where he was holding the garage door open.

"Not another animal, is it?" I asked.

"No. This one's a lot better."

I stopped at the threshold, and James pulled on the tarp and folded it over the Miata's hood.

My mouth dropped to the floor. "No fucking way."

We pulled back the rest of the covering, and I walked around the wrecked car to the passenger seats.

"I don't know how you survived this."

I picked up a jumble of bungee cords spilling out of Simone's old backpack. "I think I know how Simone survived the accident."

"Why would Hartley bring the car to the US?"

I shook my head, and my stomach tightened into a knot. I

dropped to the ground and slid underneath the car. "The breaks were cut."

"Forensics came back negative for tampering."

"Forensics also said Simone was dead." I slid back out. "They were definitely cut. On a timer. Just before we reached the mountain top."

"You think she was in on it?"

"I don't know what to believe anymore."

"Why did Hartley fly the wreck in from Austria?"

"I don't think it was Hartley."

The doorbell rang, and we both jumped up.

"What the fuck?" James whispered. "Don't open it."

"Whoever's at the door already knows we're here. Cover the car."

James pulled the tarp over the wreck, and we went to the front door, where Simone's oversized hat filled the frame.

"I thought she was at Magnet?"

"She's likely setting decoys."

I opened the door, and Simone turned on her heel to face us.

"You could have called if you wanted a tour." The coy look on her face nearly brought up my morning omelet. "What are you doing at my house, Tristan?"

"Fuck, Tristan!" Freddie screamed from the kitchen.

"That's my father's doing," she explained.

"Has the bird been living here on his own?"

"I'm not that cruel. It's fed." The indifference in her voice was new. She used to love animals, including Freddie. She crossed her arms over her chest. "What are you doing here?"

"Due diligence."

"I didn't see a car parked out front."

I looked her dead in the eyes. "My Miata's in the garage."

James's phone dinged. He checked the message and scoffed at Simone. "I was right. The woman at Magnet was a decoy."

She rolled her eyes. "Amateurs."

"I need to get back to the office. See you soon."

James gave me a knowing look and left.

"Let's take a walk." She turned around, and I followed her from the front door to the back. We crossed the property toward the shore until I broke the silence.

"What's the Miata doing here?" I asked her.

"Resting in peace," she quipped.

"I need answers, Simone. No more games. You said your father held you captive, but not really captive. What the hell happened? Where have you been the past fifteen years?"

She lowered her head, lost in thought, as I walked beside her. It was almost ten in the morning, and I was expected at a meeting in an hour. A stronger wind blew the yellowing leaves across the property. The waves crashed against the shoreline, and seagulls circled near the dock.

"Do you remember that last party?" she asked. "It was a splendid party."

Of course, I remembered. Our lives had changed that day, and not for the better.

"It was an out-of-control party."

We stopped by the swings, and she turned my way. "That was my first mistake. If it weren't for the party, my father would never have hated you as much as he did."

"I don't think the party caused your father's dislike of the Silvers. But the sex-trafficking, Simone, how can you overlook that? He broke a pact and hurt many people."

"And now he's paid for it."

"The operation still exists."

"How do you know?"

"The night he died, Jeff Hartley organized an auction of young women, some underage. He sold them, Simone. He recruited, used, and then sold them. It wasn't the first time, nor the tenth. The auctions are now organized online."

"Allegedly." She turned away from the boathouse as we approached the area and led parallel to the shoreline.

"Not *allegedly*. I was there. I saw him."

"You did? Then who killed him?" She turned around, and I almost bumped into her. "The evidence is under lock."

As it should be. Laura had pulled some heavy strings at the force to keep the case under wraps.

"I thought you were happy about his death?"

"Of course, I am. Knowing would simply give me closure."

And it would put a target on Allie's back. "I'm sorry, Simone, but I can't help you with that."

"I'm sorry too." She sighed. "I'm sorry you're as blind as you were when we were together."

"What are you talking about?"

"Your girlfriend, Tristan. She's screwing around on you."

I flexed my fingers and cracked my knuckles. "Stop making baseless accusations."

"But it's true. The guy's a chef, and he snuck Allie and her nosy friend through the back kitchen before the fundraiser. He held her hand, Tristan."

"And how do you know this?"

"I checked the security cameras. It's a miracle what a little skin can do to persuade a guard."

I scoffed. "Of course, you did. But you know what the difference is between you and Allie? I actually trust her."

"There's more. This morning I saw her outside the Langs medical building. She's been lying to you."

I was aware of Allie's doctor's appointment, but the fact Simone knew about it unnerved me. "Are you following her?"

"You should be grateful. If I hadn't followed her, I wouldn't have known her ex knocked her up."

"What?"

Simone grazed her hand over her belly as if she were the one pregnant. The gesture made me sick to my stomach.

"She calls him Cameron from Camelot, whatever that means, and she's pregnant."

Simone must have been mistaken, because I trusted Allie with my life, and hell would freeze over before I took Simone's word over Allie's.

"Whatever you're trying to pull, Simone, it won't work. I love Allie."

"You've known her for weeks, and you've known me for years."

"Simone—"

"I love you, Tristan, but I couldn't get away from my father. I just couldn't."

"Simone, it's been fifteen years—"

"And I never stopped loving you. All this time, I've prayed the sick bastard would choke on his cigars, but all he cared about were his whores and making you pay."

"He did make me pay. I thought you were dead. I've sobbed at your grave, grieved you for years, and hunted him for almost two decades."

"I wasn't supposed to be in the car. My father gave me the backpack before I left. He said it had essentials, but I think he knew I'd sneak out."

"So he gave you bungee chords?" I stood up and threw my hands up in the air.

"My father was a reasonable man."

My laugh echoed across the property. "It's reasonable to chance your daughter's life? What about all the girls he's harmed, abused, and sold?"

"Look, Tristan. I know he wasn't perfect, and I can't change what he's done, but I can bring an end to it all. Everything. I can shut down the operation, the island, give you names you don't even know exist. I can serve my uncles to you on a golden platter. I'll add in all the evidence you need as a bonus."

Vengeance swam in her eyes in a wave of determination. I

would have liked to believe her need to retaliate against the Hartleys was justified. According to Simone, they held her captive. Also, according to Simone, they didn't. The truth likely lay somewhere in between.

"What's the catch? What do you want, Simone?"

Her brow lifted.

"That depends on what you're going to do about Allie."

I stepped closer and whispered, "You want to know what I'm going to do about Allie? Let me make it clear, Simone. If Allie is pregnant, it's with my baby. Only my baby. That's how much I trust her. And I'd appreciate it if you stayed the fuck away from my family."

I stepped back. Her unwavering eyes remained on mine like she still had the upper hand.

"So the answer's a no? That's too bad. I was going to invite you to Thanksgiving, since we're family, but something tells me my olive branch would be rejected."

"The only family Thanksgiving I'll attend is the one I'm hosting for our family with Allie, at our new house. And just so we're clear, you and I are not a family, Simone. We never were and never will be. But if there's an ounce of humanity in you left, those girls' lives are in your hands. Help them escape from the Hartleys. Help us bring down your uncles."

"I may volunteer for one, but I'm not a charity, Tristan. Everything comes with a price, and I've already named mine. The question is, are you willing to pay it? And if we're being honest, my father didn't hold me captive. He blackmailed me." Her nostrils flared, and she let out a frustrated breath. "He blackmailed me, Tristan. I had no choice but to obey."

"What?"

"He blackmailed me. It's as simple as that. He told me to choose you or our baby."

Chapter 9

Allie

Tristan picked me up at the office fifteen minutes late, and I experienced the most uncomfortable elevator ride of my life. I knew he'd gone to the cove property, and from the looks of it, the day hadn't gone well. His brows furrowed, and he kept clearing his throat like he had a hairball.

I climbed into the leather seat, and he gripped the steering wheel harder. "Everything all right?" I asked.

"It is. Are you hungry?"

The aroma of Chinese takeout hit me. "I am now."

"Good. We should be home soon."

Tristan turned on his favorite eighties music and concentrated on traffic.

I yawned.

"Tired?"

"Yeah, it's been an interesting day. First Wright, then Marissa. Did you find anything at the cove?"

He turned up the heat. "More than I thought I would. I hope you're starving because so am I."

Sleep threatened me with every passing minute. I closed my eyes and lost myself to Enya's easy rhythms. I must have dozed off because when I opened my eyes again, we were sitting parked in the car.

Tristan's head rested against the seat side. He was looking at me as if he was seeing me for the very first time. The engine purred, and warm air tossed his hair like fluffy feathers. His freshly trimmed jaw curved into a slow smile, sending the scarred upper lip off center. That sexy, lopsided mouth made my heart thump.

"You're already tired?" he asked.

"It's the hormones." My hand flew up to my mouth. "You know, the time of the month coming up."

"Sounds like I should give those hormones a helping hand." The lust in his voice heated my core, and I pressed my knees together.

"A helping hand, a hard dick…" I wiggled my brows and looked out the fogged window, but couldn't see where we'd parked. "Where are we?"

He smudged the front window with his hand. He had parked on a paved driveway outside a mansion that resembled a Victorian-style country home.

"I thought you were doing take out. Do we have plans I wasn't aware of?" I asked.

"I do. Come on. I can't wait for you to see this." He hopped out of the car, walked around the front, opened my door, and took me under my arm. I checked my phone. It was already after eight. The front lights glowed underneath the porch, but it looked dark inside.

"It's a little late to visit anyone."

"We're not visiting."

He led me toward the front porch. The crisp air held a taste of salt, and I paused at the sound of ocean waves lapping in the distance.

"Are we near your parents? This feels like we're close."

Trees and shrubs bordered the property, without another house in sight.

"Patience, Allie. Patience."

Tristan took a deep breath in, and instead of ringing the doorbell like I expected him to, he lifted my hand and flattened my thumb against a keypad.

"Welcome home, Ms. Green," the intercom speaker said in a soft voice.

"Tristan, what is this?" My eyes widened, and my jaw dropped to the floor.

"Our home." He scooped me up under my knees and pushed the door open with his leg.

I squealed.

"I hope you like it."

"What are you doing?" I leaned into his body as he carried me over the threshold, then pressed his mouth to mine, stealing a passionate kiss.

"I've always wanted to do this," he whispered into my mouth.

I wrapped my arms around his neck, bringing his lips back to mine. "You bought us a house?"

Had he just bought us a house?

He set me down in the foyer and flipped on the lights. "You're right. We're next door to my parents, and I've been waiting for this house to go on the market. So when the opportunity—"

"You bought us a house?" I spun in a circle, taking in the two-story ceiling and a foyer the size of my old home.

"Please tell me you're okay with this." He stood in the same spot, watching me.

I turned around, slammed into his body a bit too hard, and took his mouth in a longing kiss. I held onto his face, losing myself in his warm lips until my bladder realized we were standing in a warmer space. I slowly slid out of his arms and down to the wooden floor. The faint sound of dripping water tortured me, but I had no time to find its source.

"Bathroom?" I stepped from one foot to another. He pointed to the right, and I rushed into the immaculate powder room.

He renovated?

After a quick relief, I stepped back into the beautiful foyer in awe. A chandelier composed of intricately enmeshed deer antlers hung above us, dangling from underneath exposed beams. Upstairs, beyond a balustrade, I saw a sitting area with plush couches and shelves stacked with books.

"You bought a house," I said to myself.

A waterfall feature trailed a steady stream down a side wall. The scent of fresh flowers drifted in the air. Blossoming arrangements in overflowing vases filled every nook and corner. The floral aroma mixed with wood and an ocean breeze floated through the house. I noted a fall flower arrangement on a stand below a mirror. Brown and orange tones stood out all around us.

"So when you say it's our home, what does that mean?"

I paced forward, trying to comprehend what had just happened, when Tristan wrapped his arms around me from behind, and lowered to my ear with a seductive whisper. "It means it's our home. For you, for me, and for our baby."

What?

I whipped my body around. My eyes grew wide as his focus lowered to my belly.

"You know?" I whispered.

"I just want the truth, Allie. Please tell me Simone's accusations aren't true."

Simone?

I swallowed hard.

"I don't know what her accusation is, but I am pregnant. We are pregnant."

I removed the sonogram from my purse and showed it to him. His hand shook, and I waited until my words sank in.

"I wanted to tell you at the work party, but then you fired me, and I've been trying to find a way ever since."

"And Cameron… Camelot Cameron—"

"What? Oh no, what did that bitch say?" I crossed my arms over my chest.

"She said you're having his baby."

"*Cameron's* baby?" I held onto my belly and laughed so hard I thought I would pee again. "I can't believe she would stoop so low."

"I can."

"Cameron's an old friend, and he and his wife are about to have a second set of twins. We bumped into him at the doctor's office, and I'm guessing that's what you meant when you said she was following me."

I took a deep breath in. This was a lot, even for Simone but judging from my earlier conversation with Emma, Simone wasn't done yet.

"You're the only one I've been with, Tristan, but if you'd like a paternity—"

"There's no need. I trust you. I love you."

He lifted me into his arms and spun in a circle while screaming, "We're having a baby!"

I held on tight, and when he stopped, I slid down his muscular body. All the hormones I'd suppressed since the shooting swarmed south. I lifted back up on my toes and kissed him hard, sneaking my tongue into his mouth with an invitation.

"I've missed you. I've really, really missed you."

A primitive growl vibrated through his chest, tightening the knot between my legs. His hands grazed over my hips, his thumbs skimming the skin. He swept my braid to the back, exposing my neck, where he left a searing trail of kisses.

"You shouldn't meet with her, Allie. She's a Hartley, and she's not the same Simone I once knew."

I winced. The hunger pangs worsened in my stomach.

"I know. She's worse. I think you'll be interested in what I found out, but I need to sit down first."

Tristan took me under my arm and led me past the Thanksgiving decorations in the dining room.

"Did your mom decorate?"

He smiled. "She did. We're hosting Thanksgiving this year."

"We are?"

"If you're up for it."

He pulled a stool from underneath the kitchen island, and I sat down. I spun on the seat, taking in the beautifully renovated home.

"Are you kidding me? Hosting Thanksgiving? I've been dreaming of this day most of my life."

"So, how pregnant are we?"

He lowered his hand to my belly, smoothing over my sweater.

"It must have been one of our first times. The doctor said my IUD discharged."

"Eight to ten weeks?"

"Nine." I grinned so hard my cheeks hurt. "It's the size of a cherry, and I'm feeling very horny and hungry."

"Hold those thoughts."

Tristan went back to the car and returned with bags filled with cartons of food. He set out the dishes of noodles, rice, spring rolls, and shrimp dumplings while my tummy let out a hungry growl.

I grinned. "That smells delicious."

"Olivier stayed back at the restaurant, so it's all fresh."

"And fortune cookies? I love fortune cookies." I sat down on the family room floor, crossing my legs.

"Leave these for last. I've heard patience brings good luck."

Tristan sat down beside me. My gaze followed his lengthy body, heating all over. His cotton shirt clung to his skin, and the sweats he'd changed into held loosely around the hips. The object of my hunger switched from Chinese food to Tristan until he swirled a forkful of noodles in front of my nose. "Chopsticks or fork?"

"Fork." I took the bite. The growing hunger in my belly held no patience. My mojo had none either, as I eyed the main course sitting next to me.

"I can't believe we're having a baby."

"So you're happy?"

"Ecstatic. My mom's gonna get drunk, and my father's gonna bake brownies. Wait—has Emma known?"

I lowered my fork. "What do you think?"

"Of course, my sister knew. She always knows."

"Speaking of Emma, I asked her for a favor, and she found out some things you should know."

"That look on your face scares me. What is it, Allie?"

The fork slipped out of my grip and clattered to the floor. Tristan picked it up and gave me a clean one.

"Simone was pregnant fifteen years ago. Papers say she had a miscarriage after the accident in Austria. I'm sorry."

His gaze dropped to the plate in front of him. "She told me her father made her choose between me and a baby. But she lost it?"

I nodded. "But—"

"I knew there was gonna be a 'but'. There's always a 'but' with Simone."

"She's seeing an OB now."

"An OB?"

"That's what Emma said."

"Sounds like I should ask for Emma's help."

"She's fantastic. She wants to be just like her brothers."

Tristan poured himself a glass of wine and a ginger ale for

me. "Her brothers are losing their touch. We're slipping. I can't find Wright, and I think Simone stashed the bastard somewhere. I just can't figure out where or why."

"Because she wants me gone. Wright can pull the trigger."

He shuddered. "Not if we get to him first. If our lawyers can pull some strings, the hard drive evidence will be admissible. Wright's value will fall, and he'll be fair game. My team will be ready for him this time."

I couldn't wait for the day I heard the beautiful news that Dave Wright was dead. "Who's got the hard drive?"

"Gabe's working on the files now. It shouldn't be long."

I finished the second plate of my stir-fried rice and gripped his arm. "So, are you going to show me around our home?"

"Let's start with the bedroom." Need sparked in his eyes.

Tristan's hands took my hips before sliding to my lower back. "I love it when you wear dresses." His lusty whisper confirmed my suspicion. We'd definitely be christening a room tonight.

He crunched my dress into his fists and pulled it up over my thighs. My skin tightened at the cool breeze, and I pressed into his warm touch and eager fingers. The fondle traveled up between my heated thighs to the back, where he squeezed my ass cheeks. I unzipped the dress in a hurry and watched as the pleased look on his face shifted to a desperate one. My head tilted back, and his lips skimmed over my exposed neck before lowering to my lacy bra and the sensitive nipples underneath. I flinched at the touch. My bra loosened at the quick snap of his fingers. He lowered his mouth to my breast, licked around rim, and snuck his other hand down my panties.

His slick fingers rubbed at my growing need. I pressed my forehead against his chest and gripped his arms. My knees locked and my ass clenched. The friction grew underneath his fingers, and his circles tightened over my clit. I wanted him inside me, but I couldn't stop him from getting me off, either.

So I came hard and fast, heaving in air and shaking in his hold. Once the orgasm settled, Tristan stripped me and carried me upstairs—to our bedroom and our bed.

He shed his clothes in what felt like slow motion. I waited naked over the crisp sheets. From the ensuite bathroom, he turned on the shower and called out, "The water's ready, Allie."

We submerged beneath the hot stream. I tilted my head to the ceiling. The water hit my face like rain, smoothing back my hair.

"I can host Christmas too," I whispered through the stream.

He lathered a sponge and proceeded to wash me, pulling the suds over my skin in a circular motion.

"We'll talk about Christmas over Thanksgiving. We're traveling, if you're healthy and up for it."

I opened my eyes past the shining soap. "Where to?"

"Away from Simone, Wright, and everything else. We're spending Christmas in Austria."

"Austria?" I swept my hand over my eyes.

"Gabe's been staying there with Sam. The whole family is coming."

"Everyone?"

"Your mother, and I believe Laura, as well. The important thing here is that you'll stay away from Wright and Simone."

"That actually sounds very nice, but you know what feels even better?" I drew my fingers up the sprinkle of dark chest hair and back to around his neck, bringing him to my mouth.

"What?" His lips vibrated against mine.

"You, inside me."

Tristan took my mouth. His possessive growl vibrated over my skin and heated my body at the core. I welcomed his needy tongue and hard body. It didn't take long before he held my leg up by the knee and skimmed his dick down my swollen folds.

"Is this safe for the baby?" He waited with the head of his penis halfway in.

I bent at the knees and sank onto him, hoping once inside me, he'd relax. He lowered his forehead to mine and closed his eyes. When he opened them again, his mouth surprised mine with a desperate kiss. He kissed me hard, held me steady, and pushed his dick deeper and faster. The scent of his desire lifted on the surrounding steam. My breaths quickened and I gripped Tristan's arms, gluing myself to his body. I rose up on my toes and squeezed around his thick cock, enticing his urgent thrusts. His ass tightened and his rhythm sped until Tristan stilled, locked his knees, and came with a loud, "Fuck!"

I waited until he withdrew. "You know I can't get pregnant twice, right?"

He looked up and laughed. "Oh, it's not that."

"What is it then?"

"I was supposed to make love to you, and that… well, that was pathetic, if you ask me."

"I'm glad I didn't ask, then. You didn't enjoy it?"

"I came like a fucking rocket, that's the problem."

"I'm sorry, what's the problem?"

We stood underneath the shower stream, lost in each other's eyes. His cheeks and forehead tinted with a shade of red, his lips parted, and the scar twisted his mouth upward.

"Why does this feel so right?" he asked out of nowhere. "Nothing has ever felt so right in my life, except for you."

"I don't know, but I feel the same way."

"I mean, should we even question all this? What's the next step?"

I pressed my finger to his lips. "Your investigator brain is overthinking. Why don't you shut up and take me to our bed?"

He scooped me into his arms in a swift move. The scar lifted on his mouth. He was stunning as he carried me to our new bed like I was his for the rest of our lives. We made love that night until neither one of us had any strength remaining and there was nothing Simone could do to claw her way back into Tristan's life.

Or so I thought until I met up with Julia Blakely at the hospital's cafeteria the next day. The same woman who'd helped me when I fell ill three years ago was not only a doctor but also the family's friend, and I was hoping she could get me more information about Simone's obstetrician.

"I still can't thank you enough for your help at the lodge."

"I helped reduce a fever. That's all."

"You urged James to take me to the hospital. I know that for a fact because I heard you. They said it could have been worse, so thank you."

"It was the nuggets, wasn't it?"

"What?"

"The chicken nuggets you had at the lodge the night before the Silvers arrived."

"I think so."

"Ha! I knew it." She high punched the air, and her scrub sleeve slid down her wrist, revealing a black mark.

"Knew what? Is that an Infinity tattoo?" I asked, and she pulled the fabric back, covering her skin.

"Ahem, yeah, it is."

"Infinity, as in Simone Hartley's non-profit company?"

Her brows narrowed, and she puffed out her next breath. "Infinity is far from non-profit."

"Simone said they help women leave dangerous situations."

She wiped away the tears filling her eyes, and blew her nose into a tissue. Her face reddened and the veins in her neck pulsed hard underneath the skin. "Infinity doesn't help women. They use them, forever. Their whole non-profit spiel is a joke."

"What do they do? Why do you have that tattoo?"

"I… I can't really talk about it. I got out, but if they find out I'm talking, I'm dead."

"Infinity? Seriously?"

"Jeff Hartley's private island is just a pit stop, and it has nothing on a secret operation. You understand why Simone volunteers at Hope for Hope, don't you?"

Judging by the look on Julia's face, it wasn't because Simone wanted to help the women, the way she claimed. Julia didn't wait for my reply. "They need fresh bodies to traffic. They look for vulnerable women with too much to lose, who will keep their mouths shut."

"Is Silver Securities aware of this?"

"I… I don't know. I really don't know, and you can't tell anyone I said anything. No one," she insisted, lifting her forefinger in a threat.

"But—"

"I said no one." Her lips trembled. Julia wiped her clammy hands on her scrubs and shut her eyes, waiting for my reply.

"All right. I won't say anything unless you want me to. But—"

"Allie, I know you want to help, but you can't. Not with this. Women don't leave Infinity alive. I wouldn't ask you if it were only my life at stake."

I didn't know what else to say because I couldn't understand Julia's reasoning. So I put our Infinity conversation on the back burner.

"So, I know Emma's been calling you."

Julia smiled. "Calling me? You tell little Emma if she tries to blackmail me again, I will be the last person she crosses."

"Emma blackmailed you?"

"I'm not exactly supposed to divulge patient information, especially on someone like Simone Hartley."

"But you found something more?"

Julia eyed the cafeteria from side to side. "Yeah, I found out something more."

I leaned in.

"Simone's documents from fifteen years ago are incomplete.

They treated her in Vienna for a broken pelvis, punctured lungs, and a ruptured spleen, but when she returned to the US, she self-admitted with abdominal pains and spotting. Paperwork said she miscarried soon after."

"But?"

"She transferred under an anonymous name to a private clinic, where she had a kid."

"What?"

"Simone Hartley gave birth fourteen years ago. Scar Wagner checked the information for me. She has a kid no one knows about. I mean, the Hartleys probably know about him, but he's been pretty much hidden this entire time."

"She had a son?"

"I called Tristan before you came in, so he's aware. DNA would confirm it, but chances are—"

"Tristan has a son."

Julia's phone pinged with a message. Her head flew up and her eyes grew wide.

"What is it?" I asked.

"Tristan Silver's in the ER."

Chapter 10

Tristan

I stormed inside Club Magnet past George. "Leave the car running. This won't take long."

"Yes, sir," he called from behind me. "She's in the diamond suite."

I stomped across the carpet. My feet sank into the plush footing, dimming my anger. Light sconces illuminated the long hallway. One of the Hartley goons pulled back the curtain as soon as I turned the corner and I stopped, watching her from a distance.

Simone was sitting cross-legged in the oversized chair her father used to occupy. My jaw tensed and my blood boiled. She'd planned to lure me all along, and she'd succeeded; but I wasn't here to stay. A civil conversation with Simone was useless at this point. She could no longer deny the secret she'd kept from me. The hard drive I'd recovered had confirmed my suspicions— photographs of Simone with my son had filled the screen, along with all the years I'd missed.

I walked across the room, fuming. "Where is he? Where is my son, Simone?"

She slowly set her phone aside, testing my patience. The

goon peaked inside the curtain, but she motioned for him to leave.

"I don't know what you're talking about."

"There was no miscarriage. Fourteen years ago you gave birth to a son at a private clinic. My son."

"And who is providing you with all these lies?"

"The least you can do is be honest."

"The least you can do is know your place, Silver." She uncrossed her legs and straightened. She reminded me so much of her father that it made me sick to my stomach. How could I have ever loved this woman?

"I want to see my son."

A playful grin stretched across her face. "How is Allie feeling? I hope Dave Wright didn't scared her on the subway."

My heart stopped for a split-second. "How do you know about Wright?"

"You've lost your touch, Tristan. Read the room."

She tilted her head and smiled with the same cocky attitude she'd carried when we dated. How could I have been so blind? At the time, I'd thought our puppy love would never end. As the tension between our families grew, so did the distance between us. I stayed with Simone because I feared she would do something stupid. And she did. Many times. I couldn't protect Simone from her mishaps any better than her father, and he blamed me for them all. She'd been using me all this time.

"Where's my son?"

"You don't have a son. I do." The spite in her voice coated my ears with bitterness.

I gripped the table between us. "I'm going to find him, Simone. You can't keep him away from me forever."

"It's worked so far, hasn't it? You're delusional if you think I'm the one who kept Tristan Junior away from you."

"Tristan Junior?"

She shrugged with one shoulder. "I'm sure it's a better name than Jeffrey. My father wanted Tristan Junior changed to Jeffrey. He was obsessed about his grandson and constantly toyed with the idea of him taking over the organization one day. My father's final jab to the Silvers was supposed to be one of their own choosing the Hartleys."

I sat down on the cushioned seat. "What happened to Tristan?"

"Your boy carries more Silver blood than my father expected. He's handsome and strong." Her smile faded.

"But?"

"But he's a teenager, Tristan. He's a fourteen-year-old with a lot of questions and enough energy to bring everything down. And I mean everything."

Oh, my God.

I was beginning to understand why Simone had returned from the dead. She had trouble on her hands she couldn't fix.

"He doesn't want to have anything to do with you, does he?"

"It's not me. It's the Hartleys." She rolled her eyes.

"You're a Hartley."

"You know what I mean. And I would have been a Silver if you'd married me."

"You died."

"I didn't."

"A technicality."

"No, it's not a technicality, Tristan. I'm not a technicality. I was blackmailed. My father stole my family life, and I will have him rolling in his grave before I give up on you or my son."

She lifted the wine glass off the table and steadied her trembling hand before she took a sip. "You cannot keep my son from me."

"I won't. If you do what's right." She leaned back in the chair, and I frowned. I would never leave Allie.

"Don't you see it? I'm a victim in all of this, just like you are.

It's all my father's fault. The accident, him keeping us apart, recruiting Wright—"

"Where is Wright?"

Her forehead creased. "I already told you the Hartleys have him."

"That's a lie. Wright is a snitch, and your uncles want him dead."

"Well, he's not dead. At least, not until they find him, and they won't find him just yet."

"So you know where he's at?"

"That depends on whether you're ready to accept my offer."

"I'm not leaving Allie. She's having my baby, and I'm going to marry her. I trust her and I love her. There's nothing you can do to stop me."

Her lip flattened.

"Fine. You want Wright, then go get him. He's useless to us anyway. You'll probably find him at the boathouse, wanking off to your girlfriend's photograph. He has a lot of those."

"He's at the cove?"

"Where else could I have kept him from my uncles? I can't believe you missed it. Silver Securities should be proud, Tristan. He's been under your nose the entire time."

I slammed my hand on the table. Simone's sudden spark of generosity had to be calculated.

"Why is Wright useless?"

"I guess you didn't hear. The snitch received a Presidential pardon for his crimes. If you kill him, you'll be doing the Hartleys a favor. Go ahead." She swept her hand through the air. "Go get him. Be my guest."

I hadn't heard the news, but then my phone beeped with the same message on our company's app.

Fuck!

Maybe Simone was onto something? Maybe I'd been going

about Wright the wrong way. If he'd already snitched, he was a liability to Kendra and Allie.

"Told you." She swayed her leg back and forth, watching me.

"What about my son?"

She stood up and paced around the table, holding my gaze until she was standing in front of me. She smoothed her palm over my chest and whispered, "For as long as you choose her, you have no son."

I removed her clingy palm. "We'll see about that, Simone. Karma is a bitch, and she's coming for you."

She rolled her eyes. "Great! I've been looking for karma as well. If you see her, tell her I'm in the Caribbean. This stress and cold weather is not good for my skin, and I have a vitamin D deficiency."

I puffed out a breath of disappointment — though I don't know what else I'd been expecting from her — and left.

Forty-five minutes later, I parked the car outside the Hartley's property gates at the cove and snuck in through the overgrown bushes. Someone had leaned an electric scooter against a tree in the front driveway, but I couldn't imagine it was Wright's. I hunched over and headed for the shoreline through the apple orchard. The boathouse door swung open with the wind. I deduced Simone must have warned Wright and he'd fled. Her cat and mouse games were getting old... and better.

I paced through the cluttered room. Garbage littered the floor, and the stench of mold and cigars overpowered the boathouse. I covered my mouth with the back of my hand and kicked through the trash until I reached the dinette. Photographs, maps, and sticky notes were scattered over the table. That, more than the smell, made my stomach twist—because all the pictures were of Allie and her mother. Allie when she was a kid, pregnant Peg, and some recent ones he must have taken when he'd followed Allie.

"Fucking bastard," I screamed, swiping the papers off the

table. The wind blew through the boathouse, lifting the garbage off the floor.

I stepped outside, and a sharp pain zapped from the back of my head to the inside of my brain. My ears rang and my vision darkened. I smoothed my hand over the aching spot and sticky hair; fresh blood stained my hand. My knees buckled, and I fell to the ground.

I wasn't sure how long I stayed unconscious, but it couldn't have been long because when I opened my eyes, I was riding in the back of my car. The sun shone through the window, and I lifted my bloodied hands to shade my eyes. The pounding in my head throbbed, pushing outward harder than a hangover. It felt like a grenade was ready to go off in my head.

"Argh!"

I lifted halfway up and focused on the young driver.

"What the hell?"

"Stay down. He whacked you pretty good, and you're losing blood." The boy turned briefly, and I gasped. His bone structure, shoulder-length darker hair, and the genetic silver streak near the bangs stopped my heart.

"You… you're—"

"Yeah, I know. I'm your son and you're my father and my family has kept us apart for years because they hate you, but I have to get you to the hospital."

It was true. My son was real, and Simone had kept him from me for fourteen years.

"I was gonna say, I don't think you should be driving a car, kid."

He glanced back again, and again, and my heart stopped.

"I've been driving ever since my grandfather bought me a Mini Porsche."

"A what?"

"One of those battery-operated ones you steer on a driveway."

My vision blurred, and the world around me appeared through a haze.

"Legally?"

He swerved to the left and laughed. "Nobody does anything legal anymore."

That wasn't true, but living with the Hartleys would paint a distorted reality. The thought of my son being raised by that bastard lifted my heart rate, and my head throbbed again. I ripped off my sleeve, folded the fabric into a square, covered the wound, and pressed the cloth over the gash.

"You're a good driver. What's your name?"

"Tristan Junior, but I prefer TJ."

I snickered. Part of me had expected Jeffrey, as Simone had said. Simone's father must have been pissed when he heard the chosen name. While I wished I'd met my son under different circumstances, and a decade and a half earlier, knowing Hartley would be rolling in his grave for eternity brought me a rare satisfaction.

"It's nice to meet you, TJ. Who hit me?" I asked.

"The asshole my mother was hiding in the boathouse. His name is Dave. My uncles were looking for him, so she hid him, because he's sick. He has this thing for pregnant women."

Wright.

"Where is he now?"

"Gone, and I hope he never comes back."

"Fuck."

"You want him back?" he asked.

"No. I want him dead."

Wright was a nuisance, and according to the Wagners, his testimony against Donaldson was weakening by the day. At some point we'd need to decide whether the evidence he could bring forth was worth the risk. We'd hang up our license if our client, Kendra, went away for a crime we couldn't prove she didn't commit.

My head pulsed like it wanted to explode. I gripped my hair, pulling hard with the hope this pain would numb the other. "Fuck!"

I slid down in the seat and lay down in the back.

"Are you okay, man?"

He must have accelerated and I must have passed out after that, because the next thing I knew, two doctors were pulling me out of the car and onto a gurney. A team of nurses and medical staff swarmed around me.

"Where is he?" I asked. "Where's my son?"

"There was no one else in the vehicle."

"What do you mean, no one else? I didn't drive here myself. Where is my son?"

"You need to lie down, sir. We'll have security check the cameras. How old is your son?"

"Fourteen. I think."

I lifted my head to look at my car and the empty driver's seat. Was it all in my head, or had my fourteen-year-old I'd never met just driven me to the emergency room?

It didn't take long before my family found me at the hospital and organized a search party for TJ and Wright. My brothers and cousins called in a few favors, and it was done. Just like that.

Wright was dead.

And I had my son.

Chapter 11

Allie

"**D**oes it hurt?" I asked.

"No" He groaned, twisting in the sheets. Tristan slept like a rock after his release from the hospital. The concussion came with fatigue, and as much as he wanted to cure his 'headache,' his body chose rest. I confined him to the bedroom, and he used the time reconnecting with TJ and gathering evidence against Simone. Karma was coming. We'd both called it.

"Liar." I checked the area at the back of his head. "Come shower and let me change the dressing."

"Not yet." He pulled me over and I straddled him. I never understood those who could sleep naked or those who slept in pajama pants. One was too cold and the other too constricting. Tristan was the former, and my choice was panties and his shirt.

I tightened my thighs around his hips. His morning wood stood tall, the same way it did every morning, eager for my full attention.

"Why do you have your panties on?" His frown slowly turned into a nefarious one.

"You want them off?"

"No, baby. *You* want them off." He wiggled his brows, and with a skillful tug at the corners, he removed them with a flick of the wrist. The scar on his lip twisted into a smile, and his cute dimple sank in. The slick need between my thighs throbbed. My favorite way to start a morning since living with Tristan was with the most orgasmic sex. Every time.

I gripped his heavy cock in my hand. He was thick, hot, and ready. His vein pulsed along my palm. I swept my thumb over the drop of pre-cum as he urged me to rise.

He lined himself at my entrance, and I lowered. His eyes closed and his lips parted as I sank onto him. I gripped his hips with my knees and took control of my ride. On the third roll, I removed my shirt and grasped my breasts. He liked that a lot because he opened his eyes and brought his other hand to my hip, trying to steal my control. The thing was that I liked his control. He knew what he was doing for the both of us. Like that lift he did, where the extra friction of his pubic bone against mine tingled all the right nerves and my clit. It spread through my body, building into bliss. He angled my hips and gripped me, rubbed tighter, rolled quicker, and pushed harder.

I bounced to the building rhythm. His hands soon replaced mine over my breasts. My head lolled back as Tristan fondled and teased my sensitive nipples. The first zap of pleasure flew through my body, and I lifted my head and opened my mouth, so fucking grateful for pregnancy hormones. He braced his arms on the bed, shifted us to a sitting position and buried himself deeper inside me. I wrapped my legs around his hips and held on as he kissed me like his life depended on mine. I melted against him, giving him every inch of control I'd thought I had, letting him do with my body as he pleased.

I orgasmed first, because he liked it that way, and he soon followed. I stayed in his hold, with him inside me until my heart calmed, until I startled at the echo of clattering dishes.

"Is somebody here?" My eyes grew wide.

"It's Olivier. Have you forgotten we're hosting Thanksgiving?"

Of course, I hadn't forgotten. We'd planned to tell Maggie and John about the baby that afternoon. Tristan's parents were to arrive with the other Silvers. I'd never hosted a large family gathering and accepted all of Tristan's and Olivier's offered help.

"No, of course not. But it's seven in the morning," I whispered, and Tristan laughed.

"I don't think he can hear you, and I'm sure your moans were louder a moment ago."

My face heated. "Seven in the morning?" I asked again.

"Obviously, he has a lot of work to do, which means he needs help."

I pushed my hand at his chest and slowly lifted off him. "You're not going anywhere until I check the dressing."

I removed the wrapped bandages and the taped ones. Wright had whacked him pretty hard, and Tristan had retaliated with full force. The doctors shaved an area where they stitched his head; Tristan was lucky his longer hair covered the spot. Truthfully, he was lucky to be alive. The doctor recommended bed rest and no straining, but Tristan insisted sex would heal him more quickly.

So it was the only activity I allowed him to do.

"I'll change the dressing and help Olivier, but you need to stay in bed. I've used you enough as it is."

"Never enough," he growled.

I jumped out of bed before he could grab me and squealed, running for the shower. He soon joined me under his own stream, and I helped to wash his hair while he helped to wash all of me. I stepped out before the need took over all senses and changed into comfortable fall leggings. I paired them with a loose sweater and hurried downstairs, where the smell of coffee and cinnamon and spiced apple wafted through the kitchen.

Today would be a good day. Yellow and orange leaves drifted beyond the window. It had been fifteen years since I'd celebrated Thanksgiving with my mother, and the expectation of a perfect afternoon lifted my spirits. Thank God for private chefs!

"Good morning, Olivier."

"Good morning, Ms. Green."

"Allie. It's Allie. I didn't know you were coming so early."

"The coffee is decaf and the ginger-chamomile tea has a touch of honey. Apple-cinnamon croissants will be out of the oven in three minutes."

My mouth watered.

"It smells delicious. What can I help you with?"

"You can have a seat and have breakfast. Tristan just texted from upstairs, insisting you eat and I'll bring something up for him as well."

My cheeks heated, but it was nice to feel he cared so much. The last three days had been rough and everything we never expected when his son showed up at the hospital. If karma had a single purpose for today, she'd ensure TJ would show for Thanksgiving.

I poured myself a cup of decaf and stuffed a croissant in my mouth. "I'm ready."

Olivier looked me over. "All right. Can you chop?"

"Yes, I can chop." I set my coffee on the counter by the cutting board. I sliced the cucumbers into eights; sweet peppers and carrots lengthwise; cauliflower, mushrooms, and radishes into bite-size pieces. The colorful hors d'oeuvres platter arranged in a pumpkin shape complemented the charcuterie board with the cold cuts. I followed Olivier's guiding voice and arranged the platters into art pieces.

By early afternoon, a blend of deliciousness filled the house and drew Tristan downstairs. Dressed in comfortable slacks and a gray V-neck shirt, he looked like a good dessert. My hormones stirred and my body tingled.

"Something you need?" He stepped in from behind and smoothed his hand over my belly.

I giggled and turned in his hold.

"The turkey and potatoes are in the oven, and the pumpkin pie is cooling on a rack."

He stepped back and eyed my outfit. "Love the apron. Do I get to kiss the cook?" He unfastened the back and slipped the apron off my neck.

"But Oliver already left."

"I meant you."

"I know." I rose up on my toes and touched my lips to his.

"Everything looks amazing," he said against my mouth.

"How are you feeling?"

He touched the back of his head. "The spot is sore, but I'm better. How is Baby Puss?"

"I hope you know we're not naming our baby Puss."

He chuckled. "No, we're not."

"Speaking of babies, any word from TJ?"

Doubt sparked in his eyes. "Nothing yet, but if he shows, it'll be a good day. The kid saved my life. He has everything we need to put Donaldson and the Hartleys away. If Simone finds out, I think he's safer staying here."

"I agree. And if she doesn't find out?"

"Then I still want him to stay here, in our home."

I smiled. "I was naive to believe she actually wanted to help the girls."

"It's sick. She used Hope for Hope to traffic the same girls she claimed she was saving."

"She won't let TJ go. Not without a fight."

"I wouldn't expect anything less, but I'll be ready. And our Christmas vacation can't come soon enough."

"Agreed."

He smoothed his thumb over my brow. "I never expected to be a father, and now I find out I have a teenager, who seems like a pretty cool boy, and another baby on the way."

"It's a lot to take in." I wrapped my arms around him and held him tighter.

"It is. Thank you for standing by me, Allie." He kissed the tip of my nose. "And thank you for working so hard today."

When Tristan told me he'd be cooking Thanksgiving dinner with Olivier, I thought he'd lost his mind. After they admitted him to the hospital, I thought he'd call the dinner off, but this was my first family celebration, and I didn't want to back out. So I volunteered to help.

"Happy Thanksgiving!" The back door opened, and Emma walked in with a platter of pumpkin- and leaf-shaped cookies.

"You're here already?" Tristan checked the time.

"Now that you live next door, I'll be over every day."

"Wonderful." Tristan rolled his eyes, and I elbowed him in the ribcage. I adored the idea of having Emma over whenever she wanted, and I loved the idea of living so close to my new relatives.

Emma slammed into me and eyed my belly apologetically. "Oops, sorry. I didn't say anything to anyone. I promise. But if I have to keep this secret any longer, I swear, I'll burst. This month has been so stressful. People, don't tell me any more secrets. I can't stand it!"

"Today, Ems. It's happening today."

"What secret?" Tristan's father walked through the front door.

"Someone mentioned a secret?" Wilma stepped in from behind him.

Emma's body whipped around to face us. "I said nothing. I promise."

Tristan took my hand, and we joined our parents in the

foyer. He lifted his chin and glanced from me to them and back. My mother looked me over from the bottom up and gasped. "Oh, my gosh, she's glowing."

"Why is she glowing?" Fred handed Tristan the bottle of wine and set the enormous plant he was carrying on the floor. I grinned like a frickin' clown. Emma held her breath, her thin lips turning nearly purple. I gave Tristan a little nod.

"Mom, Dad, Peg. We have another reason to celebrate today. Allie's expecting."

Fred caught Wilma under her arms before she fainted. "What is she expecting?" he asked.

Tristan's uncle grabbed a chair and set it behind Wilma. I hadn't even noticed when the other Silvers arrived. Where was Laura?

"You're pregnant?" she asked, and I nodded.

My mom's face paled. It was only fifteen years ago that she'd been awaiting my sister's birth. She stepped closer and took me into her arms, her salty tears dripping on my shoulder. The lump in my throat thickened and my eyes welled. My mother let me go, and my hormones squeezed out a few happy tears.

"The curse has been lifted!" Emma swept her hand over her forehead. She then grabbed her cousin James by the collar and screamed, "I'm going to be an aunt!"

He laughed and connected his gaze with mine. I recognized the stare down and felt all the blood drain from my face. The reason Emma had no more secrets was because James knew about Foxy.

"You're going to be a grandpa, Fred." Wilma patted her husband on his back before she embraced Tristan. "Congratulations, honey. I've been waiting for this day for a long time."

"And I get to name the baby!"

Tristan gave me a puzzled look.

I shrugged. "It's a long story, and she drives a hard bargain."

"And if you even think of breaking our deal, I will have you know I can find another favorite brother."

"Is Julian coming?"

Wilma shook her head. "No, he's with Kendra."

"How is she doing?"

"Better. Just not there yet. Hopefully, soon."

Worry clouded Wilma's eyes, and I took her hand.

"She's been through hell, but she'll heal. Julian will make sure she does." I smiled. It had been over a month since I'd found her at the hotel bar. According to Tristan, we got lucky that night. "But that's not what you're worried about, is it, Wilma?"

She shook her head, and Tristan cleared his throat. "Why don't you show the family around, and I'll set out the food?"

"Yeah, sounds good. We'll finish this conversation later," I whispered to Wilma. "Follow me, everyone. Follow me. Appetizers on your left and welcome pumpkin spiced bubble tea on your right. Grab your sugar poison and follow me."

I'd practiced showing off the house for three days. Everything from the library to the indoor pool and jacuzzi I never knew I wanted until I soaked off all my body aches.

"Are we boarding a flight?" Emma snickered.

"No, but you can check the attic, Ems—you know, to make sure we have no ghosts." I winked and her face went red.

Our guests hung their coats and followed me around through the home. A few minutes before dinner, I took my mother aside and showed her the guest home through the window. "It's being renovated, but we'd like you to move in once it's done."

"Really?"

"Of course, Mom. I want you close to your grandbabies. How are you doing at the Silvers'?"

"I'm down to three locks, and the rifle's tucked in a closet."

"That's good, Mom. That's amazing."

We sat in the dining room. Tristan had set the table. The stuffed turkey steamed from the pot, and the thought of the honey glazed duck made my mouth water.

My mother tapped the wineglass with her fork. "Allie, Tristan—thank you so much for hosting Thanksgiving. And I would like to say a special thank you to the Silvers for all the love you've shown both Allie and me. Thank you for the constant care and protection. After… After my husband died, I never thought I would have a family again, but you proved me wrong. This family is more than anything I could have ever asked for. Thank you."

She wiped away the stray tear from the corner of her eye, and James lifted his wineglass in a toast. "Hear, hear."

Everyone joined in a cheer.

"Bon appétit! Dig in. I want all the food gone!"

Wilma grinned, "Well, we may just have to stay the night, honey."

"It's not like you're driving home, Mom."

I sank my teeth into the crunchy bruschetta, because carbs during pregnancy tasted better than chocolate. The tomato juices fused with a touch of parsley and garlic, melting in my mouth. A hint of olive oil completed the tasty platter. I swallowed and moaned.

Tristan eyed me from the side. "If I were you, I'd save some room for dinner and dessert. You don't want to miss that."

"Trust me, there's always room for dessert." I patted my belly. "I have to call Olivier to thank him again. Everything is delicious."

The two-way fireplace crackled. I'd never been in a home with a real fireplace; you know, the kind you actually add wood to instead of flicking on a switch that magically, yet not so magically, turned on the gas. Warmth seeped through the home, and the smell of smoldering wood brought back childhood memories. I saw my mother getting lost in her thoughts as well. The before memories, when Dad was alive, were beginning to fade, and days like today brought them back.

"So, when is the wedding?" Fred asked.

Wedding? I'd barely gotten used to the fact we were having a baby.

"Dad, this is the twenty-first century. You don't have to be married to have children."

"No grandchild of mine is going to be born out of wedlock. Besides, this house is too big for two people."

"I thought you said you loved the house. You both have wanted me to buy it for years."

"Of course we love it, but now you need to fill it. With more people."

"Well, I can't get her any more pregnant than I already have, but I'm working on that too."

"Mind your business, John!" Wilma scolded. I rarely heard her use Fred's real name.

"What? Is it too much to put a ring on it?"

I chuckled.

"Yeah, Tristan, put a ring on it." Emma scrolled through her iPhone and played Beyoncé, giggling. "Can I be your maid of honor?"

"Uhm..." I looked to Tristan for help, but he appeared as dumbstruck as me.

"Well, aren't you going to raise this baby together?" James's mother, Teresa, asked from across the room. "A child should have a father in its life if the father's willing to be responsible."

"Goldie Hawn and Kurt Russell have been together for decades. They're proof you don't need a ring to make it work. "

James smiled all the way from across the table, and I knew he still loved Laura because I'd used her line. I missed her. He finally knew about Foxy, and the fallout hadn't been pretty. Hence, why she hadn't come to Thanksgiving.

From my conversation with Laura, Teresa wasn't happy

James didn't commit to Laila's mother. If that were true, she'd be furious with Laura.

My mother lowered her hand over mine. "Whatever you choose, we'll support you, but let me be the first to tell you both: I think you've found a soul mate in each other. Don't take that for granted."

Tristan set his wineglass on the table. "Of course we're raising our child together, but we should settle in before you send over a priest."

"Good idea. I knew I raised you to be a man. We can discuss the wedding date over dessert." Fred's unyielding tone gave me the shivers. Wedding date? My stomach swirled.

"That's not what I meant, Dad."

"You can get married after Gabe. The priest will be there, and you won't have to decorate again."

Emma's fork clattered to the plate. "Gabe and Sam are getting married?"

"Fred?" Wilma asked. "What are you talking about?"

"Go ahead, Jacob. Tell them."

Gabe's father removed an envelope from the inside of his jacket pocket. "I just received the official invitation on Monday. We're all going to Austria for Christmas. Gabe and Sam are getting married."

"Yes!" Emma removed her phone from her pocket and started texting.

The bruschetta swirled in my tummy.

"Why don't you get married?" I overheard Emma ask her brother. "I want to be a real aunt."

"You're already a real aunt, Ems. You just don't know it," Tristan said.

Tristan's phone dinged at the same time as mine. I opened the security camera app. A white Jaguar pulled up to the front gate. My head flew up, and I connected my gaze with Tristan's.

"What is it?" My mother lowered her fork.

"We have a guest. Mom, Dad, whatever happens, please don't freak out."

I swallowed hard and stood up. The Flintstones were about to learn they had a fourteen-year-old grandson.

"You better stay here, Allie."

"Hell, no. I'm not letting you face Simone by yourself. We're in this together."

There was no way I would allow Tristan to talk to Simone without me, simply because I didn't trust her or what would come out of her mouth.

"That's my girl!" Fred high-fived his brother Jacob. "I knew she'd make a great daughter-in-law the day she pinned Julian on our basement floor."

I shook my head and watched as James and Hunter stood up from the table and joined their cousin in the hallway.

"It's all right. I've got this."

The front door opened in slow motion to a grinning Simone on our front porch, standing beside a teenage boy who was the spitting image of his father, Tristan.

"Mom, take the kids to the backyard." I called out. "TJ, you go ahead to the back with Allie. She'll show you around."

I held the door open and waited as my curious family and my son left.

"TJ?" Simone fumbled with her car keys before dropping them in her purse.

I heard the shuffle of feet behind me, and when I was certain my parents and the kids had left, every muscle in my body tightened.

"Step the fuck back, turn around, and disappear, Simone. You won't get another chance."

She puffed out a scant breath and composed herself. "I just brought your son for Thanksgiving, Tristan. A little appreciation would be nice."

"It would have been appreciated if you'd fucking brought him to me fourteen years ago. How could you have kept this from me?"

"I already told you I had no choice," she spat back. "How could I not choose my child, Tristan? Father wouldn't give him to me until I swore my life over to the Hartley name."

"I could have helped. I would have taken you both away. I could have protected you. At least, our son won't have to put up with your fucked up life anymore."

"What are you talking about?"

"Wright is dead, Simone."

"What?"

"My team confirmed it an hour ago. Turns out, he was a greater liability than an asset for us as well. The cake topper is you can't use him to stalk Allie anymore."

She gasped and went pale within a breath. "What about Kendra? What about her case?"

"You should worry about your own business because your ass is about to be sued."

Simone composed herself. She lifted her chin high in the air and took a step forward. "You think I give a rat's ass about Wright or any business? I. Want. My. Son. Tristan!"

"All right. But you stay the fuck back, and remember, you asked for it. TJ!" I called to the back. "Come on over! He prefers to be called TJ, by the way."

That smug look of confidence faded off her face same way the Botox would when she went to prison.

"I had a chat with my son while recovering at the hospital, and he had some interesting things to say."

"You already met?" Her head flinched back slightly.

"It seems you told him I was dead."

Her gaze flew from me to who I assumed was Tristan Junior behind me.

"Well, isn't it good news you aren't dead?"

"Everything he says is true, Mother. I'm done. I've been done since the moment I googled our name when I was seven."

"You can't believe everything you read. The media twists things. It's fake news."

"The only thing fake around here are your boobs. And your ass, cheeks, nose, and chin. God only knows what else you've done." He rolled his eyes. "Silver Securities has all the evidence I've gathered over the years. If you know what's good for you, you'll leave, Mother. Go to the island or… just somewhere else. Stop making everyone's life miserable. Especially mine."

"See what you've done!" Her lips tightened into a thin line. "You've already turned him against me. It's those teenage hormones. Is that what this is about, honey? You want to go out to be with your little photography buddies? Gah, as boring as your father."

I winced. God, what was it that had once drawn me to this cruel and self-obsessed woman? Photography was calming. The activity allowed for time to think. It gave a moment of peace one rarely experienced.

TJ stepped out onto the front porch and faced his mother.

"There's nothing wrong with taking pictures, and I've been sneaking out to get away from you for years. I've been trying to find the truth at the cove—"

"That was you? You've been staying at the cove? You taught that bird to swear at me?" She jerked forward at TJ, and so did I, blocking her way. The last thing I'd allow this woman to do was threaten my family.

"Where else was I supposed to stay?" He stepped out from behind me. "And somebody had to feed that bird. I couldn't go to a normal school or the movies, so I found Freddie and made myself an escape room."

"What the hell is an escape room?"

"It doesn't matter, because I don't need the room anymore." The boy glanced back at me, and my chest warmed. "I'm gonna stay with my father from now on."

"What?" Her gaze flew from TJ to me and back to TJ again. "You can't do this to me."

"It's already done, Simone," I growled.

"Let me guess. Your Wagner boys took care of it? They're

going to get what's coming their way. You don't even know who your friends are."

"You're the last to lecture me about friends. At least, now I know my enemy. Get the fuck away, Simone. I won't ask again."

"Make me."

James and Hunter stepped in from behind me.

"All right, all right. I'm going. I know he'll be fine and you won't hurt him. But I want you back home, Tristan Junior! You're my son! Mine and nobody else's! You did this!" She pointed at Allie and stepped forward, but I blocked her way.

"Come on, Tristan Junior. Let's go."

"It's TJ, and I'm not going anywhere. Goodbye, mother." He turned around and went to the backyard.

My heart broke for the kid. He'd likely suffer from trauma for years, and hopefully, he wouldn't need the therapy fund I'd set up. If he'd allow me, I'd do anything to catch up on the last fourteen years we'd lost, and the upcoming Christmas holidays with the family were the perfect time to begin.

THE PLANE'S ENGINE HUMMED. I closed my eyes and concentrated on the spinning turbines and wheezing air. In less than nine hours, thousands of miles would separate us from Simone and the Hartleys. My son was sitting less than five feet away from me, chatting with his new aunt Emma like she was his best friend. I smiled.

The plane sped up the runway, pushing me back against my seat. I opened my eyes, squeezing Allie's hand.

"You're nervous?" she turned her head toward me.

"Excited and relieved."

The combination of the two definitely spiked the adrenaline in my veins. But how could I not be nervous? Here I'd thought I was going to be a father for the first time in my life, and I'd already been one for a decade and a half. Except I hadn't been one.

"It's okay to be nervous."

Her grip tightened on my hand. She kept me sane. She was my balance and my rock. I trusted her more than I trusted myself. If that made sense. For the first time in my life, I separated home from work, and this vacation in Austria couldn't have come any sooner.

"Maybe I am a little nervous." I grinned. "A week ago I thought I had a few months to get ready, and here I am, already a father. How do I father? They don't remember your mistakes when they're small, but they do at fourteen."

"You're a natural, and he's a great kid. I mean, how many teenagers love photography?"

"I don't know and I don't care."

"He has your genes, and he can tell between what's right and wrong. He's smart and thinks for himself. That's why he snuck away from his mother and hid at the cove. Very self-sufficient and set in his ways. Remind you of anyone?"

She was right. As always.

"It's hard to believe, isn't it? Jeff Hartley failed to convert him. The more I think about it, the more I'm convinced Jeff's mission in life was to ruin my life, and what better way to do so than keep my son away from me? I'm not sure whether we'd have this chance if you hadn't killed that bastard, Allie."

"It was self-defense."

"No. It was coming. It was karma."

She snorted and locked her fingers with mine. It felt good. She felt good, and I welcomed the support with a grateful kiss, whispering into her mouth, "I love you."

"I love you too. Are Kendra and Julian not coming?"

"I don't know yet."

"Poor Laura."

"Poor James. Look at him. He's miserable without her."

"They'll get through it, won't they?" She snuggled into my side.

I hoped they would. My cousin was happier with her than without her, and that had to count for something. I covered us both with blankets and counted her breaths until my pulse calmed, my eyes grew heavy, and we fell asleep until our landing in Vienna.

ALLIE STARED at the lodge home in the Alps like it was the castle of all lodges. Maybe it was.

"Oh, my God!"

"Better than Colorado?"

"I didn't get to see much of Colorado because of food poisoning, but I imagine nothing could be better than this."

"Nothing could."

"I can see why they want the wedding here. How many bedrooms?"

"Too many." I laughed. "The place is a maze. Four additions over the past decade as the family's grown. The cliffs make the place only accessible through the front gates, which makes this one of the most secure locations under Silver Securities."

"It's beautiful."

"Wait until you see the inside."

Emma and TJ pushed the double door open and ran inside on a search for their rooms while my parents, aunt, and uncle exchanged greetings with Gabe and Sam.

"This place is going to get busy." Allie turned in a circle, taking in the cabin.

"It's just the family and Olivier." Sam hooked her arm into Allie's and dragged her aside.

"Olivier is coming?" I heard her ask.

I enjoyed a glass of whiskey on ice, carried our luggage to our room, and stopped by TJ's on my way downstairs. He was staring at the wall filled with family photographs.

"You all right?" I asked.

"I always imagined this, but I never thought it would come true."

"I wish it could have been true sooner." I lowered my hand to his shoulder. "Hey, we should take some photos on this trip and add them to the wall. You belong with us."

"We should take ones of Allie as well. She's not up there. She should be."

"I saw your broken camera at the cove."

"Wright did that. He found my room."

Fucking Wright had to ruin something for everyone. I recalled our conversation from the day TJ came to visit me at the hospital. "The guy from the boathouse who hit you was crazy. I checked out his place once when he left, and he has all these sketches and photographs."

"What guy? Who was on the photographs?"

"I didn't know who she was until I saw her picture on your phone. It's Allie."

"Any way you know the man as Dave Wright?"

"I don't, but Mother's asked him to run errands in Manhattan. I'm not sure what errands, but he was happy to do them. Judging by the pictures, he was stalking Allie."

"So your mother kept Wright to torture Allie."

TJ confirmed my worst fears. At least, they were my worst ones at the time. If Simone had come with any good intentions, I'd have worked with her, but she became a threat the moment she showed up again. The decision to get her and Wright out of our lives for good had been easy.

And now, here I was, reaping the benefits of that perfect decision with my son at my side. TJ was everything I could ever imagine a son to be.

"That's why I thought you could use a new camera." I removed my hand from behind my back and gave him the wrapped gift.

TJ peeled off the Rudolph paper. It was probably too silly for him, but Emma pressured me to let her make the choice, and Rudolph won.

"Thank you. I love it."

"If you're up for it, why don't you take a picture of Allie and you together, and we'll blow it up? You can give it to her for Christmas. She'll love it."

"Really? I can go up on that wall?"

"I would love it if you were there, TJ. I really would. You're part of this family. It took major balls to stand up against the Hartleys. I don't know what evidence Gabe will find, but if half of what you're telling me is true, we'll have enough to help many people in trouble."

"I can tell you exactly what's there, and that's everything. My grandfather's contacts, my mother's schemes. She's the brains behind Infinity. Grandpa was too drunk half the time to know what was going on, and my uncles… they're sick and obsessed with money. Mother used Wright to torture Allie and let him live in the boathouse. She lured him with that girl Marissa."

"You don't have to worry about Simone or anyone else anymore."

"Will I have to live with her when we come back after Christmas?"

"No. You're going to stay with me and Allie. If you'd like."

He nodded, stepping from one foot to another.

"Is there something else?"

"Do I have to be a Hartley? You know, when I go back to school?"

I brought him in closer and held him against me. "We'll do whatever you need us to do. You're welcome to be a Silver."

"Thanks." He smiled. "I should go. Ems has a tight schedule. Swimming, ice bath, Swedish spa, and then she says she can work."

I laughed.

"She got me a tool belt."

"Thanks for helping."

"Dad?"

He looked up, and my eyes welled in an instant. No one had ever called me that before.

"You okay?"

"Yeah, I didn't realize how much I like you calling me Dad."

His smile stretched, sinking the dimple into his cheek. "I'm happy I finally can. Do you think Freddie will be okay?"

"I had a bird handler transfer him to our house. They'll have a look at the mass on his leg and will let me know about a treatment plan as soon as the pathology report returns."

"You're smart."

"So are you, kid."

"I don't know as much as you do."

"Not yet, but you will. Wisdom comes with age and experience."

It also came with more worry and a heart full of feelings I couldn't quite handle just yet. We spent the remainder of the day catching up with family, playing pool, and enjoying a rare moment of peace.

By midnight, our hosts had gone to bed while we remained awake. The time difference would mess with us for a couple more days. Our parents were playing cards by the wooden fireplace in the common room. Emma had started on the fairy light decorations she'd discussed with Sam. TJ was helping her, carrying around a hammer and a tool belt she'd bought for him last minute. He'd quickly rejected the 'Tool Boy' nickname but enjoyed her company as much as everyone in the family: to a limit.

Snow drifted to the ground, flying down the powdered mountains. The white peaks stood out against the night's backdrop. I walked down the hill, pulling an empty toboggan to where Allie was standing at the lookout point, admiring the town's lights in the distance.

"What are you up to?"

"Just getting some fresh air. It's hard to sleep."

"It will get easier in a few days. Can you ski pregnant?"

"You can, but I have another week in the first trimester, so I'd rather take it easy."

"I can do easy." I let go of the toboggan's rope and wrapped my arms around her, bringing her body to mine. "I can do very easy, slow and easy, nice and easy—anything easy as long as I'm with you."

"Did you have your father's brownies?" Her shoulders shook with a chuckle, and her breath trailed in the cold air.

"There's a significant possibility of that. Want to go for a dip?" I pointed to the pool's glowing light.

"It's the middle of the night."

"What happened to all that YOLO talk you give Laura?"

She looked up. "I'd have to get my bathing suit."

"No, you don't. I prefer au naturel."

"You did have brownies."

I took her mouth as soon as the accusation left hers and sealed my fate when she tasted chocolate on my lips and moaned with need.

"They don't give me the hangover booze does," I explained against her lips.

"I heard they make you horny, too. I've missed you, Mr. Silver." Her voice held the inviting note my dick had been awaiting.

"Let's do it right against that half-shaved spruce." I pointed to somewhere behind me.

"I'm willing to do you, but I'm not skinny dipping with my

mother, your parents, Emma, and TJ, and everyone else for the matter, in the house."

"Please, don't mention my sister when I'm hard and horny." My desperate kiss sucked the desire right out of her mouth. Her delicate whimper sang to my need, and I pulled on her jacket zipper.

Allie was right. Out here was much better. I could concentrate on her swelling breasts without my little sister or parents nearby. She removed my hand from her jacket.

"We're within view."

"I have a solution." I resumed undressing her. "How about I whisk you away tobogganing?"

"Naked?"

I stopped and looked her dead in the eye. "YOLO?"

Her mouth curved up, and the idea of taking her to one of the most beautiful features on this property flashed in my head. She wouldn't deny me there.

"There's a lighted trail around the perimeter. Come on." I wiggled my brows. "You sit, and I'll pull."

She zipped her jacket and sat on the toboggan. I pulled on the rope, marching through the drifts of snow until we reached the fairy lit path. I knew that Sam loved fairy lights, but judging by the twinkle in Allie's eyes, every woman loved them. Her mouth fell open, and she sat back on the toboggan, she watched the lights dance to the wind's sway.

"Tristan, this is beautiful."

"I told you so."

I kneeled in the snow and tied the loose laces on my boot. Allie sat up and gasped. I connected my gaze with hers as she choked, and then covered her mouth. "Are you proposing?"

My focus darted from her stunned face to myself, kneeling in front of her.

"Am I proposing? Ahem, no. At least, not today," I winked, though the square box burned inside my jacket pocket. I might not have timed this right, but I was ready to commit to this woman for life.

"I'm sorry. It's just that—"

"It's my mistake, Allie. No need to apologize."

"Your father's been talking about rings, and Emma's been talking secrets, and I don't know what to think anymore."

"This vacation is not about thinking, my love. This vacation is about relaxing. So why don't you let me help you do that?"

"But would you?"

"Would I what?"

"You know… marry me?"

"Allie, are *you* proposing? Wait a minute. Don't answer that —because there's no way I will have a woman propose to me."

"I wasn't proposing. It was a hypothetical question."

"I'm not a fan of hypothetical proposals; only real ones."

"Oh, good. Right now is not a good time anyway." Her voice shook with nerves.

"Why would now not be a good time?"

"It's your cousin's wedding. I wouldn't want to steal any attention from Sam."

"I don't even have a ring, Allie," I lied.

"That's why I said it was a hypothetical question."

"Well, to give you a hypothetical answer, I have been thinking about us, Baby Puss, and TJ, as a family. A real family. If you'll have me."

"Wait—was that a proposal?"

"No, just a promise to love you forever." I kissed her, and she melted into my arms. She pulled away at the sound of her lowering zipper.

"What are you doing?"

I gripped her breast through the sweater. "Look at your nipples. They're begging for my mouth."

"You excel at distractions, Mr. Silver." She laughed and grasped my hand, but I was quicker. I pulled her off the toboggan and into the snow. We rolled like a couple of teenagers, laughing, until we came to a stop. I hovered above her. The fairy lights above sparkled in her eyes. Stray snow covered her flushed cheeks, and her breath trailed in the air. She looked like a goddess. I helped Allie up and brushed the snow off her jacket.

"Ahh!" she screamed out.

"What is it?"

"I got some snow under my sweater."

I removed the packed ice from behind her back. We stood in the shadow of the shaved spruce. Strays of wet hair stuck to her cheeks, and I tucked them behind her ear, one on each side.

"Make love to me, Tristan," she whispered.

I pounced on her mouth and caught her lips between mine. She yielded to my persistent tongue, like she'd been waiting for a quiet moment. My greedy hands searched for access to her skin.

Zipper down, sweater up, undershirt, up—

"Allie?" I said into her mouth, pulling on an elastic band. "What the heck is this?"

"They're joggers."

"You mean long Johns?"

She snickered, and I found her skin. She closed her eyes, giving herself to my touch.

"Wait." She pulled away, breathing hard. "We can't do this naked. We'll freeze."

I lowered her zipper and heard my voice command from within my chest. "Turn around."

She braced herself against the tree, and I yanked at her bottoms, exposing her pink ass. It took another two point five seconds to loosen my slacks and remove my dick from my pants. It fucking steamed in the cold air, burning to be inside her. An erection was never comfortable in pants. It was even less pleasant out in the cold, but as soon as I'd slide inside her warm pussy, the world would make sense again. Ever since I'd found out she was carrying my baby, an immeasurable sense of protection flowed through my veins. I'd do anything for her... for them. I wanted to make love to this woman for the rest of my life.

I wound her braid in my hand and tugged, angling her face to the side. She opened her mouth and arched her back, waiting for my dick. I pushed just enough to make that mouth open wider.

Her wanton breath coated my face between my kisses. I slid my hands off her flushed ass, pulled away, and watched her pink skin turn red.

She leaned against the tree, and the rough bark bit into her cheek. Her whimpers and quick gasps were driving me mad. My balls gave into the pressure, my knees locked, and I stilled inside her with relief.

I slid my hand to her soaked pussy. My icy fingers found her heated clit, swollen and ready to burst. She pressed into my hastened strokes. It was rare I came before her, but I'd make this up by a tenfold. I pushed forward once, twice, three lucky fucking times, and she screamed her pleasure.

"Ahh!"

She shuddered in my grip and rode the orgasmic wave on my fingers and dick. The sound of her bliss carried through the valley and back, which, of course, made her laugh. I loved her laugh. I loved her strength and vulnerability, her trust and commitment. I loved everything about her, and I couldn't wait to show her just how much I needed her in my life.

Chapter 13

Allie

Heavy steps echoed behind me. The sound of the flappy broken soles neared, but each time I turned around, no one was there. The alley narrowed as I faced a dead end. The cigarette breath near my ear burned in my lungs. I whipped around and faced the monster.

Wright held my chin in his hand and lowered his gaze to my growing stomach.

"Don't worry, you're not quite ready yet."

"Get away from me!" I pushed at his chest, and he was gone in a puff of a white cloud.

"Leave me alone." I waved my arms through the thick smoke until someone grasped my wrist.

"Allie, Allie, wake up."

I shot up in the bed, heaving in air. Tristan encased me in his arms, bringing me back to reality, soothing my shakes. My heart pounded against my ribcage. The thought of Wright brought back the memory of his cigarette stench, and I coughed.

"You're all right now." Tristan smoothed his hand over my back. "It was just a dream."

"I was dreaming?"

"Well, it actually sounded more like a nightmare."

I shook my head and rested against the bed frame. "It was him."

"Baby, you're safe now. You're both safe. He's dead."

I rubbed my eyes. Morning had already come, and we'd actually slept through our first night in Vienna.

"It was just a stupid dream. What time is it?"

"Noon."

"Noon?"

"Don't worry. You'll adjust to the time change just in time for the wedding, and if we continue having nights like yesterday, I'm all up for you sleeping in." His brow lifted. "I'm catching up with Gabe on the files from TJ, and then we have a poker game to settle."

"The wedding's in four days. Shouldn't he be getting ready?"

"No."

"Why?"

Tristan chuckled. "Because the wedding is in four days and the engaged couple insisted on an informal, family only ceremony. They'll say their vows, we'll have dinner — do the obligatory dance — and they'll be off on their honeymoon. That's it."

"I'm sure Sam thinks her wedding day has more significance."

"What's more significant than committing yourself to the person you love for the rest of your life? By the end of the day, you're married to your soulmate. It doesn't really matter how you get there, as long as you get there. Everyone has a unique story."

His low tone sent an army of chills down my back. The good kind. We'd joked about marriage before, but this morning, his eyes and his entire demeanor were different. He was acting like we were the ones heading for the altar. Tristan had a way of shaking off my nightmare tremors. Almost all of them.

"What's going to happen to Simone and Infinity?"

"If she knows what's good for her, she'll flee. We'll deal with the Hartleys, and the Wagner brothers are taking on Infinity. If all goes well, they won't be able to hide behind a name, and if Simone is smart, she'll stay away when the organization goes down."

We dressed and joined Gabe and Sam in the dining area. The fireplace was glowing, and the smell of freshly baked pastries filled the air.

"Good morning." I hugged them both. Sam's pregnant belly poked further out than mine.

"Good morning," she chirped. "How was your first night?"

"I slept like a rock."

"She had a nightmare."

"No nightmares allowed in this home. Is there anything I can do to help you relax?"

"Don't you have a wedding to plan?"

She checked her watch. "Olivier's arriving before three, and my wonderful coordinator is half done with the decorations." She pointed to where Emma had wound string lights around the posts.

"It already looks beautiful."

"Don't worry, Allie. It's a family-only event. Very relaxed—because we all need it."

I shivered. Wright was dead, yet he still haunted me at night. Sam touched my hand where I was covering my belly.

"I totally get it. I had nightmares for weeks until Martinez… well, I guess you know how that went. You were there."

"I'm sorry about that day at your office. We should have listened to Gabe—"

"You didn't know, and I didn't know. But it's all over now. Almost, I guess. I haven't heard from Kendra since she's been back, and we're not sure she's going to make it to the wedding. James canceled his plus one request, and he wasn't happy about it."

"His plus one was my best friend, Laura. They had a tiff. Literally. His ex's name is Tiffany and they have a daughter, so I really hoped James and Laura could put their differences aside for Christmas. But I may be asking for a miracle."

"Well, Christmas is a good time for miracles, so hold on to that hope. Coffee or tea?" She reached overhead and handed me a mug as well.

The smell of pine and spice, the twinkling lights, and glowing fireplace warmed the home, but it was people like Sam and the surrounding family who made it magical.

"Tea, thank you. What do you need help with?"

She poured the herbal tea. An aroma of raspberry and mint rose with the steam.

"There's fruit in the fridge if you want to cut it up. I'm making French toast for everyone."

"Sounds perfect. My appetite's been growing these days."

Gabe and Tristan sat with their laptops by the fireplace, scrolling through. I poured them a cup of coffee each and went back to help Sam. By then, Emma had joined us in the kitchen.

"Any baby name front runners, Ems?"

"My lips are sealed." She zipped her fingers over her lips and threw away the imaginary key.

But silence and Emma didn't blend well.

"You and Tristan should get married before the baby arrives."

"I thought you said not to rush to the altar. Like Goldie and Kurt."

I saw Tristan lift his lazy eyebrow as Emma continued.

"If I'm truly going to be an aunt, a real aunt, that's the only way. You know, I could ask the minister to perform your ceremony right after Sam and Gabe's. It's really not a problem. I'm sure he wouldn't mind. And don't worry about the dress or the details. I can take care of it all. We still have plenty of time before we go home. What do you say?"

Emma was ready to take over this wedding and make it mine and Tristan's. Someone had to draw the line, and since Tristan seemed uninterested, it had to be me.

"Emma, I don't think that's a good idea."

"It's a great idea. Just ask Tristan. I'm sure he'll say yes, because if he doesn't, I won't forgive him. Besides, you're meant to be."

"I'd much rather Tristan decided on his own—if it's all right with you, that is."

"Don't you know how it is with men? They don't know how to decide. That's why they have little sisters to help them." Emma furrowed her brows and wiggled her finger. "I see what you did there. But I guess if I have to wait to help, I will. For now."

The doorbell chimed, and Emma's head flew up. She frowned. "Why do I not know who that is?"

She set her coffee aside and marched to the door, opening it wide open.

"Julian!" She slammed into her brother. Kendra walked around them, set her bag to the floor, and wrapped her arms around Sam. Laura and Foxy crossed the threshold from behind them.

"What in the world?" I set my cup aside and rushed to them. I grabbed Foxy from her and placed him over my hip.

"Should you be doing that in your condition?"

"Oh, don't you condition me. I'm fine."

The twelve-foot Christmas tree in the foyer caught my godson's attention, and I set him on the floor. Laura took in the decorations. I'd had the same jaw-dropping reaction when I walked into the enormous lodge, with an enormous wood-burning fireplace in the middle, a huge family area, and a world-class chef's kitchen with a world-class chef.

"Wow!"

"I know. It's a lot."

Teresa rushed downstairs and lifted Foxy into a grandma's spin. She covered him with kisses and he accepted them, full of giggles.

"I'm so happy you're here." Teresa magically removed his favorite chocolate from her back pocket.

"He slept the entire night, so he'll be a handful."

"Nothing grandma can't handle—right, Foxy? You go take care of what you need to take care of."

Teresa side-eyed where James was standing by the second floor railing, watching us. He had a firm frown set between his brows and his arms crossed over his chest. She then took Foxy's hand and showed her grandson all the family ornaments on the Christmas tree while I helped Laura with her suitcase.

"Leave those here." James walked down the stairs.

"Surprise!" she squinted, waiting for a hint of approval on his face. I couldn't find any either.

"I thought you were spending Christmas at your parents?" he asked.

"I was. Until they turned on me."

"Turned on you?"

"It's a long story. Kendra and Julian were nice enough to take us on their private jet. So, here I am."

"We have to talk."

"We do."

My head whipped back and forth between them.

"But I need to say hello to my son first. Meet me in our room?"

She held her hands in front and twisted her fingers, giving him a quick nod.

James lifted her suitcase and turned to the main family area with the four-way fireplace, where Teresa was showing Foxy his stocking.

"See? I told you everything would be okay." I reminded her.

"Oh, things are far from okay, but I sure as hell will try to make them okay. How are you doing? I saw the footage from Thanksgiving. Tristan standing up for you like that… It was fucking hot."

"What footage?"

"Tristan fuming at Simone on your front porch. I'm sorry I missed Thanksgiving, but I caught up by watching the security camera footage. Emma raised some hard cash. Fifty bucks per view."

"She sold our camera footage?"

"Don't you love her? It's like we belong to this family, though I may have fucked it up with James. I think they're all like that, you know—the Silvers. All protective and shit, which is great when you want your family safe and well—"

"Laura, what's the matter?"

She swept her hand over her eyes and looked up to the second floor, where James had disappeared. "Nothing. I'm here to make amends if he'll let me. But I'm pretty sure he won't."

"Have some hope. It's Christmas, and you brought his son across the world to be with him. That has to count for something."

I hugged her like she was closer than a sister, because she was. If James were smart, he'd see all the good I'd seen in her since the day we met.

"Have you seen the decorations downstairs? You said this was supposed to be low key." I tried to concentrate as I adjusted Tristan's bow tie.

"This is low key. It's just the family."

"So you haven't seen the indoor winter wonderland?"

"I have. What can I say? Emma and my mother like to decorate." He took me by my hips, bringing my belly against his side, where I felt him semi-hard.

"How long before you take this dress off?" He tugged at my lilac strap.

"Too long. I don't know how I'm going to resist all this." I slid my hands down his back and squeezed his tight behind. "But it's their wedding day, so behave."

"You keep doing that and my behavior will be the least of your worries."

I tapped at his chest. "We're going to be late if you don't stop this."

I stood on tiptoe and kissed him. God, he smelled so good.

"Where do you get that strawberry lip gloss?" he murmured against my lips. "I love strawberries, but nothing can top strawberry lips."

I kissed him again, keeping my mouth over his a while longer. My fingers and toes tingled, but I brushed the nerves aside. "I may have to tie you down and have you kiss me like this for the rest of our lives."

"That sounds more like a promise than a threat. I like it."

"I don't mean with rope."

"I know, Allie."

"Does it scare you?" I asked. "Thinking about the future?"

"Not when you're in it." He pulled me in for another taste, and I forgot where I was. My breasts squished against his chest, lifting with each breath. His arousal hardened against my hip and he pulled away with reluctance. There wasn't enough air in the room. I rested my forehead against his, and heaved in air as if we'd just climbed the Alps.

"If you keep kissing me like that, the wedding will be delayed."

"Ready to go downstairs?" He offered his arm. I adjusted my dress, reapplied my lip gloss, and hooked my arm into his.

"Ready."

Emma had transformed the chalet into an elegant venue. She had done an exquisite job of decorating. Glitter-covered snowflakes floated underneath the ceiling. Ice-blue and white streamers hung underneath the roof beams, connecting the structure in an intricate design. They had wrapped white lights around every column, corner, doorway, and railing. Hydrangea bouquets filled empty nooks, tables, and counters. Their aroma floated from one room to another, carried by a gentle breeze from the backyard. I pulled on my sweater and wrapped it tighter around my body, holding my arms around my front. The middle of winter in the Alps didn't disappoint with its frosty bite. We stepped through the back door into a winter wonderland made into a fairy tale.

Sun beamed from above, reflected by the dusty layer of snow. Underneath, thousands of lights were wrapped around the sculptures and hedges. The outdoor pool steamed through the Plexiglas holes. Glowing light cut through the fog from below, lighting the tent in blues and purples. Beams and strings tangled in sparkling lights, flowers, and delicate white streamers gave the garden a winter-like atmosphere. The snow-covered view of the town in the valley below was abso-lutely breathtaking.

Sam and Gabe exchanged their vows under the beautiful gazebo. Tristan sat beside me and held my hand in his as my heart went on a pitter-patter ride through the ceremony. Sam looked stunning with her white faux-fur rippled cape over her shoulders, mesmerized by the man she was about to marry. The couple said their 'I do's', and my gaze caught Tristan's grin-ning face. His sexy scar twisted his upper lip as he winked at me. And the room shrank, and the guests disappeared, and I felt like the luckiest woman alive, even if this wasn't my wedding.

"You may now kiss your wife," the priest said.

They locked their lips, and half the Silvers cried and the other half cheered. The happy couple walked down the aisle between the guests back toward the house, where Gabe lifted

Sam into his arms, pressed his lips to hers, and carried her over the threshold. Everyone cheered again.

Emma nudged me from the other side. "Your turn's next."

"I think the cold air has frozen your brain, Ems."

"Yeah." She rolled her eyes. "Like I've ever been wrong."

"I'm gonna grab a drink. Would you like anything?" Tristan asked.

"I've been eyeing that hot chocolate stand since Olivier set it out."

"One hot chocolate coming up."

"Make that two," Emma chirped.

"Why don't you help me, Ems?"

Tristan looked over my shoulder, and I glanced back at James. Emma shot up to her feet. "You know, you could have just said you need to talk to James." She lifted her chin and marched over to the chocolate station. Tristan followed her, and James came up as soon as they'd left me on my own.

"Hey, Allie."

"Hey, James. Beautiful ceremony."

"It was. Feels like everything this family needed. I'm sorry for yelling earlier, Allie. I know you meant well."

I'd kept Laura's secret from James, and he was hurt.

"It wasn't my place to tell her secret. She's wanted to for a while."

"So I hear," he grunted, and I frowned.

"She's a good woman, you know. And she's the best mother I've ever seen. You should be proud."

The corner of his mouth twitched. "I'm glad she has you as a friend."

"Me too, but I'll be happier when you finally forgive her. Life is too short to hold grudges."

He puffed out a breath of air as if he understood the meaning behind the words better than anyone. "You're right, Allie. Life is too short."

SAM AND GABRIEL departed for their honeymoon right after the wedding. Her mother returned to New Zealand, but everyone else was staying for Christmas and until after the New Year.

Over the next few days, Laura and James spent more time together, and by the time Christmas arrived, she was sitting in Santa's lap like it was her favorite spot.

The Christmas tree by the fireplace stood at least, nine feet tall. Ribbons were woven through the branches and between the silver, blue, and white ornaments. The white lights twinkled in the sparkling glass bulbs.

On Christmas morning, we all sat near the tree, listening to Teresa and Jacob read a Christmas story. Laura stared at James dressed in a Santa suit. Foxy sat on James's left knee while Laila sat on his right. They'd been horsing around all day and only now sat calmly open-mouthed, keeping Santa within view.

"It's family tradition that the youngest goes first," Emma said, as she passed Laila and Foxy their gifts. We waited as they each opened a toy train, a set of matching plushies, and something very colorful and crafty that Laila immediately recognized.

"That looks messy," I whispered to Laura.

"It's okay. Look at that face. She loves it."

"Here's another one for you, Ems. Ho, ho, ho." Thankfully, Laila wasn't old enough to recognize a dressed Santa as her father, but he could have put more effort into the ho, ho, ho'ing.

"He looks impatient."

"Full balls and nerves of steel will do that to you, but he's gonna blow. I can feel it."

"I gather that's a good thing."

Laura snickered as Emma removed the bootie box from its package.

"Blue baby booties?" She lifted her gaze to mine. "Are you having a boy?"

I nodded from across the room, giving Tristan a knowing look.

"Yes, we're having a boy." His full chest lifted and a boyish grin filled with pride stretched across his face. I rubbed my tummy and then welcomed the hugs and kisses from all the Silvers.

Fred and Wilma exchanged a book instead of traditional gifts. Tristan leaned into my ear. "They write nice things about each other for the entire year—wishes for their families, futures, that sort of thing—and then trade on Christmas eve. It's the only gift they swap."

I pressed my hand over my heart and suddenly missed my father. I wanted him here with us.

My mother leaned in from the other side as if reading my mind. "He's here in spirit. He's always been with us, and he guided us to meet the Silvers. I can't imagine we'd be safer and happier elsewhere."

"I feel the same way, Mom."

I'd given my mother her gift earlier that morning, figuring a bottle of the smooth Comisario tequila wasn't exactly the most traditional present. But when she saw the e-reader full of romance novels, she just sat there with her mouth open.

"That was Tristan's idea." He'd noticed the bag full of books she'd brought on the trip and ordered the gift as soon as we arrived. My mother hugged Tristan as if he were her son.

TJ snapped photographs with his new camera. Emma squeaked and cried and over-exaggerated every single surprise she opened. I didn't know what half of her new gadgets were, and waited patiently until she opened mine. When she lifted the lid off the small, elongated box, I knew she'd be speechless for at least, a minute or two.

She threw her arms around me neck in an excited hug.

"Thank you. I love you so much," she said into my hair. "It's the best gift ever."

"What did she get?" Wilma asked.

Emma lifted the pink pen out of its pouch.

"A pen? You got her a pen, and she likes that the most?" Julian stared, open-mouthed.

"The engraving says: *To the best godmother in the world.*" Emma beamed with pride.

"Ahh," Wilma cooed.

My mom blew a sniffle, and Tristan nudged me in my arm. "It's your turn, Allie. Open your gift."

"There are none left," Emma said. "Did you not get her anything? Because if you didn't, you'd better run to the closest store, if you can find one open, and buy her the one you were looking at the other day when we went out—"

"I think that's enough, Ems." Tristan gave his sister a stern look.

"Allie's gift is on the tree. I hid it because I didn't want anyone guessing what it is." He gave Emma a knowing look before he turned to face me again. "Find it." He grabbed my hands and pulled me off the cushioned seat. I searched through the branches; their fresh needles pricked my skin until my hand caught a velvet box. I pulled the gift out and asked, "This one?"

"Yes." The scar twisted his mouth into a boyish grin.

I flipped the lid open to see a beautiful platinum necklace, a bracelet, and a matching pair of earrings nestled on a cushion. It was simple enough to wear every day, and I appreciated that. I'd never worn jewelry while out in the field, but now that I worked at Silver Securities, this would really come in handy. Especially since I'd been dying to buy a set for the office.

"I love it, thank you." I kissed him, but he then reached into his pocket and held a smaller box in his palm. A much smaller one.

"Maybe this one as well?" The break in his voice stopped time, and the world disappeared as Tristan lowered to his knee, and opened the box with a beautiful diamond ring. He took my hands into his, and asked, "Allie Green, will you do me the honor of becoming my wife and marry me?"

I heard an elated 'Yes' in the distance, and my knees wobbled. Tristan caught me before I fell and steadied me. I tightened my grip on his hands and looked up into his eyes, saying. "Yes, to both."

He slipped the ring on my finger. It was a simple stone, one that reminded me of Bedrock and the Flintstones. They'd carved the glistening gem to resemble a rock, yet so meticulously that it wasn't sharp. The diamond was one of a kind.

"Your turn for a gift," I whispered, pulling out an envelope from a bag I'd held onto. I wouldn't risk anyone finding out about this. After all, what do you get a man who's just proposed to you and already has everything? He carefully tore the envelope's seam, and the Christmas card slid out.

"And I hope you keep this gift to yourself," I said to him.

"Not fair," Emma whined.

First were the coupons I'd made. He could use them anywhere and anytime he wanted, no questions asked.

Tristan's eyes widened as he flipped through the twenty-page coupon booklet of me offering sex on the spot, blow jobs, mutual masturbation, pure fuck-me-now requests, a few sixty-nines and massages: no questions asked, no out clause. I was pretty much his twenty-four hours a day and couldn't say no for as long as the coupons lasted. Not that I wanted to say no, but this was certainly a fun game to play while pregnant. He shifted in his seat and adjusted his pajama bottoms, and then opened the letter I'd written. I bit my lip, waiting for the reaction, and when the tears fell and his lips parted, I knew he'd come to the part where I'd told him we were having twins.

He ignored the hard wood in his pants, stood up, and lifted me into his arms, kissing me hard.

"This is the best Christmas gift ever."

"What's it say?" Emma pointed to the letter.

"This gift stays a secret until after birth."

Emma frowned. TJ stole her attention with a photograph of her side profile. I watched my best friend and James sharing a large mug of hot chocolate, along with their kids, and the moment felt so right, I couldn't imagine anything better.

I snuggled into Tristan's arm. "You're happy?"

He glanced down. "No, I'm so in love with you, and I... I just can't wait. Everything's going to work out now. I know it is, and I can't thank you enough." He pressed his lips to mine again.

"Get a room, you two," Julian interrupted.

And that was exactly what we intended to do.

But maybe there was one thing better than tonight, and that was New Year's Eve—and the next best surprise I should have expected from the man who deserved my heart and loyalty.

Chapter 14

Tristan

We'd booked New Year's Eve at a place in the small town in the valley. I waited with Allie downstairs while my family took their time dressing. I paced back and forth in the hallway. If this continued, we would be late for one of the most important days of my life. I was ready to take that step and make my commitment known to the world, but they were testing my patience.

I grabbed Allie's arm as she reached for her jacket and pulled her inside the closet, locking the doors behind us.

"What are you doing?"

I held her wrist and felt her pulse rush underneath my fingertips. It almost burned to hold her there. I pinned her in the back of the closet, feeling her up. The little light passing through the door slits lit up her face in glowing streaks.

"I'm using a coupon." I grazed over her earlobe and let go of her wrist, shifting my focus to the throbbing vein at the base of her neck, where I felt her racing heartbeat with my lips.

"Tristan, someone's going to hear us." But her resistance dwindled as her mouth said one thing and body something entirely different.

"Ask me which coupon I'm going to use."

"What?"

"Just ask. You won't regret it. It's your next favorite after MTP care."

"My next favorite is your cock," she panted, as I rubbed my hand over the zipper and her tight white jeans. Emma had encouraged Allie to dress in all white, and Allie had no clue why. She looked like a fucking angel who would soon be my wife. The problem was, she was an irresistible angel with a dirty mouth, and I wasn't patient enough to wait until my wedding night. So I used a coupon.

"Wrong answer."

"But this isn't the right place," she protested. Was she trying to convince me or herself?

I decided kissing her like she was mine forever would show her just how right everything was when she was with me. Her body yielded to my hold, relaxing and welcoming the stolen moment. God, she tasted like those damn delicious strawberries. It was almost hypnotic.

"What if someone catches us?" she said against my mouth.

"I'm sure nobody will need an explanation of what I want to do to you."

"And what is it you want to do?" She breathed hard.

"Much more than I have time for, but I always have time for your pussy."

I yanked on her pants and skimmed her inner thigh. Her soft flesh gave into my fingers, her hips tilted forward, and I drew over her mound. The damn jeans stood between me and her pleasure.

"What coupon?" she breathed hard.

"What do you want it to be?"

"Fast, do it fast."

"Do what?'

"Get me off. Make me come. Please."

I had lowered the front of her mommy pouch already and slid my hand underneath her pants and panties.

"You know that only makes me want to do it slow," I whispered in her ear.

"Okay, okay, do it slow."

I rubbed over her clit back and forth, stroking the nub. "Like that?"

"Oh, gosh." She drew her quick breaths through tight lips and thrashed in my grip. "Maybe a little faster, please," she panted.

I pulled up her juices and circled my fingers over the pressure, then latched onto her neck. She tilted her head sideways, giving me access while pressing into my hand. My strokes sped up, her mouth opened, her thighs quivered, and her excitement trickled into my hand. And just when I thought I had her, her warm hand wrapped around my hard dick, breaking my concentration. She stroked my length from the bottom up in a ball-tightening motion. Yet I couldn't think of a better distraction than her grip on my dick, her pussy in my palm, and my fingers inside her. She pumped me with the same keenness as her hips gyrated to my hand's motion.

I increased the rhythm and her hand responded with a tighter grip, ready for a battle of who would finish first. My toes curled without warning. She pressed her cheek to my chest, muffling her scream, and I remembered we were in the closet. I lowered my sweater over her hand and my dick twitched, soiling the sweater from the inside.

Voices echoed in the hallway, and I froze, pulling my wet fingers to my lips with a mouthed *Shh*. The smell of her excitement lingered on my fingertips.

"Where is everyone?" We heard Emma on the other side of the door.

"In the kitchen, Ems," TJ called out.

"Oh, my God, they're going to find us." Allie wiggled in my

hold. The sun streaked over her flushed cheeks and wild hair, and I realized we almost consummated early. But there was no better way to start today than seven minutes in heaven with my wife to be.

"We'll blame it on your coupons."

"You mean your coupons."

"Yours, mine, ours, I don't think it matters anymore."

She stilled and slowly let go of my dick. We put ourselves together to the best of our ability, snuck back out of the closet, and hurried to our room, where we cleaned up. The family was waiting outside, seated in a line of horse-drawn carriages.

"Tristan, what is this?"

"A little surprise." I helped her up the steps and into the carriage where she settled on the seat. I sat beside her and pulled a blanket over our legs as we set out into town.

"I can't believe you did this."

"Just sit back and relax."

She leaned in, still smelling like those strawberries. "After that little stunt you pulled off in the closet? What's next? Flicking me off underneath the blanket?"

I wiggled my brows. "Be careful what you wish for today, Allie, because I have a goal of making all of your wishes come true."

Her forehead creased, and her nose wiggled. The horses pulled on their traces, and we headed to the village square. It was the warmest winter day I remembered in a long time. The carriage dropped us off near the entrance to a festive gathering. Beer flowed and the smell of wine and burning wood floated in the air. James bought a hot chocolate for everyone, and we strolled to town square with steaming cups in our hands. I welcomed the change in scenery and my family's support. The closer it came to the task, the more my knees gave into my weight. Allie crossed the cobblestone, chatting with Laura. The few cafés in town boomed with life.

Somewhere in mid-town, we separated from the family and enjoyed our walk alone up to the old church. We scaled the steep stairs and admired the field of snow-covered rooftops. She shaded her eyes to get a better view of the postcard-perfect picture.

"This is beautiful, Tristan. I feel like I'm living in a fairy tale."

"Good. That was the whole point of this vacation."

She turned around and looked over the enormous wooden doors. "If I ever get married, I'd want it to be a small wedding, like Sam and Gabe's. But in a church like this one. You know, something quiet but still traditional."

"They have small churches in New Jersey." I tightened my grip on her hand.

"Well, it's not like we're in New Jersey, is it?" she grinned. The hint of nerves in her voice was cute. And so were the freckles on her wind-kissed cheeks. A gust picked up the flakes, lifting them off the ground, bringing back that fairy tale aura.

"No. It's not." I sipped my chocolate. "So, what do you think of this view?"

"It's perfect. This Christmas is perfect. I just wish I understood why you're so nervous."

"Am not."

"Your knee wobbled the entire ride, Mr. Silver."

"All right. I might have been nervous, but you would have been nervous too if it were your wedding day."

"What?"

"Yeah, I forgot to mention it at the engagement, but I booked this church."

"You booked this church for what?"

"Our wedding. Here. Now."

"What?"

The church bells chimed through the town. Part of their

echo got lost in the distant Alps, but part of it bounced off the buildings, creating melting harmonies. I lowered to my knee, took both her hands into mine, and asked the simplest question I'd ever had to ask her. "Marry me right now, Allie?"

She blinked once, twice, three times and tried to blubber something. Instead, her knees gave in. I caught her falling body and set her to the ground, resting her against me.

"That's not quite the response I was looking for, Ms. Green."

She looked at me from below.

"Marry you today?"

I checked my watch. "Actually, in fifteen minutes."

"Let me guess—the priest is waiting inside this church?"

"Along with our family. What do you say, Allie? Want to finish this trip as my wife?"

"Everyone's there?" She pointed, stunned. I offered her my arm and waited until the idea settled and she looped her hand.

The church door opened, and Emma stood dramatically in the shining sun. Snowflakes fell from the clear sky, timing their descent.

"Stay where you are."

The priest followed her outside. I took Allie's hands into mine and we waited as my parents, brother and cousins, aunts and uncles gathered around us. Laura handed her the white arrangement of flowers Emma had ordered. My brother held out the rings I'd picked up at a jeweler in Vienna, and we removed them from his palm. We looked at each other, standing on top of an ancient ruin, like in the fairy tale Allie described, and it all felt unbelievable and real at the same time. I couldn't wait to commit my life to her. That fierce cop inside her would protect our children with her life, and my family deserved the same from me.

The priest barely finished pronouncing us married and my mouth was on hers, stealing her breath. Peg cried, Wilma sobbed, and Laura glared at James like he had some big shoes to fill. I was one lucky son of a Fred, as my father would say, to have ended up with Allie. She was the perfect wife, and judging by the time she spent with TJ, she'd make an exceptional mother. TJ took his role as a photographer to heart and snapped every second of the day. It was a good thing he did, because I barely remembered the day. My wife was the only one I had eyes for.

We had dinner at a local restaurant. Jacob Silver bought a round of drinks for everyone. His brother covered the next round, and they took turns after that. Soon enough, we gained guests, and the wedding turned from a small family event into a dancing celebration with what seemed like half the town. Peg snuck a few tequila shots in between meals and couldn't wipe the smile off her face. Emma flirted with a local boy while TJ looked on with a guarding eye. She might have been his aunt, but the protective gene ran thick in the Silvers.

Back at the hotel, I carried Allie over the threshold to our suite. I set her down and locked the door, slowly removing my clothes, starting with my top.

She lifted her leg up to help with her white Uggs. I pulled them off, one at a time.

"What would you have done if I'd said no?" she asked.

Off came my boot, then the other.

"I don't ask questions I don't know the answer to." I gave her a coy look and removed my sweater. She reached for hers and dropped it to the floor. Her pink nipples poked through the white lace, and my dick strained under the zipper.

"Get those tight pants off your ass so I can make love to my wife." I yanked her shirt from inside her pants. Our remaining clothes flew all over the hallway, the living area, and we finally ended up in the bedroom naked.

As we lay spent in bed that night, I watched her admire the

sparkle of her platinum wedding band. It reflected the lamp light onto the ceiling.

"I can't believe we're married." She grinned.

"And I can't believe how lucky I am." I flipped over and hovered above her. "I promise to love you and cherish you forever, Mrs. Silver."

She opened her legs, and I continued consummating our marriage for the next five days.

Chapter 15

Allie

The four magically peaceful weeks after our return from Austria passed in a flash. We closed most of the cases with Hope for Hope and followed up with all leads. There was no sign of Marissa, but Tristan claimed Simone might have been using the girl's name just to taunt me. My mother used to say 'No news is good news', but to me, the no news part equated to the calm before the storm.

I took the day off work because the load of house errands was piling up, and I wasn't about to give into Tristan's offer for a personal assistant. It was bad enough we had a housekeeper come in twice every week. The construction of my mother's guest home near the pond had been delayed. Twice. First they delivered the wrong floors, broken tiles, and scratched kitchen cabinets. Then there were the furniture inconsistencies. For the time being, she was happily staying in Tristan's parents' guesthouse.

Tristan had been busy working with the lawyers on the Hartley and Donaldson cases, which left me dealing with everything else. There just weren't enough hours in a day. I went downstairs to the kitchen, poured myself a tea, and removed TJ's lunch from the refrigerator.

"Good morning, Freddie," I said as I passed the parrot a nut.

"Fuck, Freddie."

"No. I said *good morning.*"

"Morning." The bird chirped back.

"That's a good bird. I knew you could do it, Freddie."

"Fuck Freddie."

"Never mind. "

It turned out Freddie recognized spoken names and cursed out every single person. His feathers had grown back, and the lesion on his foot was healed.

TJ set two plates of scrambled eggs on the counter. "I wasn't sure if you wanted any."

"It's perfect. Thank you."

The front gate rang, and we both turned to the door.

"Are you expecting anyone?" He shook his head, and I checked my phone. Someone had set a package in front of the gate.

"It's a delivery. That's odd."

"Why is that odd?" TJ asked.

"Tristan gets deliveries at the post office."

I saw the worried look on his face.

"I'm sure it's nothing. We can get it on our way out."

I was driving TJ to school this morning before heading to Hope for Hope. I stuffed the eggs in my mouth as fast as I could, washed them down with some tea, and put on my jacket. Outside, a fresh layer of snow covered the ground. Another month and spring would be here. Two more after that, and our babies would be born.

We hopped in the car and pulled up to the front gate. TJ jumped out of the car to grab the package, but he stopped as soon as he lifted the box off the ground.

"What's the matter?" I called out from the car.

"There's no name. It's not addressed to anyone. I don't think it's even sealed."

"Put it down, TJ."

He slowly set it to the ground and backed away. I found a dry stick by the tree line and poked the box until the lid opened. We stepped closer at the same time to see a rainbow of feathers stuffed in a box and realized it was a dead parrot.

"Oh, my God!" I jumped back.

"No! Freddie!" TJ's head flew up, twisting toward the house.

"Wait, TJ!" I grabbed his arm. "That's impossible. Freddie's home. We just saw him."

His shoulders relaxed a little. "Who the hell would send us a dead bird?"

"I don't know. Get in the car. I'll get someone to run forensics on the box and the bird."

He buckled in, and I composed myself inside the car. "Okay, let's try this again."

I tuned on the ignition and the radio, pulling out onto the road and toward TJ's school. Smooth jazz settled my nerves before the top of the hour news turned on. I zoned out until the name Hartley came up. TJ turned up the volume.

"After a long delay, the district attorney's office has taken into custody this morning the Hartley brothers. The sex trafficking and corruption allegations have been growing against the Hartley family for years. Both parties have declined to comment on the case. Leaked information received by the network about the parties responsible for Jeff Hartley's death has been sent for confirmation."

"Shit," I mumbled.

"Is it too late to change my last name?" TJ asked.

"You're not going to school today," I told him.

"What?"

"I don't think you should. I mean, I'll leave it up to you, but today feels off. First it was the dead bird and now it's this news. Your mother already suspected I was there when Jeff died. It was only a matter of time before she found out the truth about that night. My gut says you should stay home. Tristan should be landing soon. I'm sure he'd feel the same."

Tristan had flown to Washington last night, and I knew the news this morning resulted from his visit.

"All right, but I'd prefer to stay with you instead of being home alone, though. Not that I'm afraid; I just think your gut is right. Something's up."

"Have you heard anything from your mother?"

"No."

"Okay. Let's do this together, then. You're coming with me."

He smiled, and my nerves settled. I hadn't realized I had so many nerves. If it weren't for his company, I might have freaked out at the dead bird more than I did. TJ was a carbon copy of his father, both in looks and calm personality, so we clicked.

Twenty minutes later, we walked through Hope for Hope's doors. I lowered the paper on the manager's desk and showed her the documents. TJ stayed by the window, watching the exit.

"We did it, Greta. I hope any damage Infinity has done to Hope for Hope can be corrected. As of now, all new staff will be screened by Silver Securities before they step a foot in this building, and the warrant for Simone Hartley's arrest is still outstanding."

It seemed money could still buy some cops.

"Thank you, Allie. We really appreciate your help with this mess."

"You're welcome."

"Hey, Allie." TJ tugged at my jacket. "I think I saw my mother in a car in front of the building."

My heart skipped a set of beats, setting me off balance.

"Let's go back to the car, TJ."

She was gone by the time we stepped out into the parking lot, but I was certain Simone wasn't far away. I buckled in and pressed my foot on the gas.

"Try getting through to your father. If you can't, text him to come home as soon as he lands. We're gonna go see what Simone is up to."

TJ did as I asked. Ten minutes later, we were sitting at a table in a cafe nearby. TJ ordered a muffin, and I opted for the fruit salad. The sound of high heels clicked moments later, and Simone walked through the door in her oversized winter hat, leather coat, and large sunglasses. She strolled up to our table and pulled out a chair, sitting between us. My gaze flew from TJ to Simone's and back to TJ's again. The boy's eyes were wide open.

"I thought you'd be hiding from the authorities, Simone."

"I do not need to hide. How was your Christmas, TJ?"

"Christmas was a month ago."

"Well, I had to go away for a few weeks so I could get better, but now you can come home."

She reached for his hand, and he pulled away.

"I'm never coming home, Mother."

"That's too bad, because you'd be a great big brother." She smirked, focusing on me. "Probably much better than a bird caretaker."

"You're the one who's sent the bird?" he asked.

"What bird?"

"Don't play stupid, Mother. You're playing your twisted games."

"What games?"

"The ones where you pretend you're not trying to torture Allie."

"I don't know what you're talking about."

"What do you want, Simone?" I asked.

She leaned back in her chair. "Given we're all going to be family soon, I think we should get to know each other. Now, why aren't you at school, TJ?"

"We know you know I was there the night your father died, Simone."

"Well, we can't all get away with the perfect murder, can we?" She rubbed her hands. "Though I believe it gets easier with practice."

"Unbeliev—"

She waved her hand in dismissal. "I mean, Tristan thought he had when he ordered Wright's murder."

A bitter taste filled my mouth, and I set aside the fruit salad.

"Wright is dead. He had it coming for years."

"I came back to life, didn't I?" That look in her eye made me shudder. "Who's to say Wright isn't rotting away in some shack? The FBI offered him a good deal."

The server brought Simone some water, and I hoped she'd choke on it.

"The bastard is dead." I felt my jaw snap. Was she playing with me?

"For now. I mean, you're not as pregnant as your mother was when he raped her, are you? That makes you not quite ready for Wright's needs. He has time before he gets to you."

"Why would you say that?" I whispered, fighting the tears welling in my eyes. My throat tightened.

Simone leaned forward on the table, lowered her chin, and removed her sunglasses. "Because he told me, Allie."

"Before they killed him?"

"That depends on your definition of killed. Well." She stood up in haste and adjusted her dress.

"You're a delusional monster."

"I prefer Simone." She shrugged and checked her watch. "I have to go. Things to do, people to scare, but I'll see you later, Allie. I'll come over to talk once Tristan settles in after his trip. See you later, TJ."

She turned on her heel and left.

"Allie," TJ gripped my hand, shaking it. "Allie, are you all right?"

"Yeah, I'm fine." But after a moment, I shook my head. "No, I don't think so. Do you mind coming to my appointment with me?"

"The ultrasound? Yeah, of course. Allie, you're shaking. Maybe I should call—"

"I don't think we have time for that. Let's go."

It just so happened that my check up was at the hospital. We arrived half an hour early, and I got a nurse to call Julia Blakely out of the ER for me. TJ waited near the vending machines, picking out a snack.

"Can you talk?" I asked her. "Because I need serious help."

"I was about to go out for a break, so I have time."

"Emma mentioned Simone was seeing an OB. Can you find out which one?"

"I checked the files already, and it's true. She is seeing an OB, and"—she paused and bit her lip as if contemplating whether to continue—"she listed Tristan Silver as the father."

"That's bullshit."

I covered my mouth as soon as I heard my raised voice.

"Are there any documents? Any backup to the paternal claim?"

"It's just her word for now, but the OB's a friend of a friend, and Simone's gloated about the in vitro pregnancy for weeks."

"In-vitro? That means she'd need to get Tristan's sperm. How would she get his sperm?"

"My guess is from his dick."

"Well, I know that. But how? What should I do?"

"Talk to Tristan. If there's anything I've learned about the Hartleys, it's that you can't make assumptions."

"Thanks, Jules. I mean it."

"You're welcome. Allie, if it ever gets out that I helped you… Ahem, I was in deep trouble with that family before, and

I don't want to go down that road again. It's difficult to escape."

"It will never get out. I promise."

We left for my appointment soon after. TJ listened to the heartbeats and was sworn to secrecy about the twins. My tummy had grown, and the pregnancy was progressing well. However, instead of leaving the appointment happy, the bile taste in my mouth remained since seeing Simone. I gripped the steering wheel hard on my way back home.

"You look pissed."

"I am, TJ. I am."

"It's my mother again, isn't it?"

"I'm sorry. I know she's your mother—"

"You've been more of a mother to me the past few weeks than she was my entire life."

My heart stopped. I pushed on the brakes, and the car's wheels squealed on the driveway.

"You can't mean that, TJ."

"I wouldn't say it if I didn't mean it." He smiled and squeezed my hand. "She's stomping all over you. You can't let her get to you. I didn't."

"You're right. You didn't, and we'll deal with anything she throws our way as a family."

Tristan's parked Bentley drew my attention to the open garage. A white Jaguar blocked its way.

"That's one of my mother's cars." TJ pointed.

"Of course it is."

"You know, you could always turn around and pretend she doesn't exist."

"I could, but I have a feeling she'd find me. Besides, this isn't only Tristan's fight. It's mine as well."

He sighed. "I wish there was no fight."

"The trial will take a while. Your uncles—"

"They'll bail, and Mother will stay out of jail."

"I'm sorry, TJ. I'm so sorry you're dealing with this crap. Because that's what it is—it's crappy. Why don't you run over to your grandparents and let me go deal with this?"

"No. I'm not leaving you. We're a family, right? And families don't leave one another when in trouble."

"No, they don't."

TJ had hit a growth spurt and was already an inch taller than me. I took his offered arm, and we went inside. Tristan was standing in the kitchen with a stack of papers in his hands. His face turned redder the longer he flipped through the pages. He didn't even notice us arrive.

"It's all there, Tristan. You're the father."

"I can fucking see it's all there. What I don't get is how! *How* are you pregnant with my child, Simone?"

Chapter 16

Tristan

I hurried through airport security, eager to get home to Allie. My trip to DC could only have gone better if it had happened years ago. Today marked the first day Donaldson and the Hartley brothers would answer to justice.

The valet pulled my Bentley up to the curb and handed me the keys.

"Have a pleasant day, sir."

"Thank you."

I turned on the radio for the top of the hour national news.

"A New York congressman, Michael Donaldson, along with the Hartley real estate moguls have has been arrested this morning on charges of corruption, sex trafficking, and money laundering. The judge has set the bail hearing for next Thursday."

As expected, my phone rang as soon as the news released.

"Hello, Simone."

"Don't you *hello Simone* me. What have you done?"

"I handed the case and all our evidence over to the district attorney's office. Donaldson and your uncles will answer to justice now."

"What about me? I'm not in the lawsuit?"

The problem with someone like Simone coming back to life was that there was no record of her being alive at all. And since you can't sue a dead person, Simone had lucked out. For now. Except she didn't have to know that. I needed her signature before they cuffed her and gave her an orange jumpsuit. I'd barely gotten TJ's legal paperwork sorted, and he took priority over Simone.

"Do you want me to add your name to the list?"

"No, of course not. I just thought…"

"Are you busy right now?" I asked. "I need to see you."

"Oh, Tristan. I knew you'd come through. Love like ours doesn't happen every day."

"Simone, I'm not doing this for you, I'm doing this for TJ."

She took longer to reply, likely stunned she'd gotten away with her crimes. She hadn't, but I'd let her think for now that she had the upper hand.

"Can you meet me at my house in half an hour?"

"Of course."

"I'll see you soon."

I clicked the end call button before she could ask me for any details. If Simone knew why I was inviting her, she wouldn't come.

Moments after I settled at home, Simone buzzed at the front gate. I let her inside, poured myself a single malt scotch, and opened the door.

Dressed in a long leather coat, matching pants, and a loose fitting top, she went in for an air kiss on each cheek. I suppressed the gag reflex. After examining the evidence Gabe had gathered from TJ's notes, voice recordings, and photographs, I'd never look at this woman the same way.

Her father's and uncles' involvement in the sex trafficking organization paled in comparison to what she had done. She'd facilitated the transactions and coerced women under false pretenses. She'd known they had Kendra and did nothing. She was their mule and Allie's polar opposite. Where my wife aimed to save women, Simone aimed to cash in on every soul.

"You look sharp." She grinned. "I guess it goes with the territory when you put notorious people behind bars."

Notorious?

"Donaldson and your uncles used their prestige, money, and power to build an empire of privileged asshole elites who not only thought they were above the law, but abused, tortured, raped, and killed."

"Potato, po-tah-toh," she mocked. "Everyone has a purpose in the world, don't they?"

What exactly was her purpose here? She must have suspected I would serve her documents for TJ's custody. Full custody, because my son deserved better, and I'd win in court.

Simone lifted her chin, and the familiar look in her eye gave me the chills. I closed the door and followed her as she sauntered through the hallway and into the family room. She sat in the armchair, crossed her legs, and waited.

I set the papers in front of her.

"You're dodging a bullet, Simone. I didn't sue you because I'm hoping you'll be civil and sign the custody papers."

She smirked. "You know I'm smarter than that, so let's make something clear, Tristan. You didn't sue me because I don't exist. You have no case against a dead person, and thus, no leverage. I'm not signing anything. Courts may fail me, but I have other ways to get my son back."

I grunted. She hadn't lost her touch.

"I assure you I have plenty of resources and evidence to prove you're alive. Like the recording in this room, for example." I pointed to the camera in the corner.

"Fine. You win. But I'm still not signing them."

"You really want to do this? Why? What's your leverage?"

Time slowed as she stood up from the chair, parted her coat, lifted her shirt, and smoothed her hand over her stomach.

I froze.

"Our baby."

I'm not sure how long I stood there, completely dumbfounded, recapping our conversations from the past. This wasn't possible. I'd kept my distance from Simone since her return. Except, deep inside, I knew Simone was capable of anything. I'd seen the level of her involvement with Infinity and all the women's shelters where she volunteered. I shouldn't have expected anything less than a calculated move.

"You're bluffing."

She opened her purse and removed a folder with papers. "Have a look. Here's the DNA report from the clinic. I used in vitro. Better chances of the embryo taking when it's the right environment."

I flipped through the medical documents, scans, bloodwork, and DNA confirmations.

What the fuck was happening?

"It's all there, Tristan. You're the father."

"I can fucking see that!" I snapped. "What I don't get is how! How did you get my sperm, Simone? How are you pregnant with my child?"

A quiet gasp registered in the hallway behind me. I turned to my right where Allie was standing at the room's entrance.

I opened and closed my mouth, struggling to find the right words.

"Allie…" I breathed.

She walked toward me and took my hand. I connected my gaze with hers, latching on the support in her eyes. "I found out an hour ago. What she says is true."

"You're sick, Mother." Focused as I was on Allie, I hadn't even noticed TJ was home as well. He turned on his heel and ran upstairs to his room. I had the urge to call out to him, but Allie stopped me. "He's going to be okay. I already talked to him; just give him some time."

Maybe it was better he didn't hear the details. Simone had scorned him enough.

"How did you find out?"

Our attention returned to Simone. Her predatory focus on Allie shook through my bones.

"There's a reason Silver Securities hired me. I don't share my sources."

"Well, then, I guess we have something in common. We always get what we want."

I stepped forward, but Allie drew her arm out in front of me. It was like she knew I would murder this woman if I got close enough. But if Simone was carrying my child, there was another life at stake.

"How did you get Tristan's sperm for the in vitro?" Allie asked.

Simone strolled to the window and dramatically looked out into the distance, watching the shoreline before she turned around again, in slow calculated motion.

"Don't you remember our night after the fundraiser?"

I shut my eyes. The night was a haze. Allie had left the fundraiser in a limo, I'd walked home, and... Simone showed up.

"You came to my penthouse."

A memory flashed from that night. Simone had made us drinks. She was flirty, and I'd had no strength to get up from the chair, so I'd told her to leave.

"That's right. It was a wild night, wasn't it? So much happened that day. I got to meet your fiancée, and for the first time in years, I could finally get out and be me. Be free. What better way to celebrate than with a couple of drinks?"

"You drugged me," I whispered.

A memory of Allie giving me a blowjob came to mind, but I was no longer certain it had been Allie. I shut my eyes and concentrated, but whatever the fuck Simone had slipped in my drink that night had done a number on me. I vividly remembered having an aching hard on that I couldn't will down in the morning. My jaw locked, and the sound of my heart pumped in my ears.

"You raped me?" The sound that came out of my mouth made Simone stand up and find shelter behind the armchair.

"I… I didn't rape you," she stuttered. "As much as I wanted to ride that cock, all I did was give you a blowjob and caught your swimmers in a cup."

I took a step toward her and she gripped the back of the armchair like she'd use it to defend herself.

"That's still rape, Simone!"

She puffed out an exasperated breath. "You can't deny it's a splendid insurance policy," she gloated, smoothing her hand over her stomach. "TJ is going to have a *real* sibling."

Allie came to stand beside me. Her freckles popped out and brightened her cheeks.

"Shut your mouth, you cunt. How could you?"

Whoa!

"You're going to bring a baby to life in such horrid deception? Tristan's in shock right now, and he has every right to be, but let me tell you how this is going to work. The police will come and cuff you, you'll have the baby in the county jail awaiting trial, and we'll raise it as our own, because letting you be near any other children would be criminal!"

Allie's sharp arm swings could chop through a bone. Her cheeks turned red and her jaw set firm.

"Ha!" Simone sneered, "Go find yourself someone who cares."

She ignored Allie, removed another folder from her purse, and stomped to the table where I was standing. She slammed the file down in front of me. "I had a hunch you'd react this way, so I had my lawyers prepare this."

I grabbed the stack and skimmed through the documents.

"You've got to be kidding me." I shook my head.

"What is it?" Allie asked.

"You want Silver Securities to have you absolved of all criminal charges?"

"That's what the papers say." She rubbed her hands, grinning like she'd already won.

"That's bullshit."

I handed Allie the documents, and she scanned them over.

"Even if I sign this, Simone, you know I have no power to enforce it. The case is out of my hands."

"You're forgetting I know just how much power you have. If you want your son and your baby then make it happen. Otherwise, our custody agreement will be void."

"I'm not touching a pen until you do, Simone. Sign over TJ's custody."

She lowered her head and studied my stare, wrinkling her brow.

Allie pulled on my hand. "What? You're not actually going to do this, Tristan, are you?"

"It's for my son," I whispered, and turned to Simone. "We can sign at the same time."

Simone's cunning grin stretched over her face. She paced from behind the chair and cautiously made her way to the table. The sound of her approaching heels drew the hairs up on my arms. I handed her the pen and readied mine. She eyed me with caution, twirling the pen between her fingers.

Allie touched my arm. "Tristan, you can't. The charges—"

"It's all right. I've got this. This is the only way to get rid of her. For now."

Page after page, I watched her pen strokes, and she watched mine, but as soon as she pulled the pen away from the last signature, relief washed over me. I had one kid, and in due time I'd get my other one away from this crazy woman. She handed me the papers, turned on her shiny red heels, and sauntered to the front door, where she paused.

"See you soon, Tristan. I presume you'll want an update on the baby's health, so I'll be in touch."

She sashayed out into the hallway, and we followed her.

"You may not be in the suit, Simone, but you're wanted by the FBI and the CIA, and your story will be featured on Most Wanted. You can't get away from this one. Where are you gonna go?"

She stopped, turned back around, walked right back toward us, and faced me.

"Work your magic, Tristan. You don't want the mother of your child to spend her pregnancy in jail, do you? What do you think is better for the baby? A cold cell or a warm paradise?"

What Simone deserved was hell.

"You don't need to answer that because you know where I'm headed."

"You're going out of the country?" I asked.

"Wouldn't you if you were in my shoes? Besides, self-care is important during pregnancy, and the world is too big to stay in one place. Try stopping me and I will ruin you and your family."

I wanted to tell her she'd already tried that once, but it was pointless. I'd stop her, but on my terms. Simone was a woman set in her ways. I had to time my move and think shit through before I acted, because I knew I wouldn't get many chances. So I let her leave.

The front door shut with an abysmal echo.

"Are you all right?"

I flinched at Allie's touch.

"Yeah, I think so. I just wish she'd stayed dead."

"Her and Wright."

"What?"

"I saw Simone earlier in the day. She implied Wright wasn't dead and he's still after me. I kind of believe her."

Fuck.

"I'm going to check on TJ. Want to come?"

"You go ahead. It sounds like I have work to do and I need to check Manhattan security logs."

Allie walked upstairs, and I pulled my fingers through my hair. I scrolled through my phone as soon as she left and rolled back the security cameras at the Manhattan penthouse. The evidence I had a hunch I'd find was all there: Simone in my apartment, slipping powder into my drink and then assaulting me. Shame and disgust coiled inside me. I slid down against the wall and sat on the floor until Allie returned from TJ's room.

"What's going on?" Allie asked.

I looked up. "How is he?"

"He put his headphones on so he didn't hear the conversation. He wants nothing to do with her."

"Good. He won't have to ever again. "

She glanced at my phone. "Are you okay?"

I swiped my finger across the screen. She didn't need to see Simone assaulting me.

"No, not really."

Allie slid down the wall, sat beside me and took my hand. The platinum band shone on her ring finger, and I smiled. If there was anything good that had happened to me the past few months, it was Allie. She had my back, and that was all I could ask for. We turned our heads to each other at the same time.

"Thank you for standing by my side."

"You're stuck with me until the end, Mr. Silver." She smiled.

"There's no one else I'd rather be stuck with than you. I can't let her get away with this. She's already gotten away with too much, but not this."

Silence. If I had to bet, Allie's thoughts reflected mine: how to get rid of Simone Hartley for good, while securing my child.

"What are you going to do? She's leaving the country," Allie asked after what felt like forever.

I squeezed her hand. "She won't leave because she can't."

"Why not?"

"She's a flight risk and won't get through airport security."

"She probably has a fake passport."

"Probably, but she won't flee. She's too obsessed with me. And with you." I reached for her growing belly. In less than three months, our babies would be here, and I had little time to straighten up Simone's mess. One of the babies kicked, and I jumped up.

"Did you feel that?"

She laughed. "Yes, I feel it everyday. Here."

She placed my hand on a different area on the belly, and a baby kicked again. I grinned like an idiot. Jesus, I wanted to grin like an idiot for the rest of my life because whenever I touched her, life made sense again. I'd never let Simone ruin our bond.

"I love you," Allie whispered from the side.

"I love you too." I turned my head toward her.

"What are you going to do?"

I took a deep breath in. "I'm going to set a trap when you go out to the casino next month, and we'll charge her there. But I need you as a pawn."

Chapter 17

Allie

Within hours, Simone had disappeared from New York. Tristan checked her coastal properties, now in the hands of the FBI, and called the hospitals, police stations, and shelters, but there was no sign of her. He found her old phone near the back gazebo, but after James sent it to forensics, it gave us nothing. As predicted, Donaldson and Simone's uncles made bail. Her brothers, Chad and Brad—or Humpty and Dumpty, as TJ liked to call them—took off into the Caribbean. The Wagner brothers and their law firm froze the congressman's and Jeff Hartley's estate assets, and Infinity's operations ceased.

We were doing great on the outside, but given Simone was pregnant with Tristan's baby, she'd make contact at first opportunity. Tristan would lure Simone to the casino with the news of my delayed bachelorette and baby shower, and we would help Silver Securities secure the criminal.

Just keep it simple.

Kendra would join us at the tables in hopes of reviving her memory. If nothing clicked, she'd leave before Simone's arrival. The days of her tortures would haunt her for a while. She needed closure, and if we all stuck together, we could put all the Hartleys behind bars.

The smell of Tristan hit me before his mouth captured mine in a surprise kiss, bringing me out of my daze. He held me in his arms in the casino hotel suite and kissed me like he didn't want to let me go. We separated with reluctance. He pulled his fingers through his hair and drew his brows, forming a narrow valley between them.

"Remember, you're being watched every minute. She won't risk getting close while you're with security, but we can make her feel comfortable enough at what she still thinks of as her father's favorite casino. We have people on every entrance and exit, so if she walks through that door, she'll leave in handcuffs. You may be a pawn, but you're my pawn. And I'm not risking any of you." He smoothed his hand over my stretched belly. Seven months down and two to go, though the doctors said twins would likely be earlier. "I promise you're all safe, and after today we won't have to think about Simone Hartley again."

"Just remember—take it easy. She's still having your baby."

"I won't harm either of them."

I relaxed and stepped forward into his arms. "She must know we're setting her up."

"Even if she does, Simone will risk facing you. She's been on your tail long enough. The dead bird was just a start. For fuck's sake, she changed your doctor appointments."

I stepped up on my toes and smoothed my fingers along Tristan's freshly trimmed hairline.

"I promise to be careful, and I trust you." I kissed him much harder than usual.

"Just follow the plan. This is a safe place," he said against my lips.

And that's how I ended up at the Casino, seven months pregnant and looking like I could pop the twins out any moment. Laura and Kendra sat at the roulette table while I stood, supporting my lower back and watching the ball roll around. I didn't believe in a perfect streak, but Laura's luck kept her on a roll. She played it safe, yet won every bet, and the stack of chips underneath her palm was nothing less than impressive. Each time she lucked out, Kendra screamed louder. I could see now why Julian had given her the nickname *Trouble*. Her cheers caught the attention we needed.

"Come on, sixty-nine. Allie needs a crib!"

Two cribs, I chuckled on the inside. Tristan was still the only one aware we were having twins.

"What are you doing? There is no sixty-nine, Laura."

"Obviously. Six-to-nine o'clock. Come on, babe. We used to have a streak on the street too. Is it the hormones?"

"It's your cryptic conversations. Sometimes I don't know if you're talking about apples or oranges."

"It's oranges and apples, and we've got security's attention, don't we?"

"I think I liked you better when you quoted pointless statistics." I eyed the area. "Looks like you've got everyone's attention."

"What's hopped in your panties?" she asked.

"Oh nothing—I'm just meeting my husband's resurrected and obsessed ex-fiancée who, oh, I don't know, is having his child."

"You know I can hear you." Tristan's smooth voice registered through my earpiece. I'd been so preoccupied with the idea I could run into Simone tonight, my nerves had taken over.

"Yes, I know. I'm fine. I promise."

"It's the hormones," Laura added, as if she could hear our conversation. "Get back on task, Green. I mean, Silver. Do I call you Silver now?"

"I haven't officially changed the paperwork."

"It's been changed." I heard Tristan in my ear again.

Laura rubbed the rabbit's foot attached to her belt and screamed louder. "Come on! Mamma needs some toys!"

Kendra placed a stack of chips on a four square area at the last minute. A slot machine chimed with a winning jackpot. The lights flashed in the distance, and the crowd's cheer resonated in waves.

"No more bets." The dealer swept his hand across the table.

I focused across the casino floor where Tristan and his crew were monitoring the area. This might have been Jeff Hartley's favorite casino, but he was dead, Congressman Donaldson no longer had any leeway in the Senate, and most importantly, Tristan's good friend from school had bought this casino a couple of weeks ago. The stars couldn't have aligned any better.

Laura stopped her happy bounce and gently elbowed me. "Jessica Hare, ten o'clock."

"Who the hell is Jessica Hare?" I asked.

The roulette slowed, and Laura eyed me from the side. "I can't exactly say redhead or Jessica Rabbit because then it's obviously Simone Hartley."

"That's obvious to you?"

"Rabbit-hare; hare-rabbit? How are you not making these connections? What happened to our streak?" Her nose wrinkled, the ball fell onto a red-twenty one, and Laura won again, screaming.

What streak was she talking about?

Laura was acting weird, and I didn't know why. Well, at least, weirder than usual, if that was possible. I stretched my legs and turned to the casino floor just as the crowd parted like the sea for Moses. Simone and four men in suits were walking toward us.

"She's here." Tristan's ominous voice in my earpiece drew shivers all over my body.

I nodded to Kendra.

"And this is where my adventure ends. I'm out, and I need to use the washroom."

She hopped off the stool like we'd planned and headed to the safe-spot before Simone saw her. Laura took her place as the target sauntered toward us, swinging her hips like a wobbling duck.

"Are we playing again, ladies?" The dealer cleared the table.

"No, thank you." Laura opened her filled purse, exchanged her chips for larger value ones, and slipped them in her pocket. We stepped away from the table and met Simone in the middle of the algebraic carpet. The bright shapes caught the eye in the fluorescent light, but nothing stole the show like Simone Hartley. Her smaller belly pointed forward; she was carrying high. While the pregnancy was obvious, she also looked like she'd missed out on a few meals. The dark circles under her eyes confirmed she'd been hiding and not sleeping well.

"Simone."

"Allie."

"Hare." Laura coughed into her hand.

"There's a warrant out for your arrest," I said.

"Tristan finally managed to bring me back to life?" she asked.

"Yes, he did. You're also wanted on rape charges. I'm sure once one sticks, the courts will dig into your past and, well, we can just leave the rest to the courts. And this one will stick and sting, Simone. I don't believe they allow rapists to keep babies."

Her lip twitched, then her eyebrow. It felt like our stare down lasted forever as she checked her position and the exits.

"The unbeatable Wagner lawyers want to take a win against me? Right. Well, this time I'll tell you how this is gonna go. The lawyers won't get a chance because I will make bail and have Tristan's baby. We'll renovate the cove house, move in together, and bond with our child."

"You're delusional," I said in disgust.

"Come on, let's make our way out." She motioned forward. Her suited guards rose to their feet, but Laura blocked their way.

"Whoa, is there a problem, gentlemen?"

Their stone faces remained intact, and I threw Laura a warning look.

"That way," one of them pointed, pushing at Laura's shoulder.

"Hey, hands off! I'm going. We're going."

Simone's sleek walk behind us echoed with glory. I headed to the spiral staircase and scaled up the glass steps. Lights glimmered, and the sounds of slot machines dinged below us.

I crossed the long bridge to the curtains where Tristan was waiting with the Silver Securities team. The velvet fabric was drawn to the sides, and we crossed inside the low-lit room. Tristan was sitting at a table along with James and a handful of federal agents. We stepped aside, and for the first time since her arrival, Simone Hartley must have realized her mistake. Her face drained of blood as she scanned the room.

"Get me out of here," she whispered, pointing to her men in suits. "They bought you out too?"

I cleared my throat. "When a criminal as large as your father gets off the street, plenty of jobs open up."

She turned on her heel, and a guard immediately stepped between us.

"Gets off the street? My father's dead, you bitch. I should have taken you down at the fundraiser."

"Stand down, Simone." Tristan's calm voice carried across the room. He stood up and crossed the space toward us, taking the guard's spot in the line of fire, protecting me. "I'm sorry, but it's all over. Gentlemen?"

One of the suits who'd come with Simone removed a pair of handcuffs and gripped her wrists at her back.

"Simone Hartley, you're under arrest on suspicion of drug smuggling—"

She tried to rip out of his hold, but he gripped her harder. "What drug smuggling?"

"It will be easier if you let them do their job, Simone." Tristan stepped back.

"Tristan, you're actually going to let this happen?" Pearl-sized tears streamed down her cheeks along with her invincibility. "What about our baby?"

"You'll have good care, and so will the baby."

"So you're just abandoning us?"

"Quite the opposite. Whenever you're ready, officers."

"Simone Hartley, you're under arrest on suspicion of drug smuggling, human trafficking, identity fraud, and kidnapping. You have the right to remain silent and anything you say may be used against you in court. Do you understand?"

The clicking of handcuffs was music to my ears. Simone turned my way. "You did this! This is all your fault." She lifted her chin higher into the air. "If you think this is over, you're mistaken. Big time!"

Tristan's phone pinged, and James's followed. I heard Laura's next and then my own. As we all checked the news, the growing silence in the room sharpened.

"What's going on?"

Simone looked around at the somber faces. I didn't want to be the one to tell her, but we all knew who should. Tristan lifted his gaze away from his phone and looked at Simone.

"Tristan? Please tell me what's going on?"

He stuffed his phone in his back pocket, approached her, and cleared his throat. "Your uncles fled on a private plane this morning... and it disappeared over the Amazon."

Her mouth curved into a slow smile as she whispered, "They got away."

"They didn't get away, Simone. The plane crashed."

"Exactly." Her smile brightened, but Tristan disagreed, and as she watched his face, that same confidence slowly faded from her eyes.

"They were fleeing the country on bail. The crash site has been checked, and your uncles were among the recovered bodies."

"Bodies?"

"Yes."

"That means—"

"I'm sorry, Simone. Your uncles are gone."

She looked up, tilted her head, and slowly turned in circle, examining every face in the room. "You people think I care my uncles are dead? I don't give a rat's ass about them! All I care about is this baby." She pointed. "And now that my creepy uncles are gone, you're all gonna try pinning everything on me, aren't you?"

Silence.

Her pointing finger jabbed the air, "Aren't you? Aren't you? Well, I'll die before I let you lay a charge against me!"

I startled as Simone doubled over, screaming. "Ahh!"

At first I thought it was Simone's overdramatic tendency, but when one of the guards caught her as she collapsed, I thought my own knees would buckle. I rushed to her side.

"Simone, open your eyes. Come on, Simone."

She slowly came to and opened her eyes. The doctor from the tactical team assessed Simone's vitals; her contractions were close and steady. Too close. We packed her up into an ambulance, and Tristan left with a screaming Simone. I hopped into James's car, and he followed the ambulance.

"It's weird, but I feel bad for her," Laura said from the passenger's seat. "All alone and aware her baby will be taken away from her? That's gotta be tough."

"They can still stop the birth," I said.

James received an incoming text on his car's screen.

Tristan: water broke.

I guessed she was having the baby, early or not.

"How are you doing, Allie?" James caught my stare in his rearview mirror.

"I don't know. I still can't believe—"

"There are a lot of things we don't want to believe in life," he said. "But living with the devil you know is better than one you don't."

I swallowed hard. Tristan was about to have a second baby with another woman since we'd met, before I'd even had my first. It wasn't jealousy, but more like the loss of our first experience. Which was silly, because we would have a lifetime of experiences to create, while Simone rotted in jail.

"Tristan may need to spend some time with Simone and the baby for now, but he loves you."

I looked up. "I know he does, but you're right. The baby needs him now."

Laura turned around in her seat and gripped my hand. "We can bring Foxy and stay with you until things settle down."

"I'd really love that. Thank you both."

I'd do anything to have a normal life again, and Laura was closest thing to normal I'd ever had.

"That's what families do, apparently." She winked, and I chuckled.

I leaned my head against the headrest and closed my eyes. It was almost over. Hopefully, the baby would be healthy, but we hadn't even discussed raising all our kids together. Late last year, I'd had no desire for a family, simply revenge against the man who ruined my mother's life, and now I was getting a family with not one, but four kids.

"You look overwhelmed." Laura reached back and took my hand. She gripped my cold fingers. "Don't worry. It will all work out. You're not doing this alone."

I gave her a grateful smile and held onto my belly. "Thank

you." I might have wanted Simone out of our lives, but I also wanted Tristan's baby safe.

James and Laura drove me home and stayed with me until Tristan called. I was sitting at the kitchen counter with Laura and TJ, drinking tea, when my phone rang with Tristan's number.

"Hey, how are you doing?"

"Okay. She had the baby. She's in the NICU and will stay there for several weeks. She's only two and a half pounds, and her lungs are tiny but strong."

"She's going to be okay, Tristan. You'll see."

After a short pause, where I imagined him staring through a glass wall at his newborn, he said, "I'm gonna finish the hospital paperwork and come home. I can't wait to see you. Simone's officially under federal watch."

As she should have been long ago.

"You do what you have to do and I'll be waiting at home."

"And TJ?"

"TJ's good; happy but a little confused about… well, Simone and the baby. He just needs some normalcy and to make new friends."

"We'll get him through this. Therapy next week is a good starting point."

"I'm sure that will help. I'll see you soon?"

"Yeah, see you soon."

Except the newborn was in distress that night, and Tristan didn't come home. That was the first of many sleepless nights for us both.

I sat in the rocking chair at the NICU with little Faith. That's what had saved my girl: our faith. She'd gained weight, but she was still small. So small I'd seen nothing like it, and I feared anyone's breath would break her. Except it didn't, because she was resilient. And I prayed... we prayed a lot. When I first saw her in the incubator, she looked like a little spider with twig-like arms and legs. I knew it looked like she had little chance, but now, four weeks later, there was no question Faith was a fighter.

"Come on, it's my turn." Emma waited in the other rocking chair as I passed her the baby.

"You look like you've just been run over by a car." My mother fixed my hair like I was still her boy. "If you want your baby to be well, you have to be well too. It works both ways."

Fatigue buzzed in my brain. What I needed was another coffee. Strong coffee.

"Yeah, but look how much Faith has grown."

"What about Allie? Are you taking care of your wife?" she asked.

"I'm doing fine, Wilma. I promise." Allie rubbed her belly. "But I am worried about Tristan."

My mother removed her glasses and eyed the overgrowth on my face. Since Simone had given birth, I'd visited daily and even slept at the hospital a few nights.

She tugged at my arm. "Well, what's going to happen to Faith when she's released?"

"Once she's well enough, she's coming home with us. I'm hiring a neonatal nurse and a nanny to help with the babies. Allie's close to giving birth, and I'm really hoping we can all go home before then."

"And Simone? She won't fight for her daughter?"

I kissed the top of my mother's head. "Don't worry, Mom. I have everything under control, and this decision is no longer up to Simone. She signed the adoption paperwork in exchange for leniency. They're taking her to jail today."

"Good. Keep that witch far away from my grandchildren."

"Do you want to hold her, Mom?" Emma asked, and Wilma took her position in the honorary chair.

I settled my mother with the baby and walked over to Allie, who was rubbing an area where one baby had pressed out a foot into her stomach. "Would you like to sit down?"

"No, I'm fine. Where is Simone?"

"She's in mental health on the third floor. They placed her on a suicide watch last week. As hard as this is for Simone, it's best for the baby. I won't allow another child to be raised by a lunatic."

The night after the adoption paperwork went through, Simone tried taking her life. She slashed her wrists, but the cut wasn't deep enough to kill.

"I'm so sorry, Tristan." She touched my arm. "When is Faith coming home?"

"They're saying a few more weeks. We're going to have a full house by then."

Allie smoothed her hand protectively over her stomach. The twins had six weeks to full term remaining.

"A few months ago, I was on my own, and now…. Now I'm going to have kids. A lot of kids."

Four, to be exact, and one of them was a teenager.

A nurse cleared her throat, and we turned to the doorway where Simone was sitting in a wheelchair. Her wrists were raw around their bandages and tied to the side rests.

"Ms. Hartley would like to see her daughter before her release today."

My family froze in their spots.

"This should have been cleared ahead," I said.

"Tristan," Allie whispered beside me. "It's okay. Who knows when she'll get to see her daughter again?"

Simone was heading straight from the hospital to jail, where she would await trial. But Allie was right. This would be the last time she saw Faith for a while.

"All right." I eyed the frail woman in the wheelchair. Simone's Botox had dissolved and her skin was blotched, her hair greasy and tangled, and her eyes shadowed with dark circles. The somber face was unrecognizable from the high-class woman she used to be. The doctors said she'd refused to eat, so they'd forced food down a feeding tube. Simone had done everything in her power to remain at the hospital for as long as possible, just so she could stay with Faith. While I empathized with her motherly instinct, that same drive had kept my son away from me for fourteen years, and today would be the last day Simone Hartley saw our daughter for a while.

I cleared the room, and I pulled my hand through my disheveled hair. The nurse wheeled Simone closer to the bassinet.

"She's beautiful." Her voice broke. A tear collected in the corner of Simone's eye, and a lump formed in my throat at the same time.

"She's a fighter," I said.

"Just like her daddy."

I lowered my hand inside the incubator, and Faith tightened her grip around my finger. "Yeah, just like her daddy."

After a long moment of silence, I sat down opposite Simone and watched her watch Faith sleep.

"She's eating well?" she asked.

"Yes. Thank you for pumping the milk."

"She's my daughter. It's what I'm supposed to do. I'm supposed to be with her—"

"Simone—"

My phone pinged, and I read the incoming message. The news would hit national channels within minutes.

"Where is the remote? Turn on the television."

"There's no television in this room, sir," the nurse said. "It's the neonatal unit. Babies don't watch television, and when their parents are here, they only have eyes for their babies."

"No, it's all right. Thank you."

"But there is one in the common area if you need it."

"Thank you."

"Tristan, what's going on?" Simone asked.

Shit. Simone.

I scrolled through the message for details. How in the world was I supposed to tell her?

"The courts will seek full justice for the atrocious crimes the deceased Hartley brothers committed," I read. "Simone Hartley will be charged for those crimes."

Simone sat silently for a long time after, and I waited until reality sank in. I assumed she'd never truly accept it, but everyone paved their own roads in life. The Hartleys had made their choices and Simone had made hers. She was the only remaining Hartley in the new lawsuit. Her charges were minuscule compared to her uncles', but I was sure they'd stick. Overconfidence had betrayed her and karma had ripped her family apart.

"It's time to go, Simone." The nurse placed Faith back into

the incubator. She had a few more weeks to go and milestones to reach before we could take her home.

"You can't take her away from me, Tristan. I've already lost TJ. She's the last thing I have and I can't live without her. I'll die without her."

I wanted to tell her we'd visit, but I couldn't get the words through my throat. I didn't want to make promises I couldn't keep, and because I was new to this father thing, my gut told me to seek a professional's advice. Faith needed a fair chance, and I simply didn't know whether a child visiting her mother in jail was appropriate. At least, not now.

"Simone, you can't take a baby to jail."

"I'm not in jail yet. You can get me out of here, Tristan. We can do facial surgery and prosthetics and they'll never find me. I'm sure we can find a body double if there's a need, but you're the only one who can help me, Tristan. Please," she begged.

"I'm tired, Simone. I'm tired of dealing with everything, and I just want some peace. That's all. We could have done this differently, but it's too late now."

"It's never too late. You loved me once, remember? There has to be compassion in there somewhere." She pointed her finger at my chest. "I didn't come here for nothing. I came here to get my baby."

Legally, Faith was no longer Simone's, and the sooner Simone accepted her reality, the quicker she could move on.

"You're in a hospital because you're hurting yourself. I know you've been wanting to stay with Faith, but she'll be leaving soon as well, and... you know they're discharging you today."

"What about my baby?"

"Faith will come home with me. I will take care of her."

"And that's it? That's my life from now on?"

"You have good lawyers, and with cooperation—"

"What? I'll visit my baby through a glass wall? If you even

decide to let me? No, Tristan. You can't let them do that to me. *You* cannot do that to me."

Except it was already done.

She pulled on the restraints until they cut into her wrists.

"Simone, you need help—"

"I need my baby!" she screamed. The nurse filled a syringe with white liquid and added the medication to the IV.

I didn't know what would happen to Simone after the trial, but the likelihood she'd remain in jail for a while was great. The chances she'd go crazy sooner were even greater.

"I'm sorry."

"You can't! This isn't over!" she cried. Two more nurses came inside the room, sedating her. As I watched Simone wheeled out of the room, limp and sobbing, my heart broke in half. Actually, it shattered into a thousand pieces.

"WHERE ELSE DOES IT ITCH?"

Allie sat halfway up on the couch with her belly high in the air. The sky turned orange in the window behind her as evening set in.

"Right there." She pointed near the navel, where one twin liked to stick its foot. I scratched the area and applied a gooey cream Allie gave me.

"It's green. Why does it have to be green?"

"It's organic, and it helps with the stretch marks and the itch. Fifty to ninety percent of women develop stretch marks during pregnancy."

"Is that what Laura said?"

She threw me a dirty look. I tickled near her ribs and she squealed before settling down. Her presence soothed every-thing that had gone haywire during the past several months. TJ was in his room organizing baby pictures in an album he'd made for Simone of him and Faith. My girl was coming home tomorrow afternoon, and the courts had set Simone's trial in three weeks. The state's case was solid, and TJ knew his mother would need something to ease the blow.

Allie shifted on the couch and winced in pain.

"Everything all right?"

"Yeah, just getting a little tight in there."

"It could be any day."

"No, they're not ready."

"Yeah, but it could be, and if the twins come, we'll do great. Look at little Faith. She's coming home tomorrow afternoon."

Allie's eyes widened, and her lips quivered. "Oh, my God. She's coming home."

"Hey, hey. It's all right. We've got this. I'm taking time off, and I'll be here."

"You need to do guy stuff."

"What? What do you mean?"

"Once the baby's here, you won't have time to spend with your brother and with your family. We're going to have three babies. That's three, if you didn't hear me. Three. You need to go fishing."

"Fishing?"

"Yeah, fishing. Isn't that what guys do?" She sat up on the couch.

"You're panicking. Lie back down."

"I've never had a baby before, and now I'm going to have three. For goodness' sake, your parents don't even know we're having twins."

Never mind my parents. I worried that when Emma found out we'd kept this secret from her, she'd tighten her reins. We were adding the cribs, changing tables, and accessories to the nursery last minute because Emma would have snooped beforehand.

"They'll know soon enough, and I'm sure they'll be ecstatic.

My mom is a stone's throw away and so is Emma, and Peg is moving in this weekend fifty yards from here. There's nothing to worry about. We'll have plenty of help."

Her nose wiggled, and she rose up on her elbows. "Says the man who's rubbing guacamole on my stomach."

"I thought it was the stretch mark cream?"

"That's the stretch mark cream." She pointed to the tube on the table, then a small bowl. "This is guacamole Olivier left from the nachos."

"It's still organic, right?"

She chuckled. "And you're saying you're okay with handling three babies?"

I went to the kitchen, moistened a towel, washed off the guac, and sat near her feet.

"Okay, I hear ya. But I've taken on government criminals and the mafia. I'm sure I can handle three babies. Now give me your feet."

"What?"

"Come on, lift them up. You need to relax. And I promise I'll take that fishing trip. Tomorrow morning. How's that? Julian's been fixing his motorcycle and taking care of Kendra. He needs a break too, so I'll go fishing with my brother and we'll do the guy thing. We'll take TJ with us down to the shore and catch… fish. Hopefully. And do the guy thing."

She smiled. I loved her smile. I would do anything for this woman. She lifted her foot, and I pressed my fingers into her soles, soothing the pain from the daily weight she was carrying. She closed her eyes, moaned, and my dick hardened.

She opened her eyes as fast as she closed them. "I'm gonna make waffles for breakfast. I haven't made waffles in a long time."

"I know. Your mom told me. But you need to relax."

I rubbed the foot harder, and she settled into the couch.

"You told her over tequila?"

I nodded. Since Allie was expecting, I'd taken upon myself to visit my mother-in-law and ease her worries. She was down to one lock on her door, and we planned to buy her a puppy when she moved in. Because three babies weren't enough.

"I'm looking forward to waffles, but you know what else I'm looking forward to?"

I scanned her from the bottom up, and she writhed on the couch. The image of her naked on our bed flashed in my mind.

"What?" she whispered.

I lowered her foot and shifted higher on the couch, my mouth meeting her swollen lips.

"You."

Chapter 19

Allie

Tristan and Julian were standing on the shoreline with their fishing lines in hand. TJ was snapping photos of a family of ducks nesting near the back pond. Morning breezes swept through the kitchen window, replacing the waffle aroma with warm spring air. It was only nine in the morning, but already heat had collected into a sweat on my back. The boys had another hour before the store delivered the cribs, and Faith was coming home in the afternoon. My breasts lactated at the thought, and both babies kicked at the same time.

I propped the second batch of ingredients against my stomach, resting most of my weight on the counter, and swirled the batter. Olivier had sent me his best waffle recipe, so after fourteen years of relying on frozen Eggos, I braved the impossible: homemade Belgian waffles.

The smell of baking dough brought back memories from before my father's death, when my parents danced around the kitchen floor, laughing. The dusty cloud of flour hovered in the air, settling over my father's black jeans.

I smiled at the memory and poured the batter onto the checkered skillet, closed the lid, and twisted the handle.

"Batch two, here we come."

I missed my father, but now that my life had settled and my family was whole, I would share his legacy with my kids. The waffles steamed, and I opened the window wider. A low knock echoed from the front door. I glanced through the back window to where the brothers were standing by the shoreline. The babies kicked harder, and a second knock came on the front door, this time louder.

"Delivery," I heard from the outside.

The cribs must be early.

I set the bowl aside, wiped my hands on the apron, and wobbled to the front door.

"I'm coming." But when I pulled on the handle and the door swung open, I froze.

Time stood still as I stared down at a loaded barrel. The rewind button played in my mind to fifteen years ago, when Dave Wright had attacked my mother. Suddenly I was back there again, shaking and crying, snot dripping down my nose and fear creeping through every bone. I couldn't stop the shaking then and I couldn't stop it now as Dave Wright pushed a pistol against my stomach. My knees softened as I backed away, watching the aimed gun. I lowered my hands to my belly, their span and my spread-out fingers not even close to being big enough or thick enough to protect my children from a bullet. He closed the door behind him and followed me inside, catching up.

"Hello, Allie. It's nice to see you again."

"What are you doing here?" My voice trembled and my body shook as I slowly backed through the hall all the way to the kitchen in the back. How the hell was he alive? More importantly, how the hell was I going to get away alive?

"You mean, how am I alive?" He grunted. "It's good to have friends in high places, and prosthetics have come a long way.

Your men shot a body double. Ms. Hartley promised me she'd find you. And she delivered."

Simone?

I should have known she'd have a back-up plan.

Oh, my God! We'd killed an innocent man instead of Wright.

"I should have shot you that day," I whispered, holding onto my stomach. I should have pulled that trigger the day Tristan took me from Charleston and we drove into the mountains, where he'd found my secret. That day, Tristan gave me the chance to end everything, and I bailed. David Wright should have been in an urn years ago. Instead, he was standing in front of me, threatening my babies. My mind spun. Or maybe it was the room. My thoughts and vision drifted in and out of focus as I searched for a dark staircase, but there wasn't one. The sound of my heart thumped in my ears, along with those of my babies. My mother's cries and pleas for help carried back from the past. Memories of the blood, the hospital, the funeral, and our narrow escapes rushed on a fast-forward film. Adrenaline pumped through my body. I couldn't stay under that staircase if I wanted to save my babies.

"Get the hell away from me." I pushed the gun from my chest and heard my voice shake, even though I didn't mean it to. I wanted to be strong, yet I backed into a wall because he pushed the gun into my ribs.

That gun controlled everything at the moment, not me.

"I came to claim what's mine, Allie, and you're it." He closed in until his cigarette breath burned in my lungs. He lifted the gun to my forehead, and I shut my eyes. The cold round tip pressed hard into my skin.

He's going to do it. He's going to pull that trigger.

"I thought you were dead. How are you not dead?"

Life was so much better when he was dead, but Wright didn't seem to hear me. I could imagine Simone gloating from jail. She'd never stop haunting me. I should have seen this coming, but I'd missed it.

"You had a double as well, my darling. Don't you remember Marissa? Marissa was the perfect bait, and so, so good, but she wasn't you. I knew I couldn't get you at the auction. You had security, so I took the next best thing." He reached for my belly and I shoved his hand away.

His bushy brows furrowed. "You know what I also found at the auction? That I could get close to you, and when Ms. Hartley told me she'd find you for me, showed me where you worked, gave me direct access from her boathouse to yours, it made all the years spent looking for you worth it. Who knew a little girl from the farm would find her way in Manhattan?"

A drop of courage spread through me, along with a mouth full of disgust. "Get the fuck away from me," I barked.

Wright pressed the gun harder to my temple, forcing my head sideways. If he pulled the trigger now, my waffles would be ruined. They were nearly ready.

"I should turn off the waffles. They'll burn."

But he ignored me, looking around the house, "You set yourself up nice."

His hand and the gun shook against my ribs.

"Tristan will be back in a minute," I whispered.

Please be back in a minute.

The surprise from Wright's visit was slowly wearing off, and I felt my instinct scramble a plan.

"He's just outside. There's a security camera here, and the police will arrive any moment," I lied. With the babies on the way, Tristan was installing a new system, but during the two days it would take to complete the job, Wright had found me.

He motioned me toward the kitchen counter by the back door. "You look just like your mother. And with a belly, too. I love baby bellies."

My stomach squeezed. I forced the nausea down and held it in. A cramp flew through my lower back.

"I have some fond memories of that day." His grunt released a stench of dirty teeth and an empty stomach.

He eyed me up and down with a smirk. "Peg loved it when I touched her."

Shit, shit, shit. I cursed in my mind. This wasn't happening! Where was he going with this?

"I'm sure you'd love it too, my darling."

The cocky shadow on his haunted face darkened.

I would die before I let him rape me and kill my children.

Think, Allie. Think!

He moved forward.

"Don't you dare touch me, you sick motherfucker! I swear if you take another step closer, I will kill you with my hands before you shoot and bury you myself," I threatened.

The smirk returned. Wright drew the gun slowly down my nose, then the side of my neck. I felt my jugular pulse against the metal tip. He lowered it to my chest and then my belly. My heart raced, and I held my breath. The low click of the gun held me in my spot, and I slid my hands forward, wrapping them tighter around my stomach, fearing for my babies' lives.

"Take three steps to your left and turn around," he ordered.

"Fuck you!"

He whacked me across my face with his free hand. The slap stung, ringing in my ears. The sweet smell of waffles rose in the air as my backside hit the doorway's edge.

"You think I'm kidding?" He dug the gun deeper into my belly, and I shuffled my feet into the kitchen to get space.

Oh, my God! He's going to shoot me, then rape me!

I couldn't let this happen. I'd sworn never to be afraid again and promised not to give in and to fight. In seconds, the instinct I'd nurtured to return for my entire life flashed in my mind, and adrenaline flooded my veins like a rushing tsunami.

I would settle this today, and David Wright would not walk out of this house alive.

"Fine, fine." I put up my hands, palms facing forward, and moved to where he wanted me, against the counter.

"What are you going to do after you're done?" I stalled.

His voice softened. "Marry you, Peg, the way we were years ago. I had plans for after the prom, and I won't let you leave this time."

Did he just call me by my mother's name? Something had shifted in the air.

"I've been looking for you everywhere, Peg, and when your daughter said she knew where you lived, well, that was just a bonus."

He was confusing me with Marissa. He'd bought Marissa because he thought she was me.

"I almost settled for your little girl, Peg. The girl was tight and giving. But she had the baby, so she's spoiled now. It's good that I have you, Peg. It's always been good to have you."

Bile built up in my throat. What had happened to Marissa? Where was she? What did he do to her?

Get away from me, I repeated my head. *Get away from me.*

"But there's no one who can ever compare to you, Peg. We'll go to our prom again and have the family we always wanted." His stinky mouth came closer to my ear, and I turned away in disgust. His hand slid to my belly as if I were carrying his child. My stomach twisted into a knot. He gripped my chin with his free hand and turned my head sideways. His three-day stubble raked against my cheek. "All you have to do is stay still, Peg. Just. Stay. Still."

The sound of his lowering zipper echoed forever, and I shut my eyes.

Tristan. Where are you?

The smell of waffles filled the kitchen, and I looked out through the window, but I couldn't see Tristan or Julian. Pigs would fly up in rainbow patterns before I'd let my family suffer at the hands of this man again.

"Why don't we sit down in the family room, Dave?" I changed my voice to my mother's.

Arguing with the son of a bitch wouldn't help. Nothing would, but maybe my mother's voice could buy me the time I needed.

"Come on, Dave. We haven't seen each other in so long. Let's sit down."

For a moment, I thought he'd respond to the suggestion.

"We can sit afterwards. All I want is you, Peg. Just you. Right now. Then we can sit."

My throat tightened. I might not be my mother, but if I played his game, maybe I could turn this around.

"No, Dave. I'd like tea first. You're a guest in my home, and guests always have tea. Why don't I make us some tea?"

He jutted the gun back at my stomach, and my plan evaporated. The tears fell freely down my cheeks.

"I'm carrying a child, Dave. You need to be careful. I... I can't have them hurt. Please." I whispered through the sob, and braced my hands on the counter, searching for Tristan out the window.

"There's no need to bleed like last time if you just listen." He grunted, pressing his front into my back. "No fighting. Now lift your fucking skirt."

I did as he asked, but my mind was racing at a thousand miles per hour. The stench of his cigarette breath, along with something burning, filled the room as Wright positioned himself behind me. The sound of him fumbling with his pants again gave me chills. Disgust collected in the back of my throat.

This isn't happening, this isn't happening!

I took a deep breath in, calming my nerves, but the gun at my ribcage held all the power. One wrong move and the bullet would fly through me–through us. I exhaled slowly and gripped the counter, giving myself enough space for my belly and then some, just in case he pushed too hard, like he had against my mother.

What are you thinking? Fight!

I jolted.

"Stay still," he barked, and I jumped.

"No."

I had to fight, and it had to be done now because if I didn't, he'd kill my babies when he was done.

"What did you just say?"

"No," I said louder.

The smell of burning batter intensified, and I remembered the waffles. "We're going to set the kitchen on fire, Dave. Let me take them off the skillet. Please. Before the fire spreads." I slipped out from between him and the counter and went straight for the waffle maker. I twisted the grids streaming with black smoke and turned off the machine, eyeing the kitchen knives. I'd have to throw one and not miss. And if I missed, he'd shoot. The only problem was sliding the blade out of the compartment without making a noise. I glanced back at Wright, to where a tiny red dot appeared in the middle of his forehead. Then everything happened all at once. The window shattered, the red dot on Wright's head exploded, and I collapsed to the marble floor.

Moments later, Tristan appeared above me and helped me to a sitting position, propping me against the cupboards. He blocked the doorway where the glass had shattered and checked over my body. "Don't look, baby, don't look. It's all over now."

I didn't have to look to see blood splattered over our kitchen floor. "Is he dead? Is he really dead?"

"Yeah, he's dead."

"Do you smell that?" I tried to get up, but the pain around my hips intensified.

The smoke alarm went off.

"It's the waffle maker. Hold on."

Tristan shot to his feet, unplugged the waffle maker, and opened the kitchen window wider.

A cramping ache shot through my stomach.

"Ahh!" The scream tore through my lungs. I grabbed my belly, and he hopped over my legs to the other side, cupping my face. "Allie, look at me. What's wrong? Did he hurt you?"

"No, no. He didn't get to it... I... I think I'm okay." I shook my head, feeling the swell of tears building on the inside. A breakdown was inevitable, but the unfamiliar ache streaming around my lower back and the navel drew my attention to the babies.

Julian walked through the back door, stepped over the pool of blood, and kneeled at my other side. He had a sniper rifle braced against his shoulder. "The ambulance is on its way, and so are the police."

"You killed him? You shot Wright?"

"No, it wasn't me." Julian removed the rifle from his shoulder and lowered it to the floor.

I looked at Tristan. "It was you?"

"No, it wasn't me either," he glanced over to his brother.

"Are you gonna be ok?" Julian asked. "I should go."

"Go." Tristan said and Julian hurried out the back door.

"If it wasn't you two, then who was it?" I asked.

The brothers looked at one another, but just when Tristan opened his mouth, I screamed. My stomach cramped. Pain shot throughout my body, centering at my pelvis. The next contraction tightened so hard, I nearly broke Tristan's hand with the scream. A pool of liquid collected between my thighs, trickling out of my panties.

"What's hurting? Are you all right?"

"Tristan, I think my water just broke."

Chapter 20

Tristan

The sound of ambulance sirens was outdone by Allie's pained cries. Her grip tightened on my hand, turning my fingers white. I sat on a small seat next to her gurney while she breathed in an odd sequence. This wasn't what I'd read about, and I thought we'd have more time, but by the looks of it, the twins were in a hurry.

"Breathe, baby. Breathe."

"I am breathing," she said through gritted teeth, and I summoned all my patience and strength for her. "The babies are coming, Tristan. The babies are coming."

"I know they're coming, and you're doing great."

"There's nothing great about this. They're early." Her face contorted as she fought through the pain. It made her look like a… well, I'd better not even think it.

"They're right on time, baby. Everything's going to be fine. Just breathe."

"It's normal for twins to be born early," the paramedic said as he clipped an oximeter on Allie's finger. "Concentrate on one breath at a time, Mrs. Silver. Breathing is good. Just breathe, and we'll be at the hospital in three minutes."

"Stop telling me to breathe. I can obviously breathe because if I wasn't breathing, I'd be dead, and I'm alive, so stop telling me to breathe."

I exchanged a look with the paramedic, and we both chose silence over admitting my wife was breathing like a fire dragon.

She turned her head my way in between contractions, pouting.

I assessed the mood shift with caution. "What's the matter?"

"My waffles are ruined."

"It's okay. We'll make more waffles."

"They were supposed to be a surprise, and now they're ruined."

"The pancake aroma saved your life, Allie."

"It did?"

"Yeah, it did."

"How?"

"We all smelled them from the shore. After the babies are delivered, we'll come home, and we'll have a large family breakfast with all the waffles you want."

"We can't have a family breakfast." She lifted on the gurney. "There's blood all over the kitchen. I need to go home and clean."

"Stay still." I smoothed her hair back and gently pressed down on her shoulder. "We're almost there."

"Ahh!" She pulled her knees up on the next contraction and crushed my fingers in her hold.

I looked at the paramedic. "They're close. It's our first baby. Well, third and fourth if you want to be technical, but first together, and I thought we had more time."

"Everybody's body is different, but we're almost there." The paramedic re-checked Allie's vitals, recording them on a screen. "And by the looks of it, your labor team is all set."

"Team? We have a team?" Allie gasped.

"Apparently we do. I'm sure Emma mentioned it the other day, but I wasn't paying much attention."

"Holy crap, it hurts. What about Mom? Did you call my mom?"

"I called everybody. Laura, my parents, Peg. Everyone. I called Emma first, and she had the duty to call everyone, so I'm sure she did."

"Okay, good."

"Now, brea…" I stopped before she breathed fire again.

"And Laura? Is she coming? Where is Julian? Julian was at the house."

"They're all coming, and you're doing great. Julian's getting Kendra."

I didn't want to remind her of the scene at the house where my brother was answering police questions.

"Everyone will want to see the babies."

She smiled and sucked in shorter breath. "Okay, okay. I need drugs. Lots of drugs. The babies are coming. I don't know if I can do this." She smiled before screaming through another contraction.

"Yes, the babies are coming." I brushed the hair off her face. "And I know you can do this because you're strong. Break through the pain."

She gripped the sheet. Her lips thinned into a line, pausing her labored breath. "There's definitely something I want to break right now, Tristan, and I beg you to move away because I cannot control this."

"I'm not leaving you for a moment. Not now and not ever."

"Even if I break you."

"Even if you break me. Now breathe. He-he-haw."

"That's not it. It's hee-hee-hoooo."

"Good, then just do it that way: hee-haw-hoooo."

The ambulance came to a soft stop, and the door opened wide to a group of doctors. I followed them as they wheeled

Allie out on the gurney and inside the hospital. We sped through the hall, turned a couple of corners, and then someone handed me a blue gown. It was all happening so fast. The contractions, the rush of doctors and nurses, and Allie's labored breathing. Her frightened eyes met mine. "I know these are my first, but they're coming, Tristan. They're coming now. I need to push."

The next few minutes passed in a haze. The nurses and doctors moved around the room like a coordinated army, but had no time for an epidural because Allie was fully dilated and pushing hard.

"Mr. Silver. Can you move up a little?" the doctor asked. "You're about to have a baby."

"What about my drugs? I need drugs." Allie pushed with the contraction.

"There's no time, Mrs. Silver. You're fully dilated."

"You're doing great, baby. You're doing great."

"The pressure." She steadied her breath, gripped the bedside, and braced herself into the bed, pushing. "Ahh!"

Jesus, there sure was a reason God made women for this because I couldn't imagine shoving a basketball down my… oh God! he room spun. My vision tunneled and I almost blacked out until I heard the doctor again.

"Okay, Mrs. Silver. The head is out, and I need another hard push on the next contraction. Ready?"

Allie nodded with haste, clenched her jaw, shut her eyes, scrunched her shoulders forward, drew her chin down to her chest, and pushed. Once the shoulders passed, the rest of the baby slid out, and his cry was the happiest sound I'd heard in my life.

"Congratulations, Mr. And Mrs. Silver, you have a baby boy."

The world around me disappeared. Somewhere in the distance, I heard our first baby being handed to the nurses where they cleaned him, but I couldn't let go of Allie's hand. I wiped the sweat off her forehead and kissed her. "We have a baby boy. One more to go, Allie. A few more pushes and you're done."

"For Emma's sake, I hope she didn't settle on Barney," Allie snickered, before her next contraction hit. I let her squeeze my hand hard because that was the least I could do when she was pushing two melon-sized babies out in the same day.

"You're going to feel that same need to push, Mrs. Silver. When you do: push."

"It's coming," she screamed, locked her jaw, tensed her upper body, and pushed.

The second baby's cry made the world disappear again. My focus drifted from Allie to the baby and back to Allie again.

"Congratulations, it's a girl," the doctor said.

"A girl? We have a boy and a girl?" I asked as she handed the baby to the nurse.

"He's an eight on the Apgar," I heard the other nurse say, and snuck a peek as they cleaned, measured, and weighed the kids.

"She's an eight as well."

"That's good, isn't it?" I asked, but the doctor was concentrating on Allie.

"That's very good. Now I need one more gentle push, Mrs. Silver." The doctor concentrated on Allie's lower section, and Allie's eyes grew wide.

"There's a third one in there?"

"No. It's just the placenta now."

Allie strained once more, gave another solid push and then slumped in the bed with relief. I wiped the sweat dripping down her forehead. Both babies cried out, forcing a fresh stream of tears down her face.

"They're here," I whispered, scanning over their little bodies, then glanced back at Allie. "They're pink and perfect."

They weren't exactly pink—more like peachy, with white gunk in the elbow creases—but they were still perfect: small but healthy. And they were the most incredible two little things I'd seen in my life. I'd fallen in love with them when they slept inside my wife, and now I fell in love with them all over again.

Allie grinned from ear to ear. Flushed spots scattered along her arms.

"Are they all right? They're early. Please tell me they'll be okay."

"The babies are doing great. You'll both stay at the hospital for a few days, but everything else looks good so far."

"Thank God!" I tightened my grip on her hand and kissed her forehead. "Are you all right?"

"Yeah, I think so."

"You did it, Allie."

"We both did." She closed her eyes. "We both did."

👣

"Two! You knew you were having twins and didn't tell us?" Emma swung her arms through the air. After that, she couldn't get a word out. Her mouth opened and closed without making a sound, like a guppy, as she stared at the twins in the incubators.

"We wanted to surprise you, Ems," I told her.

I fought the urge to take a picture of my speechless sister. After all, I knew I'd need babysitting help. My mother sat in the chair beside the two incubators while smoothing the back of her hand over Faith's arm. Peg sat on the other side, staring at her grandkids and wiping away the tears as they surfaced every few moments.

"You have two babies. I'm a double aunt," Emma said.

"Triple aunt." I pointed to the bassinet with baby Faith. "Technically—"

218

"Please, no more technicalities. Just say it how it is."

I stuck out my hand with the thumb tucked in. "If you include TJ, we have four kids. You're a quadruple aunt, Ems."

"I'm a quadruple aunt?" She sat down in the chair beside Allie's bed, staring into space.

"You're the best aunt these babies could have asked for." Allie shifted in the bed. She'd lost a lot of blood during the birth, and her tired eyes could barely stay open.

"You know, Ems, you're slipping. I'm going to have to rethink some of your training." I checked over Allie's chart and latest blood work.

She shot off the chair and came to stand over my shoulder. "What do you mean I'm slipping?"

I closed Allie's chart and set it aside. "The blood work you forged when Allie first found out she was pregnant showed higher levels of hormones than expected in a regular pregnancy. You should have been the first one to know we were having twins."

"What forged blood work?" my mother asked. "Emma, what did you do?"

"I promise it was not a big deal." She fluttered her lashes at our mother. "The important thing here is that we have two healthy babies. Three. You're a grandma now, Mom, and I'm a quadruple aunt."

My sister seamlessly diverted Wilma's attention back to the babies. The door opened, and Julian peeked through, motioning for me to come out.

"Excuse me a moment." I left my family in the room and stepped outside into the hall, where Julian was pacing back and forth. Blood had stained his jeans and shirt.

"The cleaning crew was supposed to take care of that mess." I pointed.

"I slipped before the clean-up, and we came straight to the hospital once I got done with the police."

"How's Kendra?"

"Under observation. What if she relapses after this?"

"She saved Allie's life."

"I know, but what if she… what if she doesn't forgive me?"

"For what? Keeping your word? Protecting her all these years and keeping her out of trouble?"

He braced his bak against the wall and lowered his hands to his knees.

"I didn't really keep my word, did I? I took my best friend's daughter and ruined her. I wasted years fighting her, but she was so young. She's still young, and I'm the asshole who fell in love with her. I don't know where to draw the line anymore."

"What you should ask yourself is whether to draw a line at all. She's gone through more than people twice her age have. You should forget any line even exists."

"You're probably right." He stood up. "But we have more problems on our hands."

I couldn't imagine what they were because I had three healthy babies across the hall and an exhausted but happy wife. Not to mention an excited sister who had just become a quadruple aunt.

"What is it?" I asked him. "It wasn't Wright in the kitchen?"

"No, it was him. I know that for sure."

"His head was splattered, and I'm sure DNA is not back that fast."

"What does Allie say?" he asked.

"She says it was Wright. He told her we killed a body double back on the farm. Simone orchestrated the whole thing."

"Speaking of the devil's spawn, they've admitted her."

"As in, to this hospital?"

"Yeah. This time she slit through enough skin that they have to keep her here."

"Are the guards with her? I want increased security."

"Already done."

Julian rose to his feet and paced from where I stood to Allie's door and back. He looked like he'd run a marathon.

"What's the other problem, Julian? What aren't you telling me?"

He stopped, looked up, and exhaled out a long breath, like he'd been holding it for years. "Kendra remembered."

"What?"

"I think she remembered. She said little, but no, no... I'm sure she remembered."

"Okay, okay. We've been expecting this, right? You've been wanting this."

"Right."

"Donaldson is in prison, and the Hartleys are dead. Everything will be okay. Now, would you like to see your niece and nephew?"

"Wait, what?"

"Allie had twins. Come on. I know the babies will put a smile on your face, Uncle Julian. Today is a happy day. We can worry about everything else after at least, a few minutes of peace."

Our father and TJ returned with trays of coffee, smiling and joking around. Julian finally relaxed a little. I had a feeling everything would work out.

"What are you two discussing?" my father asked.

"Nothing, Dad."

"You can cut the crap, Tristan. Now, both of you stop talking business for a moment and take a break to enjoy the miracle in that room." He pointed to the door, pushing it open. "Come on."

I lifted my brows at my brother and he snickered. "I wonder who you take after."

We followed our father back inside. Allie opened her eyes. It wouldn't be long before she fell asleep again. She'd already pumped the milk for the babies twice and seemed spent.

"So, Ems. Have you named the babies yet?" my father asked.

"Names? Oh, my God! I totally forgot about the names. Well, I have one, but I didn't know about the other one, and now they won't match—"

"It's okay, Emma. Do you have one name?"

"Well, you told me you'd have a boy."

"We did."

She turned to Allie, saying, "So I thought that perhaps Raleigh, after your father—Ray Green."

Peg choked, and Allie broke into a river of tears. "I love it, Ems. It's perfect."

I handed her a tissue, and she blew her nose.

"What about the girl?" Emma fumbled with her fingers. "What are we gonna name the baby girl?"

I nodded to Allie.

"How about Rose?" Allie asked.

"Rose?" Emma's head flew up. "But I'm Emma Rose."

"If you don't mind, we'd like this little one to take after your second name."

"After me?"

"After the best aunt in the world, because our little girl is as unique, loving, and beautiful as you, Emma."

There it was again: that rare moment my sister's mouth didn't release a sound. But it didn't matter because she'd make up with lullabies, alphabet songs, and riddles. As my family laughed and cried, I realized the woman I wanted in my home and in my bed, and who I'd soon have there, gave me the kind of love and fulfillment I'd never expected.

Chapter 21

Allie

I opened my eyes at the faint knock on my hospital door and saw Laura's head pop in.

"Hey, you decent?" she asked.

"Come in. Thank you for the flowers and stuffies. Where's Foxy?"

Her smile brightened. "With James."

"Good. That's fantastic." My best friend and her baby daddy made the perfect stubborn pair, completing each other.

The sound of flushing water distracted Laura.

"Emma's in the bathroom. The excitement gave her diarrhea."

"I can hear you," she called out. "And it's not funny. I don't think I can go home like this."

"Why not?" Laura asked.

"Because I'll shit my pants."

"I can get you some adult diapers, Ems."

"Not funny! Ouch!"

"Should I call a nurse?" Laura asked.

"Not yet," Emma called out. "There's more coming."

"That does not sound good. This hospital doesn't have nuggets, does it?" Laura made herself comfortable beside me.

"None that I know of."

"How are you feeling, Mamma?"

"Good. Sore and weak, but good. Tristan finally went home to change, but should be back soon, and the family's been taking turns staying with me. What about you? I miss you. I miss Foxy."

"I'm good too. I think. We're figuring things out. I thought you should know Wilma and Fred are planning a party when you come back. They said it's just the family, but everybody's invited. And I mean everybody. Even the Wagners."

I sank back into the pillow and closed my eyes. "Almost like three and a half years ago in Colorado."

"Except without the avalanche."

"I missed out on a lot that Christmas, didn't I?"

"I caught what you missed out. My Silver Fox."

The thing was, I was sure I didn't miss out on anything. I might have taken a different route to get there, but I had my own Silver boss with golden experience and very gifted fingers.

"Allie? Are you listening to me?"

"Ahem, no. Repeat, please."

"Marissa's fine, and so is the baby. She's at a shelter, receiving help and counseling."

"Oh good. I was hoping you'd say that."

"Jesus, do you ever look tired."

I was beyond tired. I was exhausted.

"Thanks. They ripped me with no mercy. It will take a couple more days before I can walk, which is fine because they're not ready to go home yet. I'm not ready to go home yet either, but for the first time in my life, I feel like it's finally over."

I glanced at my sleeping angels. Gosh, my heart had never felt this full. And anxious. They were awesome when they slept, but when they were hungry, they all cried at once. Then came the diapers and charts. I wasn't sure how I'd keep up at home.

Laura touched my arm, and I flinched. "You have every right to feel overwhelmed, but you're not alone, and you're fierce."

"Thanks. I think I'll work from home for a while."

She laughed, then rolled her eyes. "You're joking, right? Listen, with one baby, you barely get enough time to ingest enough crap to sustain the sleepless nights and smelly diapers. With three…Jesus girl, I feel for you."

"I thought you just said not to feel overwhelmed?"

"That stays. You shouldn't, even when you are. Just sleep when the babies sleep. I'm more worried about you returning home."

"You mean because of Wright?"

She nodded.

"He's dead, Laura. I saw him die, so I know he'll never get up again. He's finally dead. That bastard doesn't deserve another second of my time. These babies deserve all my time and attention."

"That's my girl."

"I just need to rest while I can." I closed my eyes.

The hospital's intercom clicked on. "Code yellow, code yellow."

"What's code yellow?" Laura strode to the door and opened the blind covering the small window. Beyond, a commotion of doctors and security bustled through the hall.

"It's a missing patient," Emma called out from the bathroom.

"I'll go check it out and be right back. You stay here."

"Okay."

Like I could go anywhere! I had trouble sitting up, and hadn't tried standing, unless I went to the bathroom. The alarm beeped overhead, repeating *code yellow*, and I must have drifted to sleep quickly because when I opened my eyes again, Simone was standing by the IV at my bedside. Her wrists were bandaged, and a cut ran through her cheek, held by fresh stitches.

"Simone? What are you doing here?"

"You took my baby," she whispered.

Her lips were cracked and bleeding, and her eyes had sunk in deeper than when I saw her last.

"I don't think you should be here, Simone."

A tear ran down the side of her nightgown. Her hands were bloody from the open wounds she'd uncovered, and her forehead was smeared with dirt and blood.

"I want my baby." She stepped closer.

"Let's get a doctor and see what we can do about that." I reached for the call button, but she yanked the cord before I could press it. I pushed up on my bed until a stitch busted between my legs. A stabbing pain slashed at my insides.

Simone tilted her head sideways. "Are you a cat?"

Had she lost her mind already?

"What? No, I'm not a cat."

"You have nine lives. No matter how many times I try, you stay alive. You steal my life, my fiancé, and my baby, and nothing I do will kill you."

She shuffled her feet closer to the bed and reached inside her pocket. "Except this."

"You need help," I whispered. "We can get you the help you need."

But she ignored me and removed a syringe from within the pocket.

I shook my head.

"We used it on your friend Kendra." She snickered. "A little will knock you out. The girls called it the miracle drug because it knocked them out. It helped them pretend they weren't my whores."

My stomach twisted, and I wanted to throw up.

"But this much"—she tapped the plastic tube—"you don't wake up after something like this."

She attached the end to my IV and pressed the end, pushing the liquid inside. I watched as it flowed from the bag and into the drip.

"Simone. You can't." I pulled on the IV line, trying to rip it out of my arm before the fluid made it through, but she grabbed my hand and held it firm.

This isn't happening. I can't let her do this.

"Help! Somebody, help me!" I screamed.

She grabbed the additional pillow off a chair and threw it my way."

"Shut up! Shut up or I'll strangle you."

"I need hel—"

A loud thump sounded from where she stood, and she froze. Simone's mouth opened and her eyes grew large like saucers. She let go of my arm, and her knees buckled as she collapsed to the floor. Emma stood behind her with the top of a toilet bowl in her hands.

"I never liked that bitch. Simone Hartley, you have the right to remain silent." Her grin faded, and she looked up at me. "Are you okay?'

I nodded fast and ripped the IV line out of my arm. Emma dropped the ceramic to the floor and rushed to the door. "Security! I found your missing patient."

A swarm of nurses, doctors, and security filled the room. They checked my vitals. More doctors hovered over Simone before placing her unconscious on a gurney. Security cuffed her to the bed.

"If my brother doesn't change that woman's hospital, I will."

"Thank you, Ems. You saved my life."

"That's what sisters are for. And you're my sister, now and forever."

She sat beside me while the nurse poked me for a new IV

line. The doctors rolled Simone out of the room alongside security just as Tristan and Laura burst through the door.

"What the hell happened? Looks like somebody did her in well. I leave for one minute and you make an arrest?" Laura came to stand on the other side of my bed.

"It was me. I did her in. We didn't make any arrests. She tried to kill Allie, and this time she's going away for good," stated Emma.

"I'm not leaving your side again." Tristan stood beside me.

"This isn't your fault. It's no one's, but Simone needs help. Actual help." I stared at him, watching his eyes and waiting for the reply. "She has no one, and she's lost."

"All right. I'll make sure she gets the right help. I promise." He bent down and brought my head against his chest, holding me there. "I don't know what I would have done if I'd lost you."

A knock sounded on the door, and the security chief stepped through.

"Everybody all right? The doctors tell me Ms. Hartley had an assault wound on the back of her head."

"That's right." Emma stood. "I whacked her before she killed my sister-in-law. That's self-defense."

"Not quite," Tristan whispered, giving her arm a pull to be quiet.

Emma's frightened face turned to Tristan. "Are they going to charge me?"

"No one's gonna charge you. It was their mistake to allow a convict to escape. You did great, Ems. You both did great."

Tristan stayed with me and the babies from that moment until the doctors cleared us all over a week later. He had Emma do coffee and sandwich runs while he bathed and changed the babies. Watching his big hands handle their fragile bodies did something funny to me. It hit that mommy nerve where I found my husband so attractive. My toes tingled. Except I couldn't have him, because I was sore and swollen. And horny.

"I got this life-saving thing that's supposed to ease your…
seat." He fumbled with the inflatable donut and I laughed,
prepping the babies for their feedings.

"Thanks."

"Maybe you should sit. You've been on your feet since…"
His arms flopped at his sides. "I don't even know when you sat
last."

"The doctor says I'll heal more quickly if I move." I set the
baby bottle down, walked over to Tristan, and kissed him hard
on his lips. Ahh, that mouth and tongue messed with my head
better than tequila. When I pulled away, the scar on his lip
twisted into a smile.

"I see," he growled. "If walking is what you need, you'll get
the chance when we go over to my parents' this afternoon."

"Wait, what?" I stopped. "Is that the party Laura mentioned?
Where everyone's gonna be there?"

"Likely."

I slumped. "I'm gonna be so tired. We have three babies.
Well, I can carry two, and if they cry, you'll take one. I guess
between the two of us we could manage. My point is—"

"I don't think you're seeing the point, babe. We're going to a
party with a keen aunt and two grandmothers who won't let
our kids out of their sight. This is an opportunity to relax: lift
your feet high in the air and do nothing. But if you'd rather
walk around, you can walk around. There's a hammock underneath the wisteria blossoms in my mother's backyard." He
wiggled his brows. "It's just a family gathering. Easygoing."

It would be lovely to unplug for a moment and enjoy the
change and all the blessings we'd been given.

"Okay, let's do it."

"Not yet." He grasped me by the hips, spun me around, and
pinned me against the fridge. Air whizzed out of my lungs.

"Mr. Silver, if you're trying to seduce me—"

"Not seduce."

His hand lowered down my thigh, and he scrunched my dress upward, dragging his fingers along my skin. "I'm going to make you come."

My next breath hitched and my body stiffened at the thought of him where I was raw from birthing twins. As much as I wanted him to, I couldn't have him touch me yet.

"Relax, Allie," he whispered in my ear. "It won't hurt. I know what I'm doing."

He withdrew his hand from underneath my dress, generously licked the tip of his finger and slipped it back under and down my panties, right over my clit. I shuddered at the feel of his cold skin on my heated flesh.

"Oh, my God." I closed my eyes and succumbed to the gentle circles over my swelling.

His mouth trailed kisses from the strap on my shoulder, up my neck and along the jawline, until his lips found mine and took me for a spin. I lifted my hands to draw him in closer, but he gripped my wrists, pinning them above my head. I writhed under his mouth's pressure and tantalizing tongue strokes, giving into his guiding fingers and pressing my need into his hand. The pressure exploded and relief spasmed through my body. I trembled in his hold as the orgasm settled with his slowing rubs. My eyes felt heavy and my body spent. I gripped Tristan's arms for support.

"Why don't you lie down? I'll wake you in time to change before the party."

"What about the kids?"

"I've got it handled, and I can ask for help if I need it." He kissed my forehead and my eyes closed by then. I might have been exhausted, but I had never been this happy and fulfilled in my life.

SILVER DECORATIONS TWIRLED between the blues and pinks. Emma must have ordered flowers from every shop in the state because the bouquets stood out in every entrance and every room.

Wilma and Fred had hired private catering to welcome us all home, and everyone was hanging out in the backyard. I lifted my feet to the cushioned wicker lounge under an umbrella. Faith was sleeping, and the grandmas were cuddling the twins.

Gabe and Sam had flown in for the occasion from Austria with their newborn, and Sam was nursing the baby upstairs. Tristan stood alongside his cousins, each one with a scotch in his hand, sneaking a peek at the babies every forty-five seconds.

"Look." Laura started her stopwatch. "It's like he's got a clock in that brain."

"Don't you have anything better to do than time how often my husband checks the babies?"

She set her phone aside. "Of course I do. I'm elbows-deep in cases and files. The Hartleys might be gone, but the damage has been done. The Wagner lawyers have been great, though, because Infinity is a monster."

Hartley's organization had created an unstoppable crime ring, and the Wagner brothers were right in the middle of the operation. Laura found work for Marissa at the downstairs coffee shop. They added a daycare section, and the business was blossoming from the support it provided to the community.

Simone's sentencing was coming up next week. She'd taken a plea deal for a few years in jail with the hope she'd see Faith and TJ. Tristan ensured ongoing therapy, and maybe one day when she was well, she could join the same family who had opened their hearts to me.

"And how is working with James?"

"It's… he's everything I never expected."

She glanced across the deck to where the Silvers were chatting. The dreamy look on her face was new, but it suited her.

I caught Tristan's attention. He'd trimmed his stubble and looked absolutely delicious in his white shirt. He lifted his glass in a cheer, and I smiled. "I know exactly what you mean."

The sudden rush of bodies at the side yard startled us both. We watched as Julian passed the sandbox, rubbed Foxy's head, and headed straight for the group of boys.

"Come on. Something's up." I hurried off my seat as fast as my body would allow me, and we strolled semi-casually toward them.

I worried I'd bust a stitch when I saw their somber faces.

"What's going on?" Laura asked.

"They've arrested Kendra." Julian's face darkened.

"For what?" I asked.

"Murder."

Chapter 1

Julian

Trouble was Katherine's middle name, and it followed her like a puppy follows its mama's lead. The first time I babysat, I learned that chaos flowed through that girl's blood. I was only eighteen, and she choked on a Lego just before her baptism. My Lego. Jake and Ashley would have killed me if anything had happened to their baby girl, but I saved little Katherine because the hero complex coursed through my blood. It turns out that's not such a bad thing when you're a bodyguard. And Jake and Ashley never found out. They also never found out about the sock she flushed down the toilet. I spent half a day unclogging the throne. Or the time she fell in the pool because maintenance left the gate unlocked.

Like I said, they would have killed me. Over the years, Katherine grew, and I eased Ashley and Jake's busy schedules by babysitting. I walked through the park with a stroller while Jake completed his political whatever-Ph.D. alongside his wife, studying somewhere on the bench. I graduated from NYU and did what all the Silvers do best: built relationships. Plus schooling. Lots of fucking schooling because that's what it took to be a good private investigator. And tonight, all that prestige earned me a late night emergency phone call from my best friends.

I scanned my card at the front entrance and hurried down the long hall to my corner office, where the night security guard was waiting by the door.

"They're inside."

"Good. Inform me immediately if anyone buzzes downstairs."

"Yes, sir."

I pushed the door open. Jake and Ashley launched from the couch toward me, Jake in a pair of sweatpants and Ash in leggings and Jake's sweatshirt. The power couple from D.C. were on their way to another Congressional nomination and a win, and they looked like someone had dragged them through the trenches.

"What's going on?" I asked. "Is Katherine okay?"

Ash shook her head, crying, while their fifteen-year-old daughter sat behind my office desk, looking out the window into the night. The sky was clear, and the moon outlined Manhattan's beautiful horizon, but if I had to bet, my goddaughter wasn't paying attention to the city skyline. I glanced over at her. She was picking at the skin near one nail, and she looked like an absolute mess. Her plaid skirt was shorter than I remembered. She must have hemmed it, and Ashley must have freaked. But the spunky girl I'd known since birth seemed off.

"No. Nothing's okay. Nothing."

I passed her a tissue. "Start at the beginning."

"It's Katherine," she whispered. "She's in trouble."

Katherine drew her thumb to her mouth and chewed on her nail, staring at where Lady Liberty's flame lightened the night. Her lifeless posture combined with that stare gave me the shivers.

"Why is she in her school clothes?"

"We found her four hours after school was out, in our back-yard. It had rained, and she was soaked and didn't want to change."

"Are those blood stains?"

I hurried to the corner basket and picked up a white plush blanket, a gift from Stefanie. The psychiatrist gave my office a facelift last Christmas—and gave me a blowjob the next morning. I draped the blanket over her shoulders, and Katherine looked up. My body turned numb when I saw her features. Her long, tangled brown hair stuck to her face and neck.

"She's been asking for you. She says you're the only one who can help."

I picked her up off of my chair. A pack of bubblegum fell out of her pocket as I carried her to the other couch. Once there, she lay in a fetal position, shaking.

"Hey, Kay. You're safe now. Whatever happened, we'll fix it." I turned to her parents. "Did anyone hurt her?" The words barely passed through my throat.

"I… I don't know. I don't think so." Ashley's tiny sob broke my heart in half.

"I can make things right. No matter what it is, we can make everything right."

Katherine twisted my way in slow motion and looked up at me. The spirit I recalled in her saucer-shaped eyes had vanished.

My heart picked up speed. Jake's desperate glance over at his daughter punched me in the gut.

"What the fuck happened?"

"I need to speak to you privately." Jake stood up.

It was that serious.

"All right. Come with me. Ash, we won't be long, and you're safe. You're both safe. I promise you that."

"I know." She smoothed her hand over Katherine's arm, whispering softly, "I'm sorry."

Jake followed me through the revolving bookcase. I poured us both a scotch and handed him a glass.

"What's going on?"

"We've already spoken to Fred and Jacob. All the Silvers are on board with the plan. I called you earlier, but you weren't available."

I left the office early today for a date with Stefanie. Jake called, I answered, and thereby guaranteed myself a pair of blue balls.

"I had a date." I waved my hand. "It doesn't matter. What plan are you talking about?"

"Julian, you're her godfather. You've taken care of her since she was in diapers."

"I love her like my own."

"That's why I know we've made the right decision."

He handed me an envelope I hadn't noticed him holding. "In case something happens, this is a key to a safe deposit box. You'll find the instructions with documents. Tristan and James are setting up the operation for tomorrow, and I hope you agree…to this. We both hope you agree to this because we need you to become Katherine's guardian. Temporarily, of course."

Where the fuck did that come from, and why hadn't I woken up yet?

Blood drained from my face, and I set my glass aside. I knew the Moores were in the middle of a Congressional fight, but I had not not realized they were in trouble. "What the fuck happened?"

"We need to disappear for a little while."

"You're going into witness protection?" I guessed.

"Yes, but we can't take Katherine."

"What? Why?"

"The profile of a couple with a teenage daughter will draw everyone we need to avoid. It won't be possible to give her a normal life, or as close to normal as we'd like."

"The Federal Witness Protection program deals with this every day. I'm sure they can handle Katherine."

"But you're the only one we trust to give her what witness protection won't: a life. A normal life."

"What about New Zealand? She was born there."

"But her life is here."

"What life, if she's in hiding? You haven't thought this through, Jake. I'm a single man without kids for a reason." Work was my life, and dating was an extra-curricular activity I enjoyed mostly in bed. Or against the wall.

He shook his head. "It's the only way to keep her safe. Your father and brother are already prepping for tomorrow." He lowered another thick manila envelope to the table. I refilled my glass and emptied it in one painful but extremely satisfying swig.

"What's happening tomorrow? And what happened to Katherine?"

"There was an accident at the school, so she can't go back. She'll have a private tutor from now on, and we'll keep in touch. Maybe not immediately, but soon. She'll stay with you, close to your parents. She loves your family, and I know you love her too. We should be back by summer." He said it like they were going on a vacation.

"Jake, I don't even have a kid. I don't have a wife or a girl-friend. How am I going to explain having a teenager?"

"The great thing about you, Julian, is you know how to adapt. And you're a good best friend and a great godfather. If everything goes according to plan, it won't be long before we're back. The FBI will find the evidence against Donaldson, and we'll be in the clear."

"Congressman Donaldson?"

"The one and only." He gripped my shoulder like the deal we'd made to take guardianship of my best friend's daughter, all in secrecy, was final.

Wasn't it?

She was my goddaughter, and I'd vowed to protect her when her parents couldn't. The answer to that promise was simple, and Jake must have seen it in my eyes because, along with my hero complex, flowed a tsunami of courage.

"Thank you. I knew you'd come through."

"I didn't say yes."

"Your eyes did, and that's enough."

He handed me the other envelope with a thick stack of papers, marked *Kendra*, he'd been holding under his arm until now. How many of those did they have?

"Who's Kendra?"

"Ashley liked the name as a new one for Katherine. For now."

"And does your daughter know it?"

"Obviously not. We're not paying you the big bucks to do all the work, Julian. She'll need a psychiatrist, and I know you know a good one."

I couldn't get Stefanie involved in this. The reason we worked was because we were free of drama.

"Jake, I know we've been friends for a long time, but—"

"But there's no one else who can do this job better than you, and I trust no one else. You're her godfather, and it's only for a few months, Julian. After you hear the plan for tomorrow, you'll agree you're the best thing for Katherine. She already knows you, and she's comfortable with you."

"What's happening tomorrow again?"

"It's in the envelope. We have to find a place to clean up and hide out for the night, but if we're alive come morning, I'll see you then."

He turned around and went back to my office. I set my glass on the counter and hurried behind him to where Ashley was sitting beside her daughter. Katherine lay curled in a fetal position. I'd never seen the bubbly girl so frail.

"She fell asleep," Ashley whispered. "I gave her my Xanax."

"You gave her what?" I stopped mid-step. "Ash, those are addictive. I'm not sure a fifteen-year-old should take Xanax."

She turned to Jake and anchored her gaze to his. "Didn't you explain what happened?"

"I had no time for that part," he replied.

"What part?"

"We have to leave and hide before tomorrow."

"Okay, just give me a sec to catch up."

I pulled out the papers from Jake's envelope and flipped through the pages. "Oh, crap."

"You see our problem?"

I saw their problem, but I couldn't see a way out of my predicament even if I tried. No matter the choice, there'd be trouble. Lots of trouble.

"Where are you guys going tonight?" I asked. "Where are you staying?"

He pulled his fingers through his hair. "There's a contract on our lives. Donaldson hired a hitman… His name is Martinez, but that's all we know. I'm not even sure whether the security out there is sufficient." He nodded toward my office door. "I don't know where to take my wife and my kid to keep them safe."

I lowered my hand to his shoulder and gave enough pressure so he could sit beside his wife and daughter.

"You're already where you need to be. You can take Tristan's bedroom by his office. There's a shower there, too. I'm sure he won't mind. I'll move Katherine to my bed when she wakes up." God, what sounded so innocent at the time would become one of my dirtiest fantasies. Had I known the trap I was setting for myself, I would have never agreed to the arrangement.

I pointed to the stack of papers from my father. "Looks like I have some reading to do before morning. There's food in the staff room; I wouldn't risk ordering out. Don't make any contact. Turn off your cell phones. In fact, hand them in right now."

"We already gave them to Tristan."

"Good. Well, maybe we should have started with that."

I wanted to explain the task they'd asked of me would be hard; pretty much impossible. But Silvers were great at the impossible, and I couldn't let my friends down. I'd hide Katherine in my house, and... yeah... impossible.

Fuck.

I didn't know it then, but I wasn't ready for the trouble my best friends were handing me. I was totally out of my mind, thinking Katherine could stay with me.

Then again, I hadn't been ready when Ash and Jake came over to my penthouse when Katherine was four. That emergency evening of babysitting ended with little Kay applying makeup to my face. The smeared lipstick stains over my bathroom counter weren't as appreciated. Katherine washed them off with my toothbrush. Dipped into the toilet.

"Wait a minute. What about her godmother?" I asked. "What was her name—Jodi? The one from your mother's side, Ash?" I waved my finger in the air like it was a wand and I could make Jodi appear out of thin air.

"Jodi passed away from cancer three years ago."

"Shit."

Ashley lowered her cold and shaky hand over mine. I could ask my parents, but Emma was only eight, and they had their hands full. Besides, I wasn't about to cop out. That wasn't in my blood.

"Julian, we wouldn't ask you to do this if we didn't have to."

Ashley's raw voice and pleading eyes broke through the thick wall around my heart. I covered her hand with mine and gave her a comforting smile. Katherine had definitely inherited her mother's beautiful eyes.

"I already said I'll do it," I whispered. "I'll do whatever you need me to. It's what families do, and we've been a family for a long time."

"Thank you," she sobbed, slobbering into another tissue.

I stood up and loosened the top button on my shirt.

"You two know where to find Tristan's office, and I'll have Greg show you the private quarters. He's waiting out in the hall with your security, which I assure you you don't need in this building. We've got plenty."

"Thank you, Julian." Jake handed me one more envelope. How many of those did he have?

"What's this?" I asked.

"Details about tomorrow's plan."

I scanned the papers all the way to the end, where my father and uncle had signed off on an agreement with Jake's crazy plan. We were taking a private train ride across the mountains, and tomorrow, we'd throw off the search for the Congress members and their daughter with a single flick of a switch.

"You've got to be fucking kidding me."

"It has to be real, Julian."

"You're dying?"

"Best way to stay out of the way is from six feet under. Katherine can't come with us. She needs a normal life, and you can give that to her."

They had no clue what they were asking, but the point was they'd asked, and I couldn't say no.

Ashley and Jake left for their room, and I moved Katherine to my room and my bed. I removed her shoes, coat, and sweater and tucked her in before settling back at my desk. I read over the plan my father and uncle had put together more than a dozen times that night. It was an ambitious plan with too many holes and moving parts, and it nurtured my insomnia until the morning.

I watched Katherine sleep that night, completely clueless it would be the first of many nights I'd spend with this girl. And not a single one of them would be easy, because Trouble was her middle name.

Silver's Trouble, Book 5 in the *Silver Brothers Securities Family Saga,* follows Kendra and Julian's forbidden love story and has a happily ever after ending.

ALSO BY LACEY SILKS

Silver Brothers Securities

Silver Santa

Silver's Rebel

Silver's Pawn

Silver's Secret

Silver's Trouble

Silver Fox

Silver Hunter

Dirty Deeds Series

Dirty Cowboy

Dirty Mechanic

Dirty Con

Be the first to know!

Visit www.laceysilks.com

ABOUT THE AUTHOR

USA Today Bestselling Author Lacey Silks crafts riveting romantic suspense filled with heat, spice, and pulse-pounding tension. Many of her endearing characters are inspired by her own life, and her loved ones often find themselves playfully woven into her tales. Her two children and her dog, Kygo, keep her days lively with homework queries and affectionate slobbery kisses (courtesy of Kygo, of course).

Outside of penning intense love stories, Lacey is an avid camper and skier. Naturally an early riser, she often finds herself reaching for coffee over water, crediting her billionaire heroes for her packed schedule.

Lacey's characters, replete with flaws and quirks, evoke laughter, sass, and emotion on every page. She cheekily measures men by their foot size, has a penchant for sultry lingerie, and harbors dreams of exploring the nation in a motorhome.

MYLIT
PUBLISHING

ACKNOWLEDGMENTS

Silver's Secret was never meant to have so many twists and turns because I have a rule. It's called KISS (keep it simple stupid), and I broke it. But if I'd kept it simple, the story would not be completed.
I guess some rules are meant to be broken ;)

I couldn't have done the work without my reader support or the ever-inspiring indie author community filled with a wealth of knowledge. The continued encouragement and faith in my work, along with the outpouring of love, replenished my muse.

To my amazing editor who always finds the time for me, thank you for making my life easy and my writing understandable. I will chuckle over those 'silver eyes' for a while.

To my beta readers, thank you for your keen eyes! Once I read a story twenty times (or more), the details aren't easy to spot. Your feedback is invaluable and makes the novel what it should be.

To my family, the past few years have tested us in more ways than we would have liked, and I could not do what I love without you. Thank you for your support, faith and encouragement.

Maya, thank you for your artistic eye and cover design. I'm honoured to watch you grow and develop as an artist. Alex, your loving heart and sense of humour are a constant inspiration.

To my parents, this book would not have happened without you. Thank you for believing in my dreams.

9 781998 306213